ALSO BY RACHEL LOUISE SNYDER

*Fugitive Denim:*
*A Moving Story of People and Pants*
*in the Borderless World of Global Trade*

*No Visible Bruises:*
*What We Don't Know About*
*Domestic Violence Can Kill Us*

# WHAT WE'VE LOST
# IS NOTHING

A Novel

## Rachel Louise Snyder

SCRIBNER

*New York    London    Toronto    Sydney    New Delhi*

Scribner
A Division of Simon & Schuster, Inc.
1230 Avenue of the Americas
New York, NY 10020

First Scribner trade paperback edition June 2020

SCRIBNER and design are registered trademarks of The Gale Group, Inc., used under license by Simon & Schuster, Inc., the publisher of this work.

For information about special discounts for bulk purchases, please contact Simon & Schuster Special Sales at 1-866-506-1949 or business@simonandschuster.com.

The Simon & Schuster Speakers Bureau can bring authors to your live event. For more information or to book an event contact the Simon & Schuster Speakers Bureau at 1-866-248-3049 or visit our website at www.simonspeakers.com.

Manufactured in the United States of America

1   3   5   7   9   10   8   6   4   2

Library of Congress Cataloging-in-Publication Data is available.

ISBN 978-1-4767-2517-8
ISBN 978-1-4767-2520-8 (pbk)
ISBN 978-1-4767-2522-2 (ebook)

*To my gang of five: Ann Maxwell, Don Rutledge, Julie Gibson,*
*Soleak Sim, and Yasmina Kulauzovic*

*And to Caroline Alexander, who made so much possible*

All things are in the hand of heaven, and Folly, eldest of Jove's daughters, shuts men's eyes to their destruction. She walks delicately, not on the solid earth, but hovers over the heads of men to make them stumble or to ensnare them.

—Homer, *The Iliad*

# Contents

PART TWO: WEDNESDAY, APRIL 7, 2004

# WHAT WE'VE LOST
# IS NOTHING

# Prologue

---

## Wednesday, April 7, 2004, 3:20 p.m.

Mary Elizabeth McPherson could feel Caz's hand slide down her lower back and into her back pocket. He surreptitiously handed her a joint, and she took a deep, adrenaline-fueled toke, cupping it in her palm as she'd seen him do. She held the cough until her eyes watered, looking away from Caz, toward the Tasty Dog, where she and her friends sometimes shared milk shakes and hot dogs on the weekends. A wallet chain jingled against Caz's hip. His faded jean jacket quietly shifted on his shoulders, made him seem bigger than he was. She slid the joint back to Caz and exhaled. He took a hit, held it a second, then leaned in and blew the smoke gently across her face in what she interpreted as deeply romantic.

Caz was known for cutting class, known for his rap sheet, which included multiple school suspensions and carrying around a dulled fishing knife with a broken tip; he was also known for maintaining a deep and abiding contempt for anyone with authority. Once, back in his freshman math class two years earlier, he'd fallen asleep and Mr. Fonseca came up and squeezed his wrist tighter and tighter till he woke up. Without lifting his head, Caz had said, "Get your fucking hand off me, dickwad." Fifteen years old. He got slapped with a three-day suspension, which only amplified his reputation, the hushed reverence with which kids approached him. A god of anger and contempt. Also: gorgeous. Mary wondered if he was this way at home, with his parents, or whether it was all for show.

Keep the conversation going, she told herself, keep him talking about things that mattered to him. *But what mattered to him?* Having never before been the object of a boy's fascination, *any boy*, let alone a boy such as Caz, left Mary flustered. She recognized this moment as one of those rare opportunities in life where one might shuffle one's standing in the high school caste system, and she knew it was only the burglaries the day before that catapulted her into Caz's periphery at all. When he'd sidled up to her that morning in class and said simply, "See you at lunch," a revelation had presented itself to her. It was the first time Caz had acknowledged her in their two years at Oak Park River Forest High, all because of the burglaries on her street. News reporters had flocked to their house the day before, and her whole family appeared on television. A garden-variety home invasion wouldn't have boosted Mary's social capital, but one element of the story had spread through the halls before the first bell even rang. During the burglary Mary Elizabeth had been home.

She fielded a flurry of questions between classes.

Mary, were you scared?

*Not really.*

Did you see them?

*No.*

Did you hear them break the door down?

*No.*

Where were you when they came in?

*Dining room. Under the table.*

Wasn't it, like, during school? Didn't you cut class?

*Wink, smirk.*

She was surprised by her proclivity toward self-editing as the questions flew at her. Was she scared? Hell, yes, she'd been scared once she knew what was happening. But copping to her fear would not have won Caz's affection.

"What street do you live on again?" she asked him now as they walked in step.

His wallet chain hit a rivet on his jeans. "Madison and Austin."

Mary stopped walking. "An apartment? Which one? Across from the bank, or . . ." She shut her mouth when she realized her enthusiasm was suspicious. Caz was glaring at her. "Sorry," she said. Thankfully, his arm was still around her. She hadn't lost him yet. "That's one of my mom's buildings. I mean, not hers, but she shows the apartments in that building. I only know because she's always bitching about it." Had she worded that right? Was *bitching about it* the right phrase?

Caz said nothing. Mary recognized that a fine line existed between conversation and chatter, between interest and disinterest. She pulled him by the pocket loop, began to walk again. "My mom works at the Housing Office, showing apartments to try to have diversity and all that. Like the buildings that want Diversity Assurance."

"Diversity what?" His voice was rough, distant. They passed the joint back and forth again.

"Diversity Assurance? Integration and all that. You know, the east side. How it was so dangerous, like, back in the seventies or whenever and Oak Park created this program to get people to live together again?"

"No idea what you're talking about."

"I mean, you know, blacks and whites? White people didn't want to live on the east side, and businesses wouldn't open up there, and now it's like got racial diversity?"

Mary knew all about the sordid history of race in Chicago, the stuff her mom talked about, like she was some sort of social crusader. Mrs. McPherson even came to Mary's school sometimes to talk about it, how investments weren't made in black communities and so the neighborhoods fell into disrepair. Then gang warfare and poverty from the west side of Chicago had supposedly trickled into Oak Park. The Housing Office, where Mrs. McPherson worked, tried to shore up the difference. Mary knew more about it than she cared to admit. She had never been warned to stay away from the west side of Chicago, from Austin Boulevard, yet still she'd instinctively avoided it. Never once had she wandered over there.

Caz had caught Mary Elizabeth on the local news the night before and suddenly remembered her as the head of hair that blocked his view of the blackboard in composition class. Until now, he'd only ever thought of her as *hair*. The burglaries were interesting not only because she'd been home, but because they'd spanned her entire street. Caz was mildly impressed by the audacity of such a crime (admittedly, a small part of him wished he'd thought of it). Looking at her on the news as she stood half-hiding behind her father, Caz saw something he'd never before seen: a girl who was . . . not bad-looking. A cheerleader, if he remembered correctly. And he wanted to see the street, see the houses themselves, see from his own view what lay inside the homes he'd wandered past, but never visited, those manicured lawns and pristine paint jobs he'd always lived near. The apartments he'd lived in his whole life were a mass memory of punched-out walls and broken mirrors, grates over the windows, and stale cigarettes crushed into carpets.

So he'd asked her to lunch, which was how he thought of it (not quite making the distinction between a statement and a question: *See you at lunch* versus *Would you like to sit together at lunch?*—the latter of which would never come from Caz's mouth). But then she'd asked that crazy question, thrown him that complete left hook: *What's the worst thing that ever happened to you?* Where had she thought of such a thing? What stranger asked that of another stranger? He'd worked hard to keep his own *worst thing that ever happened* out of his day-to-day consciousness, and he was largely successful. He couldn't remember a girl ever just asking him that, the worst thing. Even *he* didn't want to remember. And in his quieter moments—not that there were many—he was pretty good at not remembering at all. That's how it went in his house. Kill off the shit that could kill you.

He could hardly remember his mother now. She had brown hair. She watched soap operas. Her belly protruded when she lay on the couch. She called alcohol her "medicine." He remembered finding her one night weeping in the corner of the basement, holding the phone to her ear.

"I need to disappear," she said to whoever was on the line. "I got nothing. I got nothing here. Not a fucking set of dimes to squeeze together." She was crying, her face slick and wet, and Caz, who was still little Chris back then, had snuck glances around the doorframe.

He started collecting change for her after that—little, glimmery shards on the sidewalks, or money tossed into fountains. He tried to find abandoned coins that would keep his mom from disappearing.

When she died, he was six years old. She'd tried to shoot Caz first, but missed. Tried to set him free, she'd said, but his father made a run for her, and all she could manage in that split second after missing her son was *not* missing herself.

Caz was six years old. He'd scavenged $41.07 in change.

A decade had passed since that day, and Caz had survived. He wasn't into all that psychobabble bullshit about trauma and memory. Caz's mother had been too weak to hack it. Simple as that.

Caz shivered for a moment, and he felt Mary look at him. Her eyes held a kind of need, bottomless and also a little alarming, her thick, curly hair like rope. He managed to stop thinking about his mom and start thinking about the girl beside him, and how good her ass seemed to fit inside the palm of his hand. He gave her a squeeze, and a grin, and she squeezed right back.

Mary felt Caz's hand in her pocket. For a moment, she imagined reaching around him and yanking on his wallet chain, forcing him to spin in a circle. With another guy, this might have been funny, a lighthearted moment of young love. But not with Caz. He was all bluster and sharp edges. Much later, years later, she would know what it was to carry a smile on your face while the whole rest of your body frowned, and she'd remember that Caz had been the first person she'd ever seen do this. He was like a city under siege, full of broken buildings, and yet, inexplicably, light still flickered from some unknown source. She wondered what he normally did after school; she could hardly imagine him plopping down in front of the computer with a bowl of cereal, as she usually did. Maybe this could be the thing he did, come home with Mary. At least for a time.

"When my mom comes to school," Mary said, "it makes me want to die." It didn't, of course. "She always comes to talk about integration, and the Housing Office and all that. I bet she even talks about your building."

Caz gave a guttural grunt in response. This past year had, in fact, been the first time Susan McPherson visited a class Mary attended. Until that day, Mary had never heard her mother talk about what she did for a living in such an idealized way and had thought of her mother more or less as a Realtor for renters. When Susan spoke of the importance of a diverse community, of empathy and tolerance, of the people who once risked their lives to break the cycle of injustice, Mary's teacher had called Susan one of Oak Park's local heroes, and Mary had begun to wonder, could her very own totally annoying and overly righteous mother also be a hero?

Mary didn't share any of this with Caz, of course. Mercifully, they'd reached her house through the back alley, and Mary pulled her keys from her backpack. Her large, pink, fuzzy heart keychain flashed a purple light at the center when you clicked a button. She didn't know if news vans still lined the street from yesterday's burglaries, and she certainly didn't want to be caught on camera, but part of her hoped Caz might see a reporter or two and think it cool. Day-old yellow police tape fluttered from an oak tree beside her house, and her parents still hadn't cleaned up the mess in the den, or entirely sorted out what had gone missing from the garage. They'd met with the other neighbors the night before. Everyone had been robbed. Everyone was freaked-out. But honestly, the whole thing felt to Mary as if the world were granting her the possibility of a brand-new version of herself. People who'd never before noticed her at school had been *so nice* to her. Teachers, the assistant dean, even a bunch of the popular kids. And now here was Caz, who'd acknowledged her in class for the first time ever, then sat beside her at lunch with the *whole school* watching, then promised to come hang out with her at her house after school. It was dizzying.

She shut the door. The house was silent and Mary Elizabeth felt reassured.

"Well, it's not like the black people in my building are chillin' with the whites," Caz said finally, as if he'd spent the entire last five minutes of their walk conjuring up this brilliant response. "Doesn't sound like that diversity program is any kind of anything."

Mary dropped her keys. She felt a surge of anger as she bent to pick them up. What was so bad about people getting along? About trying to include all kinds of people into your world? She was apathetic about her mother's work, sure, but she'd never heard anyone insult it, and she felt a sudden, unfamiliar desire to defend her mom.

"I mean, people are people. Blacks, whites, whatever . . . we're not going to stop hating each other," he said.

They were standing in the kitchen. Mary Elizabeth felt a flutter on the top of her head, the light touch of fingertips. She looked up and Caz flashed a grin at her, then signaled down to his crotch with his eyes. Mary blushed and looked away. She tossed her keys on the counter, harder than she'd intended.

"Speak for yourself. I don't hate black people."

"Me either. I'm just saying. It's a stupid program."

"Your building is full of white *and* black people."

"I guess so."

"So it's working. I mean it worked. Think about what it would have been like in the seventies with all that crime. You're just ungrateful." She thought of her mom, how frustrated she'd get when she'd spend a day showing beautiful apartments to people who would turn around and tell her they felt "unsafe" near Austin Boulevard, as if all those decades of creating community were for nothing. Fears, her mom called them, that were the impossible-to-excavate kind. Fears that just had to "die with the bigots who hold on to them," she'd sometimes say.

"Well, maybe you're changing my mind, Mary Elizabeth McPherson," Caz said in a quiet voice. A low, gravelly baritone, the voice he'd used at lunchtime. "Maybe you can teach me to be a little grateful."

Mary forced herself to look into his eyes. Brown and dark. She understood why people called them chocolate-brown eyes, but to her they were more like the brown of fall leaves, misted with the change of seasons. He reached over and flicked on the radio, stationed to the Loop. Foghat streamed through the kitchen. Caz's hands found her hips. She felt the countertop to her left, the ocher curtains hanging at the glass door. She felt his hands move around her, rounding her ass, down, slowly, and then back up. Her chest rubbed against his jean jacket as he pulled her in close. She wanted to get him up to her room, but that could wait just a minute. Then he bent his head, just an inch, and he leaned in to kiss her.

# Part One

———

# Tuesday, April 6, 2004

*Chicago Tribune, Breaking News*

# Multiple Homes Burgled in Western Suburb, Suspects Sought

**By Donald Rutledge**
*April 6, 2004*

What appeared to be a well-planned mass burglary occurred around 2:00 p.m. on the 100 block of Ilios Lane in west suburban Oak Park. At least four homes have been identified in the burglary with other Ilios Lane residences still under investigation.

Police currently have no suspects.

Electronics, keepsakes and antiques were among the stolen items, though a formal tally is not yet complete, said Police Chief Brian Mazzoli.

Two residents were home at the time of the theft, but were unharmed.

Ilios Lane resident Michael McPherson said his daughter had been home from school, ill. "We're just so thankful our daughter's safe," he told WGN news.

This is the largest residential burglary on record for the near-west suburb.

"This is someone looking for attention," Michael McPherson said. "For us, what we've lost is nothing compared to what we in this neighborhood, on this street, will always have."

Chief Mazzoli is asking that anyone with tips call the Oak Park Police Department at 1-708-555-2300.

# Chapter 1

———

## 3:10 p.m.

S usan McPherson ignored her husband's phone call. The couple sitting at her desk were in a rush. Away from work for a long lunch break, only a few minutes to sign the lease and write the check. They'd managed to convince the landlord that the two-cat policy could be stretched for their three kitten siblings. What can you do? Heartless to separate them and so forth—and Susan had subsequently ignored the phone. She had no other clients scheduled for the afternoon and had toyed with the idea of going to Buzz Café down on Harrison just to relax and read the paper for an hour. It would have been a rare moment to breathe, except that half the people in this town knew her, and so if she really wanted to get away, she needed to go into the city, to an anonymous café in Wicker Park, perhaps, or the Ukrainian Village. She stapled the security deposit and rent receipts to the couple's rental application and tried to place the stapler back in the exact dust outline from whence it had come.

Her husband was insistent on the phone. She smiled, nodded at the clients. The man handed the lease to his wife to look over. Michael would call again, Susan knew. And he did. Again his number popped up on the caller ID on her desk phone. After a moment, she heard her cell phone vibrate in her purse—a desperate move since she so often left it at home, or forgot to charge the battery.

"It's supposed to *help* us," he'd once yelled at her, "these modern conveniences. Make our lives *easier*." She suspected he'd bought it for her so it could make *his* life easier. ("Can you pick up some steaks on the way home?" "Can you drop the tax returns at the post office so they're not late?" "Cable guy's changed his appointment window. Can you run home to meet him?") The combination of having a cell phone and working a mile away from home often worked against her. But his insistence this time was unusual. So she held up one hand in apology and took the call: "Housing Office, Susan McPherson."

"Robbed. The house. Arthur, too." His voice was midsentence, harried, higher than normal, and angry at having had to call and call and call, she suspected. Robbed. It took her a moment to connect his broken sentences. Their house. *Her* house. It was the middle of the afternoon, on a sunny April day, one of the first nice days they'd had since winter. *Who robs a house in the middle of the afternoon?* She could hear the turn signal blinking in his car, a distant car horn.

She'd soon learn that the afternoons were prime time for home invasions. That crime spiked in the first warm days of spring. She'd learn their neighbors had also been robbed, and that *robbed* was the wrong word. *Burgled* was what had happened to them. Robbery was just stealing, but burglary was breaking in *and* stealing. But of all the things she'd come to learn about burglary, none mattered to her much at all when she heard the next thing Michael said.

"She's fine."

Susan hadn't understood at all what he meant. Who was *she*? Fine . . . ? Michael repeated himself. Susan couldn't seem to make her mind process the words. *Mary is fine. Mary is fine, though she sounded a little funny on the phone. You need to get home, Susan. You'll get there sooner than I can. I'm in the car now.*

*Mary is fine Maryisfinemaryisfine . . .*

But the words got stuck somewhere after *fine.* Mary?

"Why wouldn't Mary be fine?" She noticed the rectangle of dust, the inexact placement of the stapler, thought for a moment how the office had scaled back the cleaning crew. Budget cuts. The clients began to fidget, the woman checking her BlackBerry. A lawyer type in a dark blue suit and trench coat, her brown hair in a tidy ponytail at the base of her neck. Why did this woman want to live in Oak Park anyway? Wasn't she more the Gold Coast type? Susan knew the reason, though, even if this woman didn't: kids. The couple were testing out the most urban of suburbs, seeing if it fit, seeing if it was a haven to raise your kids and walk your dogs and cultivate your garden. Susan herself had chosen to raise her kids here, one of whom was at this moment *fine.* Which is another way of reminding one of luck and chance.

Then she finally heard Michael. "She was *home*, Susan."

Susan looked down at her desk at the three-cat clause in front of her. The air felt thinner suddenly, as if her office were lifting, hurtling toward deep space. "Mary was home?"

"Jesus, *hello!* This is what I've been telling you."

"Home? During the robbery?"

"She's fine. The police are there now, but you need to get home, Susan."

She began to feel her daughter's presence underneath her own skin. Why had Mary Elizabeth been home? Was she ill? How close had she come to . . . ? No, this was not the place to go. If Susan allowed herself, she could picture all kinds of grim scenes for her daughter, and her stomach would fill with dark, gnashing fear. When Mary had been a baby, Susan had a recurring dream about the two of them swimming in a pool, and as they swam, the pool got deeper and deeper, falling away from their feet until they were treading water. Only they didn't notice. They were laughing and splashing, weightless and graceful, and then Mary said she wanted to show her mommy how she could hold her breath, how she could go under, and Susan laughed and nodded and watched her daughter bounce up once, take her lungs full of air, and disappear underneath the surface. Susan kept laughing, and waiting, and in a few seconds she, too, went underwater and watched her daughter's tiny legs as she was sucked into an enormous vent far away on the side of the pool, and when Susan began to swim toward it, the hole of the vent slowly began to shrink back to its normal size, the tiny feet of her daughter kicking furiously, disappearing to a place unreachable. Susan would wake, suddenly, in a cold sweat and have to go into Mary's room and make sure the little girl was still sleeping. And always, always, she was, sleeping peacefully, curls stuck to the pale skin of her forehead. But the image of those legs slowly receding, kicking furiously, the tiny feet in the crystalline water as they vanished—all the images stayed with Susan. As the years passed, she had forced her mind to stop when such grisly, terrifying scenarios filtered into her consciousness. Now though, this moment was like her dream, her daughter being taken away from her by forces too strong for Susan to fight, watching, her own call for help silenced. It didn't matter that Mary was fine. What mattered was how close she had come to *not* being fine.

The clients to Susan's left faded from her periphery; a single loud laugh from the break room melted into the background. She grabbed her purse to go. She thought she could feel her heart begin to work more quickly, to keep her conscious, yes, that's what hearts did, pushed the blood around your body when you weren't quite capable of keeping yourself upright.

Susan pictured Mary's bedroom, the posters of rock stars who were hidden behind $1,000 jeans and push-up bras, pink hair and thick lipstick and airbrushing, so unapologetically stylized. The unmade bed, the clothes spanning the entirety of the floor, one wall painted a dark purple that Mary had been threatening to paint black. She pictured sealing herself in the house with Mary. This was the great secret of parenthood. As the childless couple sitting beside her began to contemplate their next move, what they were really asking was "Where is the safest place I can raise my child? Where can we go to keep the world at bay?" Susan apologized to them. She had to leave. Parents knew the world offered no such place. Not here in Oak Park, not in Chicago, not in the state of Illinois, not anywhere across America or beyond. The world had a way of reaching that child. And Susan knew that the world had just reached hers.

She scanned the office for her boss, Evan. She would remember the sunlight streaming through the plate-glass window of their shared office space, the silk roses gathering dust in a thin vase on her coworker's desk, a tape dispenser shaped like a cow; she would remember the angry looks on the faces of the clients and how she wanted to slap them out of their selfishness, slap them into knowing—before they were quite ready—what vulnerability *really* felt like, slap them into recognition of their own safety; she would remember searching for her purse, her head darting around the desk, under the desk, atop the desk, until she realized she'd been looking at it the whole time. She would remember thinking just how far a single mile felt, as if gravity had suddenly become something other, something to fling her away, rather then keep her on the ground. How close? How close had Mary come?

# Chapter 2

---

## 2:10–5:00 p.m.

During the burglaries, Mary had been cutting class with her neighbor Sofia. They were high on ecstasy they'd gotten from a fellow cheerleader named Chelsea. ("Why do you think I'm always fucking smiling?" she'd said, handing them a tiny baggie in a school bathroom that smelled like matches and face powder.)

Mary and Sofia lay on a faux Oriental rug under the McPhersons' dining-room table, holding hands, letting the drug flood them with warmth and softness, wondering aloud why the underside of the table wasn't stained to match the top.

"Don't you think it's a rip-off?" Mary said. "To not stain the whole thing?"

"Who cares?" said Sofia (whose actual name was Sophea).

"I'm just saying." Mary lifted her hand, felt the bare wood with her fingertips. It was rough to the touch. "Adults are so stupid."

An intruder was in the study, tugging a Dell laptop into a cloth gym bag, or maybe it was a pillowcase, snatched from the house next door. While Mary crawled under the table, listening to Coldplay and Aerosmith, the intruder slung Mr. McPherson's iPod into a pocket. The stranger wore Nike Air Max gym shoes (size ten, pebble dash soles). That's all they knew for certain. He swiped Susan McPherson's silver platter off a bookshelf. Mary Elizabeth rolled around in the other room, giggling, beneath the table, completely unaware. Her vision had tinted fuchsia. As she reached for the hand of her sometimes friend Sofia-but-really-Sophea, the intruder snatched Mary's father's engraved Parker pen set (black ink, roller ball tip). No reason to take this except that it could be taken. Computers, iPods, electronics. These had monetary value. Engraved Parker pen sets? That was pure malice.

Little shits, Mary would say to her neighbor Arthur Gardenia later, and he would laugh because he didn't mind her swearing, even though he was old and she was young. *The little shits even took my dad's pen set.* They'd also taken a gold-plated paperweight globe, Michael's brushed-pewter pen/laser printer/flashlight from Brookstone (he was prone, consumeristically speaking, to combo packages), and one collection of silver-dollar coins kept in a ceramic, green bank shaped like a dollar sign. In the garage, two baseball mitts and a baseball, an electric drill, and a bag of beach toys.

They had not noticed anything amiss at first. And they hadn't heard a thing. Thirst drove Mary from under the dining-room table, where they'd been lying for a half hour. Sofia, curled up and giggling, waited for Mary to return with their Diet Cokes. A warmth rose up from Mary's belly and radiated down to her fingertips, everything in soft focus, wrapped in silk. She didn't walk, she danced, she floated, she *sashayed.* Suddenly she was aware of her beauty. *Stunning,* she thought. *I am absolutely stunning.*

She saw the police car outside Arthur's house and the warmth ebbed. Were they looking for her? Had someone from school narced on her and Sofia? Were the police now simply going door-to-door to find kids who skipped school? Was there some new underground truancy unit?

"Sofia," Mary hissed. "Get over here. Sofia!"

"Okay, love," Sofia sang.

Mary shushed her, though something in her brain managed to confirm there was no way the police could actually hear them. Instinctively they hunched beneath the window.

Sofia gasped, suddenly sobered up.

"I know! WTF!" Mary said. "What do we do?"

The girls spotted two police emerging from Arthur's. One walked next door to where the Francophile chef lived, while the other headed in the exact direction of Mary's front door. Neither girl knew, yet, that it was standard procedure for police to check with neighbors in the immediate aftermath of a home invasion. Once the police established that the McPherson home and the Lenoir home had also been targeted, they wouldn't take long to widen their search area, to cordon off the whole of Ilios Lane, to see that the Rutherford home had been targeted, and the Kowalskis and the Oums and Coens and Pappalardos, one after another after another in lightning succession. But in this moment, Mary was sure these serious-looking police officers making their way toward her home at a jog had been called in by the Oak Park River Forest High School to track down two truants. Sofia cried out and bolted for the back door, leaving Mary standing alone, holding two Diet Cokes. She didn't know whether to wait and answer the door, to run, to ignore it, or to stand stock-still. So she did what any unthinking, terrified teenager might do: grandly attempted to reverse course. Carrying the Cokes, she dashed back to the dining room and, under the table, lay with her arms splayed out sacrificially, breathing like a trapped gazelle.

Then the doorbell rang.

Over the next couple of hours, the police found shoe prints: the Nike Air Max with a pebble dash bottom. Size ten. The prints were twenty feet from where Mary had lain, a radio in the kitchen still turned to 97.9 The Loop. The items taken were only surface things. Things that lay atop shelves and desks. No drawers, no closets, nothing that opened.

He, she, they, those . . . Mary didn't know how to grammatically refer to them—*those* people had robbed the house next to hers, and next door to them, and across the street from her, and next door to him, and next door again, and again, and again. Eight homes in total. The whole of Ilios Lane. Those people would wander across the world, skittering, careening is how Mary imagined them, those people would offer no penitence, no remorse that she would ever see. It didn't matter that crime was down if fear was high. And Mary would learn, not right then, but soon, how one meanness can spur another.

"A crime of opportunity," one detective told her after he'd arrived at the scene.

*What crime isn't a crime of opportunity?* she wanted to ask.

The police asked her what she remembered, and she laughed. She was still rolling hard on ecstasy. What did she remember? She remembered thinking, as she lay beneath the table, how odd it seemed that something as warm as the sun was yellow. Such a thin color, yellow. So layerless. Fuchsia would have been a much better color choice for the sun. Sunsets were God's indecision, Mary had thought. Her mind had then skipped along a series of randomly connected thoughts: She didn't really know if she believed in God. Maybe, Darwin screwed up. But Darwin didn't create the sun. Who did, though? This clover of thoughts had made her laugh so hard tears had rolled down her face, her temples, and disappeared into the Oriental rug, into her crispy hair as she sometimes called it, and her cheeks had started to hurt. Not because there was anything humorous at all in those disjointed meanderings, but because the questions only led to more and more and more questions, and so the asking of the one felt as endlessly futile and frustrating as utter silence itself.

But she knew enough not to tell this part of the story. She stopped at fuchsia. If the world could be calculated mathematically as Mary's algebra teacher always insisted, what was the equation for colors? Darwin would know. What had Darwin looked like with a smile? she wondered. She only remembered pictures of him stern-faced and serious, like that soccer player's wife from England, who always looked to Mary like a cardboard cutout. Thin, sharp-angled, speechless, smileless. No one smiled in pictures from Darwin's time. Not like now, when people smiled all the time, smiled even when they didn't feel like smiling. She noticed this about Sofia's mom, who was Cambodian and didn't speak English, but still she smiled so much she appeared simple. It unsettled Mary. Made her consciously not smile back, which seemed the wrong response.

So many police milled around Mary's house she couldn't count them all. One man in gloves spread white powder everywhere searching for more prints. An enormous gray toolbox sat outside the door to the basement. Mary and her mom were stationed in the dining room, at the table, told not to disturb the "ongoing investigation." Mary imagined herself melding into the chair, starving, dehydrating, while a funnel-shaped investigation raged around her. She imagined the detective returning the next day to find her still there, waiting for her dismissal.

She expected her mother to cry. Not because Susan McPherson was prone to tears, necessarily, but because this seemed like the kind of thing that might elicit the waterworks, and indeed Susan had rushed in the door red-rimmed and hysterical. She sprinted toward Mary and threw her arms around her in a kind of suffocating, boa-constrictor way.

"Um. Mom? You're cracking again." (Which was Mary's code for "crying." As a toddler, she'd once looked at the blood vessels in the whites of her mother's eyes and declared them "cracks." Tears, logically, were simply the cracks leaking. Over the years, *cracking* had become a kind of familial shorthand.) Susan kept grabbing at Mary Elizabeth, wiping at her cheek, putting one arm over her shoulder, just *looking* at her over and over as if they were long-lost relations separated by the ravages of war and time. Someone turned off the radio. Susan reached over and touched Mary's hair, pushed it back from her face.

"Mom. Please!" Mary shrugged away.

Susan had always loved her daughter's hair, the thick mass of it. "Strong as Samson," she used to tell Mary as a child. "That hair makes you *unbreakable*, sweetheart." Mary had believed it far longer than she should have.

Detective Wasserman interrupted, bent over Mary as if she were hard of hearing. "You just never know how a small thing can be the very thing we need for our big puzzle here."

A puzzle metaphor. Did he think Mary was an idiot? Did he think she was nine?

She shook her head. The color was still there a little, framing her peripheral vision. A fuchsia mist melted around her mother's worried gaze. Mary saw her mother hold her face in her hands for a moment too long, rub her eyes and grimace for a fraction of a second, washing away an unwanted thought.

Mary's father appeared in the doorway, trench coat slung over his arm, tie loosened, cell phone in hand. "I called State Farm," he announced in a general directive, as if this were the paramount task that needed to be tackled in that moment. He hugged Susan, and then Mary, but then followed the sound of the detective's voice to the kitchen. Mary heard the footsteps of the investigating police everywhere, clomping on the hardwood. It sounded like ten men, a dozen, two dozen. It sounded like a house party of footsteps. She wanted to go and watch them.

Her father came back into the dining room and asked Mary, "What did you do?"

"Nothing."

"Nothing?"

"Nothing." *(Popped E and rolled around under the dining-room table.)*

"Why were you here, honey? At home?" asked Susan, reaching again for her daughter, then stopping short of a touch, catching herself and retreating.

"Why?"

"Why weren't you in school?"

That's when it escaped. A bubble of air rising to the surface. A kind of hiccup. A giggle. A gigcup, you might say. Things had been just fine until then. But there it was, unmistakable. It would come to be a great regret. Proof of an inability to control her own body—what came out, what went in. The gigcup had been a result of Mary's flummoxed mind, and in moments it would dawn on the McPherson parents.

"Mary Elizabeth McPherson, what did you see?" Michael McPherson glared down at her with angry, parental eyes.

A shrug. "Fuchsia."

Detective Wasserman put his hand on Michael's shoulder, compelling him to sit down. Michael reluctantly sat.

An officer peeked his head into the dining room. "Corey in here?"

Detective Wasserman shook his head. The officer disappeared.

"Fuchsia what?" Susan McPherson asked. She appeared to believe this was a clue, something they should perhaps tell Detective Wasserman.

"Just fuchsia."

"Mrs. McPherson," the detective said, "please let us finish up here, and then you can ask her anything you want."

"What do you mean? What does that mean? Were they wearing fuchsia?"

Mr. McPherson's home office and the garage appeared to be the only rooms disturbed in the house. "It's possible that the perpetrators were startled by Mary's presence and fled," said Wasserman. Mary had seen nothing, sensed nothing. It didn't help that her dad's office was separated from the dining room by both the kitchen *and* the living room. With the radio on, it hardly seemed surprising that Mary had nothing to offer the police.

The evidence technician dropped his brush and it clattered across the wood floor.

Mary Elizabeth put her forehead on the table.

"Are you all right?" Susan put her hand on Mary's thigh. (Mary remembered Susan telling her once that a mother knows the answer to this question before she ever asks. But a mother always asks anyway.)

Michael McPherson was surveying the room. Nothing had been taken. Wasserman told them dining rooms weren't big targets, not like a few decades back when there was a market for secondhand silver and crystal. Now heirlooms were practically worthless. Brides these days wanted exotic vacations, kayaks, pink Cuisinarts. Thieves wanted iPods.

"Where were you exactly?" Detective Wasserman asked.

"Here," Mary said, tossing her hand vaguely toward the floor, nodding once at the space under the table. Her voice was thin, as if her vocal cords had temporarily walked out on her.

"Where?"

"Here. Right here."

Two chairs, pulled out slightly. The minute he'd walked in, Michael *knew* there'd been something off about the room. So subtle. But he noticed these things. Once, as an undergraduate, he and some friends had moved every piece of furniture by a single inch in his roommate's bedroom. The roommate never guessed what they'd done. He knew something was wrong—he'd banged his knee on the bed frame when he came in—but he never knew what it was. All semester long it irked him, until he eventually grew used to the difference and the difference became the habitual. One single inch. Could change nothing. Could change everything.

Michael followed Mary's pointed finger to the floor. His mind calculated:

*On the floor.*
*Under the table.*
*Feeling fuchsia.*
*Not in school.*

"Jesus Christ, Mary," Michael McPherson said. Now fully aware. And pissed off.

# Chapter 3

___

## 1:58 p.m.

Arthur Gardenia had been the first to call the police. He'd heard noises but was too terrified to go downstairs and actually *find* something.

"The police are going to come right in," warned the dispatcher. "Stay right where you are, sir."

He stood behind his desk. Not breathing, pressing his heels together as if the action might diminish him in some way.

The police swarmed Arthur's house in a small army, lights flashing, stationing themselves in both the street and the back alley. Arthur could hear snippets of words through their radio static. *Canine . . . burglary one . . . Detective . . . in progress.* They yelled up to ask if he was okay, told him not to move, not to touch anything, to wait for their all clear. He heard the clunk of heavy gear, jiggling metal, and a single hard pounding as if something had been dropped. One set of feet bounded up the stairs.

"In here," Arthur said.

Detective Wasserman followed the sound of Arthur's voice to the study. He came in the door and flipped on the light switch. Arthur gasped at the sudden burst of fluorescence and covered his eyes, and the detective drew his gun and squatted. Three or four confused seconds elasticized the two men, until Arthur waved one arm toward the detective saying, "Turn it off. Turn it off. The light."

The detective turned off the light and adjusted his eyes to the darkness, and Arthur quickly told him he had day blindness, and both men began to breathe again.

"Wasserman," the detective said by way of a more appropriate introduction. He took a single stride toward Arthur, holding out his hand, gun still drawn in the other, and he swiped his forehead with the back of his hand so that the gun arced through the air. Arthur did not think to shake the detective's hand until the gun was back in its holster.

The police cleared one room at a time, checking closets and under furniture. They sounded like a whole platoon. Wasserman sat Arthur down in his study to take the report once the premises had been checked. Arthur had not yet established those things missing from his house and he had not witnessed any perpetrators, despite feeling nearly sure he'd heard *something*. Wasserman advised Arthur to buy curtains for his downstairs windows. *Invest* was the word he'd used. Arthur might want to think about *investing* in a set of curtains, as if a dividend might be available on such a purchase. Arthur had lived without curtains for so long, lived without the ability to see past a reflection for so many years, that he'd forgotten—or else never considered—that his personal security might have been jeopardized by that one angry, fiery afternoon when he'd burned them all in a fit. Occasionally, he had to remind himself that while he could not see well, most people could see him just fine.

The police downstairs were loud, shouting to one another over their radios and their own lumbering movements. The lights in the hallway were dimmed low. Detective Wasserman wore a light cotton golf shirt with a blazer. Arthur thought detectives were required to wear ties.

"What I'm offering," said Arthur to the circling detective, "is simply that the pumping of several arms through the air might suggest a professional outfit. Organization."

Detective Wasserman stopped. "It might, Mr. Gardenia."

Was Arthur being patronized? Who was this small man? He wasn't even wearing a tie.

Arthur was fairly sure of what he'd heard, and the noises had alarmed him, but he *had* been listening to the radio at the same time. Maybe there'd been no sound at all, just disturbed air, the sensing of a presence other than his own. Live alone for long enough and you get to know just how much oxygen one small person can take up. He'd been in his study, in an oversize rocking chair, eyes closed, bookshelf blocking any possible light from the window, listening. His back door was propped open to let in some fresh spring air. He had a fence around his yard and took for granted his isolation. He listened as he always had, headphones on, but with one side pushed back, behind his ear, so that the outside world wasn't gone, exactly, but muffled. He knew the radio schedule by heart. He woke at noon with *Worldview*, then took a break for breakfast, and started up again with *Fresh Air* and then *All Things Considered*, and if he hadn't tired out, he stayed around for *Marketplace*. It whittled away the time, gave his days a kind of shape and heft. But it also offered him a vast array of dialects and speech blueprints, which he sometimes wrote out using the linguistic pattern he'd developed over the years. Arthur believed that the way people spoke was as individual as a fingerprint. There were subtle differences, the hiss of an *s*. The softness of an *f*. A jarring *ch*. He'd noticed some years ago that so few Americans used the letter *t* when it came in the middle of a word.

He'd heard *something*, though he could not identify what that something had been. He had no physical recourse against an intruder, against a threat of any kind, really. What could he do? Wave an angry bat toward a blur? Once he may have been able to fend off an intruder, when he was young, in his early thirties, just a few years after he'd finished his PhD. That was before the colors of the world had begun to fade, reds to pinks, pinks to grays, oranges and reds, purples and blues, blues and greens, all melting, washing into one another until they were a mass of nothing. Palimpsests of color, indiscernible as layers.

"It seems like it might be difficult to hear an arm pumping through air with headphones on," Detective Wasserman said. Arthur didn't tell him that he listened only through one side. He'd always done it, he reasoned, as a *precautionary* measure, a way not to be fully absent from the world. The irony was not lost on Arthur.

The point of entry had been Arthur's back screen door, wedged open with what Detective Wasserman suspected had been a screwdriver. Screwdrivers were the weapon of choice for break-ins.

"It was Terry Gross," Arthur said. "On the radio."

He imagined the way she spoke in reconfigured language and punctuation. Sometimes she'd throw two or three words together so they sounded like one. *Terrygross*, for example. Arthur believed personal dialects and idiosyncrasies and idioms were reflected in our letters and e-mails, and he aimed to capture it, the individual language of every person on earth.

"I'm Quite Sure I hearD twothreemaybemore arms. I'm guessinghere. At the arms. Twothreearms in The Air. Pumping intheair."

Arthur both said *and* envisioned these phrases. He peered at the detective's thick, wiry hair. The man had pockmarks on his nose, thin lips, and high cheekbones, but mostly what Arthur saw was an indistinct blur.

By the age of thirty-five, Arthur had gone entirely color-blind. So he gave up driving. Then he noticed the headaches, the eye aches. They came more often in summer, when the sun was high and bright, a phosphorescent light spearing his eyes. On winter days the sun glinted off the snow, casting shards of glassy light into his pupils. Sometimes those days were so bad he'd stumble into bed and stay there all day. During the school year, he began going to his office early and staying late; he never turned on the lights. He used overhead projectors in darkened classrooms and wrote in large letters on transparencies.

The doctor told him he had cone dystrophy; *self-destruct* was the term Arthur remembered. His foveal cones, responsible for day vision, for fine detail, for color—for so much of the world—were *self-destructing*. Such drama happening in silence discomfited Arthur. He slept, he walked, he worked, and all along he had this terrible feeling of unconscionable physical theft. How, Arthur wondered, had such imbalances begun?

He was officially diagnosed with hemeralopia. It was rare in American adults, rare among those not nutritionally or genetically predisposed to such a condition. So he had, at first, hoped that the color could be restored to him somehow. That he could take some pill, some vitamin, some exercises, that might restore his vision. The ophthalmologist gave him photo-chromatic glasses, which darkened in bright light, and told him to make sure he got Vitamin A.

The doctor suggested Arthur carry a portable magnifying glass and a clip-on polarizer filter to wear over his glasses. Instead, Arthur went numb. In rebellion against what he believed was his physical doom, he tore down the curtains on the first floor of his house and burned them in his fireplace. The fire made him squint. Pride had kept him from replacing the curtains, and eventually he took to living mostly upstairs. He took a leave of absence from his tenured position at the College of DuPage, where he'd spent seven years teaching eighteen- and nineteen-year-olds, who couldn't have cared less, how to diagram sentences. He refused to get large-print books. He tried to go on afternoon walks, but he could barely open his eyes; he had begun to blink, on average, four times a second, and eventually the pain was too great and he simply went to bed in a darkened bedroom for one entire summer. He was thirty-eight years old. Unmarried. Just tenured. And pissed off.

One late-August afternoon, lying on his unwashed sheets, he began to hear the far-off voices of young teenagers returning from a day at the public pool. As their voices grew closer, he began to distinguish them not only by pitch and audibility, but diction, by the way they said certain words and phrases. By the emphasis of letters and how some words ran together and others seemed separated by more than a mere breathy pause. (Angela, *cudid* OUt! YOU cuDID out!) Arthur sat up in bed and listened. He began to wait for these kids each day, to listen for them, with a notebook beside him. He never saw the faces of the children, but their voices became as familiar to him as his own mother's had once been. He listened for the rhythmic properties, the frequency and pitch, and tried to create a visual analog, a sort of written language, for the sound of a voice. The girl, Angela, seemed to front-load her sentences, emphasize the beginnings and then trail off. Her friend—Linda was it?

Lynn? She spoke more quietly, but rose in tone the longer she went on, as if gaining confidence at the sound of her own voice. John ran his words together and had staccato phrasing, sometimes separating a two-syllable word with as much time as wholly separate words. Arthur ignored how words were spelled and instead wrote how they sounded, not phonetically so much as rhythmically. He realized, one day, that maybe this could be his purpose, maybe hearing the world in a whole new way would someday justify going blind. He brought his ideas to the dean and she was supportive. The college gave Arthur disability pay and a small pension to continue his "research," and he never taught another class again. He learned he was also eligible for more disability pay from the federal government, and for Medicaid, and so, before the age of forty, Arthur found himself semiretired and spending his days listening to the voices of the world around him. That was twenty years ago. He'd managed to publish one small and not particularly well-received textbook—really just a vanity project—on his research. He called it, unsurprisingly, *The Music of Language*.

Now, the police milled around in Arthur's house, and Detective Wasserman took Arthur by the elbow to lead him downstairs. Arthur needed his glasses. The light was sharp, stinging his eyes. He was so rarely on the first floor of his home in the afternoons. He had hired Mary McPherson, his teenage neighbor, to clean once a week, but her cleaning afternoons had turned into reading sessions—she was unwittingly receiving a literary education as Arthur enjoyed the sheer pleasures of language and story. She'd read *The Invisible Man* and *Encounters with the Archdruid*, and he'd gotten her to start *Anna Karenina*, though after the first three days she'd put her foot down at that one and they hadn't cracked a Russian since. The downside of this arrangement, of course, was his continued existence in filth.

"Terry Gross was speaking with Oliver Sacks," Arthur said to Detective Wasserman. "On her show." Arthur squinted, blinked repeatedly. He saw flashes of dark uniforms like apparitions. "Her guest. The neurologist. The famous neurologist." He pictured the pattern in his mind: herGuest. (the)neurologist, The famous NEU-rologist.

He overheard one officer say to a second, "These kinds leave shit for evidence."

Arthur held a blank form given to him by Detective Wasserman.

"It's called a supplementary property list," Wasserman had told him. "You'll need to fill out what's missing and bring it by the station."

"You really need to keep those doors closed and locked," one policeman said. "It's an invitation. I'm not blaming you. The victim. Sir. But really. You've got to keep your doors locked."

At the back door, the evidence technician was dusting for prints. He held up a gloved hand to stop them from coming too near. The powder floated around the room, settling on every possible surface. Wasserman warned him that the dust practically turned the floor into an ice rink.

"What are the chances here?" Arthur said. "The chances for me . . . for my . . ." He felt a hand on his shoulder and fought the urge to brush it away. Part of him did not want to catalog the stolen items, as if the not knowing somehow postponed the loss. He wouldn't care about the handheld voice recorder, once he realized it was gone, or the music CDs, or even the electronic photo album his sister had made for him one Christmas in a misguided attempt to secure their childhoods in his visual memory. He'd wonder at the half-full bottles of liquor that were swiped, and at the first-generation answering machine that was no longer on his counter, where it had lain dormant for years. But it would be his notebooks that would shatter him, the loss of years and years and years of work, one man's attempt to slow down his own crushing erosion.

"We'll do all we can," Wasserman said. "We'll check the pawnshops, run the prints. But I'll be honest with you here, Mr. . . ." He struggled to remember the name, trailed off for a minute. "Mr. Gardenia. These are tough cases," Wasserman said, his voice confident again. "Tough cases. Guys get in and out pretty quick. Something like this . . . quiet, easy entry. No locked—and I'm not blaming you, I'm just saying—no locked doors. It's tough."

The policeman coughed. "Sir, we've got another hit. Right across the street."

# Chapter 4

---

## 4:00 p.m.

The Kowalskis were on vacation in the Florida Keys. Their dog, Chester, was on vacation at Dan Kowalski's in-laws' house—George and Arlene Dixon's—in Naperville. Both canine and couple ate well on their respective vacations.

# Chapter 5

——

## 4:15 p.m.

Sary smiled, nodded, wadded tissues. She sat on an embroidered pad atop a wooden chair. Lilacs with a tea-stained background. Her husband, Dara, stood behind her, his hand on her shoulder, trying to comfort her, as if they were posing for a portrait. He had the voice and confidence of a prepubescent boy, it seemed. Something about it all was unsettling.

"My daughter. My daughter. *Kone srai,*" Dara said. "I, little little English." He held his finger and thumb in the air two inches apart, the universal sign for small. Insubstantial. He knew tiny, tiny English. "My daughter, Sophea."

Sophea was hiding in the sunlight, by the untidy boxwood shrubs. She was still high on ecstasy. Torn between helping her parents navigate the linguistic terrain, as was her duty, and keeping the secret of where she'd been and what she'd been doing. It was never easy to watch your parents suffer. She couldn't be her parents' translator in this moment, not for the police.

Sophea had always been the conduit between her parents' lives in Cambodia and their lives in the United States, and she wondered how they'd ever survive without her. Once, when Sophea was still in elementary school, she and her mother had been rear-ended in Sary's Toyota Camry by a young man driving a rusted-out Gremlin. Sary had briefly inspected the damage—lots of scratches and one largish dent—then waved the young man away. Wasn't that what was meant by *accident*? The other driver knew the law, knew he was getting lucky, and quickly sped away before Sary—through Sophea—changed her mind. What was the point of laying blame, Sophea's parents had said to her later. No one was hurt. Why did it matter to make sure someone was at fault? Wasn't the lesser of the two the victim? they wondered. Richer should pay poorer. That was the way it worked in Cambodia most of the time. Blame was rarely the center of the debate, particularly when all parties tended to agree that it was an *accident*. Didn't the very word offer amnesty?

"Just tell us what's gone. What's missing?" Detective Wasserman asked.

Dara shook his head. "I don't know."

"You don't know what's missing?"

"My daughter."

"Your daughter is missing?"

Nervous laughter.

"You're laughing?"

But Dara didn't understand the conjugated word. He knew *laugh*. He knew *smile* and *loud*. He did not know *laughing*, *laughter*, *laughed*, *chuckle*, *grin*, *howl*, *cackle*, *shriek*, *giggle*, *chortle*, or *guffaw*. He knew only that a man of authority was standing in his living room, so he stooped a fraction lower. The policeman's little, white notebook had just a few notations. Another policeman milled about their kitchen, looking at their back door and into the enclosed back deck. Sophea squeezed herself smaller behind the boxwoods. A translator, who'd been called in by the first responding officer, stood by the detectives, admiring a nylon cushion of the Hello Kitty variety on the unpadded sofa. The translator was Chinese. Dara and Sary were Cambodian.

"Did someone take the other cushions?" Wasserman pointed with his pen, clicking the spring in and out.

Dara was confused. He followed the point of the pen to the couch. Did he want Dara to sit on the sofa? Did the man himself want to sit on the sofa?

"The cushion. Padding. Pillows. You understand? Only wood here. Was the padding stolen?" Wasserman spoke slowly.

"Who the hell would steal cushions?" growled a policeman from inside the kitchen.

"Same kind of asshole who'd steal half a bottle of liquor," Wasserman snapped.

Dara took a half step toward the couch. He was being ordered to sit on it, perhaps. That seemed so. Maybe he didn't like Dara standing behind Sary. Maybe Dara should show more respect for his authority, sit while the man stood. Then, confusingly, the man pointed to the television. Dara knew he'd misunderstood.

"You see? TV on floor, okay. So what's gone?" Outside, Wasserman could hear vehicles pulling up, voices. He recognized the din. The press had arrived.

"We.

"Need.

"To.

"Know.

"What.

"Is.

"Gone."

Dara understood *TV, floor, see*. Should he sit on the floor? Turn on the TV? He often sat on the floor. He recognized the peculiar tone Americans took when they realized they weren't being understood, separating words slowly, carefully, into linguistic pileups. It happened at work every day. Dara was ashamed of his lack of English after all these years. He believed himself too old to learn, and his daughter's fluency had made it easy for Sary and him to avoid taking the time to study. Dara's eyes followed the silver-blue point of the pen from the wooden, nearly cushionless sofa to the television sitting on the floor, and then around the room. There was the chair holding Sary. A picture of their wedding on the white wall, a portrait, Sary beautiful with white skin in red, fine silk, a patterned orange sash going from her shoulder diagonally across her chest. Beside it a picture of Sophea from her first year in American high school, a dynamic blue background with white streaks as if she herself were a grand announcement. Sophea, now an American named Sofia. So. Pee. Ah. She had tried to explain to her parents, it was embarrassing, the kids laughing at her. "So go pee ah, So Pee Ah," they taunted. Her teacher, that first year, gently suggested the slight alteration.

"We've got to get another translator in here," Wasserman said. "Call down there, see if they found someone."

Sofia, hiding in the boxwoods near the far corner of the house, listening through the screen door, picked up a twig and began to scratch at the surface of the caked dirt. She traced her own name, then wondered how many thousands of grains of soil she'd displaced, how long it would stay. The ecstasy was wearing off. *We are Cambodian*, she thought. *Not Chinese. Fucking Cambodian!*

"I think his daughter's missing," Wasserman said, and took the picture of Sofia down from the wall. A bland square showed on the wall underneath. Sary blushed, ashamed of the filth they'd allowed to build up. She stood up. She'd planned to go get a damp cloth and clean the wall before he put Sophea's picture back. But the men were moving toward the door, holding the picture. Had they forgotten it? Did they want the picture? She began to panic. She made a noise like *suh* and pointed to the picture with a worried look on her face.

"Yes, ma'am. I know. Don't worry. We're going to find her."

Sary responded in Khmer. "Where are you going with my daughter's picture? If you wait a few minutes, she'll be here to translate."

She and Dara thought they had escaped this kind of chaos when they left Cambodia. They never guessed that more *bad* lay ahead when so much *bad* had already happened to them. Sary knew, though, that even then, with American police milling all around, lights flashing, people yelling, it could never be as bad as what they'd already lived through.

Dara took out his cell phone to call Sophea. He thought she was at cheerleading practice.

In the boxwoods, squatting in the dirt, her cell started to ring, and Sofia felt her heart drop. Confusion bloomed on her parents' faces as they turned and looked out their back screen door, in the direction of their daughter's ringing phone.

# Chapter 6

——

## 5:17 p.m.

When the detectives knocked on the back door of Étienne's restaurant, Frite, he knew exactly why they were there. He'd intended to call them in four days. Just four more days. Long enough to have returned from a vacation that he never actually took. He'd already cataloged what was missing from his house: a leaded-crystal vase from the middle of his white, Louis XIV–style coffee table. The vase had had a note card inside of it for his weekly cleaning service: NO WATER! NO FLOWERS! The vase was gone. Also missing: one set of Bosch speakers; a Tissot watch from his bedside table; a music box—baroque, of course, which played "La Vie en Rose"; a bouquet of lavender made from blown glass from which several purple-bud and green-leaf shards littered the doorway and the backyard grass; his television; and his collection of European travel DVDs (though, curiously, the DVD player itself had been unplugged from the television and left). His laser printer and fax machine were both gone, as was his backup hard drive (perhaps the first time he'd felt relieved over his laziness—he'd never bothered to use the thing). He was missing an eighteen-karat chain-link bracelet and a set of mother-of-pearl-and-gold-leaf coasters that had been sitting next to the vase.

The knocking was insistent, but not obtrusive. Étienne considered not answering, but his car was parked in the lot just behind the door, and the door was unlatched. He wore an old, gray T-shirt and a pair of jeans. He wished he'd taken the time to put on his chef's uniform and hat, but settled on his bib apron instead with the yellow stains down the front. Details mattered. His T-shirt was faded along the seams, and tiny holes had begun to form across his shoulders like moth bites. He hadn't showered since the day before.

Étienne grinned, then swung the door open widely. "Yes! Yes! Do come in. Sorry. I was in the lockup and didn't hear you. The freezer! I mean, we call it a lockup. Ha-ha! I was going to call you, yes, I've been terribly busy."

The restaurant was dark. Closed. One pan on the stove held cooling caramelized shallots. Sliced mushrooms and chopped leaks sat on a carving block.

"You're aware of the burglaries, Mr. Lenoir." He pronounced it *Len-Or*.

"That's *Len-wa*."

"Mr. *Len-wa*," the detective said (did he have a hint of sarcasm? Étienne wasn't sure). "So, you're aware?"

Étienne rubbed his palms down the front of his apron and shook his head. "Terrible. Terrible. I can't imagine. We have such lovely neighbors."

"Do you suspect a neighbor?"

"Oh, certainly not. No. I just mean . . ." Étienne didn't know what he meant.

The man introduced himself as Detective Witkowski, his partner was Detective Dadek. "We work with Detective Wasserman, who's coordinating the investigation." Étienne recognized the Cicero accent. Nasal, and hard-voweled. Southside Chicago. Born and bred. He'd had it once himself.

"Experimenting," Étienne said of his presence in the kitchen with the restaurant closed. "Menu changes, you know. Playing around."

"I see. What's in the freezer?"

Étienne was suddenly aware that no frozen goods were apparent. He looked around the kitchen as if a bag of peas or hard fist of frozen duck breast might suddenly appear. He had nothing to hide, in the freezer nor out, yet suddenly he had the overwhelmingly absurd urge to keep them from looking in the freezer. As if, somehow, a body might unwittingly have ended up there, as if Étienne might be an accomplice to a dastardly crime about which he knew nothing.

"Veal," he said.

"So you're the owner here? Of Frite?" Witkowski used the long vowel. *Fright.*

"It's *freet*," Étienne said, nodding. "It means—"

Witkowski interrupted, "And you're the cook, too?"

"Chef. I'm the proprietor and the chef."

"Mrs. McPherson thought you were out of town."

"Yes. No. I'm not. Out of town. Ha-ha! Of course, as you can see."

"Paris, was it? I believe Mrs. . . . McPherson mentioned Paris."

Ah, Susan. She loved Paris, too, Étienne thought. "Indeed, I was supposed to go, but sadly had to cancel at the last minute."

"That's too bad. Springtime in Paris."

"Oh, yes, it certainly was. Paris in April."

"When was that?"

"When was what?"

"The cancellation. The trip."

"Oh. The cancellation. Of the trip." Étienne saw that his shallots were congealing. He'd have to start again. "A few weeks ago. I was so far behind on this year's menu change, I mean, you might think a menu change would benefit from my having gone!" He offered a single laugh. Étienne stopped suddenly. Was he rambling?

Overhead, the fluorescent light buzzed and Étienne could feel a thin layer of sweat on his forehead. The mild smell of old, hardened butter permeated the kitchen.

"I have a list of what's missing," Étienne said brightly. He reached into his pocket, unfolded it, and handed it to Dadek, who didn't so much as glance at it.

"We have you down as Edward Lenoir. Not Étienne. Is that right? Edward?"

Étienne didn't say anything. Here was the truth of it, he thought. Didn't we all have something to hide? Wasn't Edward his own secret? After all, he wasn't the one they were after. They had to know that.

"Yes," Étienne said finally. "It's Edward. My real name. But I prefer Étienne."

"Why is that? The preference? Edward."

Étienne reddened. "I just . . . do. The food . . . and every-thing . . ." His voice melted into the kitchen fan, melted down into his abdomen. It was one thing to be aware of the quiet shames in one's life, but quite another to have to own up to them publicly. He had learned from a pamphlet left behind on the el one day of the need to "brand" oneself in order to succeed in the modern age, and so the name change had merely seemed an extension of this exercise.

Étienne ran his hand over his hair, which thinned more every day; time surging at him in seconds, one tiny loss after another. His hand, unsurprisingly, came away with dozens of gray hairs. This loss, even this, was just another in an endless line. A particle of loss, invisible but open to measurement nonetheless. Suddenly the crystal tulip-bud vase, the one he'd never filled with flowers, meant much more to him than he'd realized; its sudden absence without his ever having used it for its intended purpose seemed inexpiably wasteful.

"Okay, Étienne, the *chef.*"

Dadek waved the paper. Étienne's list. "We'll look into this. Add it to the others, but you'll need to fill out a supplementary property list."

They made their way to the back door.

"And Edward," said Witkowski, "look around for that canceled-Paris-trip stuff . . . travel agent receipts, reservations, anything. Give us a call when you find it. We'll need to include it in our case files. Just a formality." He smiled.

Étienne nodded. Of course, he wouldn't find the paperwork they wanted—no receipts, no vouchers of cancellation, no lost deposits. There was nothing. There had never been Paris. And Étienne knew they knew it, too.

**Listserv: Oak Park Moms**

**Messages in This Digest (6 Messages)**

**Messages**

1. **VAL HALLAS spring CD sales events**
Posted by: "Val Camilletti" no_reply@yahoogroups.com Val
_Camilletti
Tues Apr 6, 2004 6:45 a.m. (CST)

Val Hallas wants to help celebrate the coming spring (we're
sure it'll come Oak Parkers! Just keep the faith!). Stock up on
CDs, albums, magazines and all things musical. Buy one CD,
get 20% off the 2nd and 50% off the third! Mix and match old
and new releases. This weekend, April 10th and 11th all day.
7231/2 South Boulevard, 708-524-1004.

**Reply to sender | Reply to group | Reply via web post |
Messages in this topic (1)**

2. **POLICE ALL OVER ILIOS LANE?????**
Posted by: "Deb_ST" deb_ST@yahoo.com Deb_ST
Tues Apr 6, 2004 3:45 p.m. (CST)

Anyone know what's happening on Ilios Lane? Just drove past
on Erie St and there's police everywhere! Cars, police tape, etc.
etc. Very scary! Please give info asap . . .

**Reply to sender | Reply to group | Reply via web post |
Messages in this topic (1)**

### 3. Help with finding upholsterer?
Posted by: "Ellen" elancaster7211@resourcesdev.org Ellen Lancaster
Tues Apr 6, 2004 5:10 p.m. (CST)

Anyone know a good upholsterer in the area that doesn't cost a fortune?

**Reply to sender | Reply to group | Reply via web post | Messages in this topic (1)**

### 4. Free train table and Legos
Posted by: "blabbingmums" blabbingmums11@hotmail.com blabbingmums
Tues Apr 6, 2004 5:20 p.m. (CST)

Our little one has outgrown the train table and complete set of starter Legos. Free to first one who gets in touch . . . very good condition. Contact for pics: 708-555-3275

**Reply to sender | Reply to group | Reply via web post | Messages in this topic (1)**

### 5. New kids dance cooperative in river forest
Posted by: "OPRFdance" info@oprfdance.com OPRFdance
Tues Apr 6, 2004 5:45 p.m. (CST)

Come join the fun in our brand new studio on Lake Street, just across from the Jewel. Open house this Saturday from 10 a.m.–5 p.m. Classes from toddler through teen! Jazz, gymnastics, ballet, movement, music and yoga. New schedule starts May 1. Drop off or stay and watch. Combination packages available. We'd love to see you! Check our website for discounts and news about new classes.
www.oprfdance.com
708-555-4227
info@oprfdance.com

**Reply to sender | Reply to group | Reply via web post |**
**Messages in this topic (1)**

**6. Mass robberies on Ilios Lane!!**
Posted by: "Stevenson/Blair" sbfamilyop@yahoo.com Robert
Stevenson
Tues Apr 6, 2004 6:30 p.m. (CST)

Not sure of the whole story, but apparently residents of
Ilios Lane have had a number of robberies this afternoon.
Mostly electronics taken . . . watching breaking news now on
television. Police chief is asking all to be on the lookout for
suspicious behavior, or dumped goods in alleyways, etc. seems
there aren't any leads yet, but just a reminder to keep doors
locked, and make sure alarm systems are up to date. No one
injured, but v. scary. Will post more as I learn more.
Robert Stevenson/Mandy Blair
Washington Blvd.

**Reply to sender | Reply to group | Reply via web post |**
**Messages in this topic (1)**

# Chapter 7

## 7:10 p.m.

T ruly, honestly, we are people who have a lot," Susan had told a reporter whose name and newspaper she could not remember. Was it the *Sun-Times*? The *Defender*? The *Tribune*? They all arrived at once, parking just beyond the yellow police tape that ran from her house all the way across the street to Arthur's. The whole of Ilios Lane blocked off. A makeshift press conference set up in the McPhersons' front yard, Detective Wasserman presiding, offering updates on the investigation: "At this time, we believe every home on the street to be affected. Eight in all. The investigation is ongoing; at this time there are no leads. Anyone with information leading to the arrest and prosecution . . ." It was the standard press release. He took no questions.

"To live here," Susan had said, speaking sometime after Wasserman as she stood beside her husband, Michael, "the place is special."

Oak Park. The spirit of the place electrified her. People such as Hemingway and Edgar Rice Burroughs had lived here. Frank Lloyd

Wright and the dancer Doris Batcheller Humphrey. The writer Carol Shields, the actors Bob Newhart and John Mahoney. Oak Park wasn't a *place* to live, it was a *way of life*. A COMMUNITY OF LIFE, so proclaimed a banner at her office.

Susan worked at the Oak Park Community Housing Office on the village's west side, across from the train tracks that split North and South Boulevard. She was officially titled an *escort*—a name that had never sat quite right with her. She wasn't merely showing people places to live, she was showing progressivism, tolerance, community in idealized form. She was showing that the present *could* right the ills of the past. If those she escorted could grow to love the village as she had, they'd stay. They'd put their kids in the respectable public school system here. They'd become community activists. Oak Park was not one of those molded, socially conservative suburbs awash in chain stores.

She kept her showings to the east side, the side that began with Austin Boulevard near the west side of Chicago. The *bad* side of Chicago, so many believed. The gang-dominated, drug-addled, violent (and, no one said it, but it was implied, black) side of Chicago. Austin Boulevard lay at the seam. Ilios Lane just three blocks west of the seam.

Susan McPherson spent her days convincing young, semi-urban white kids (she thought of anyone in his or her twenties as a kid) that Chicago's west side offered no threat to their potential idyll in Oak Park. How many times had she cited the statistics? How many times had she talked about the beautiful homes that lay east of Austin Boulevard? But inevitably, they'd have a friend of a friend who'd been mugged on Austin, or they'd heard the story of a carjacking from those Austin gangs. She constantly fought against fear and perception.

Back in the late sixties and early seventies, Oak Park became the site of a curious social experiment, an attempt to get whites and minorities—mostly blacks—to live together in harmony. Diversity Assurance, it was called. Oak Park's west side was predominantly white and affluent. The east side was populated by minorities. The village trustees devoted significant resources to encourage east-side integration, to get whites to move to these predominately black apartment buildings. Susan's own street, Ilios Lane, was another matter. One couldn't force homeownership, but devoting her working life to diversity in rental units, then returning home to her nearly homogenous cul-de-sac, had irked her for years. Back in the early twentieth century there had been no great visual separation between east Oak Park and west Chicago. Not like now, when flowers and plush green courtyards populated Oak Park's once-notorious east side, and just across the street, from Austin Boulevard east, trash and rusted iron gates announced the start of the city. Slowly, in the wake of the Great Depression, when people and banks and businesses were terrified, Chicago became one of hundreds of urban areas redlined, where mortgages weren't given to anyone wanting to live in neighborhoods—so read the literature Susan gave to her clients—"in decline," where Realtors and developers, block by block, created white flight by convincing them their neighborhoods were being overtaken by blacks. Insurers often rejected black residents seeking mortgage loans while community reinvestment funds dried up. And so the marginally poor, marginally black areas became poorer and blacker as the suburbs of Chicago, of Philadelphia, of Atlanta flourished.

Diversity Assurance was supposed to be one antidote for redlining and blockbusting. Indeed, the program, and others like it, had cleaned up Oak Park, solidified it with gardens, trash-free lawns, young urban professionals all over the east side. Susan McPherson guided would-be residents through all the beautiful vintage apartments the Austin Boulevard area had on offer. Susan sold her clients on the history of the buildings, architecture that had survived Chicago's race riots, a famous doorway where one of Al Capone's midlevel henchmen was found with a knife protruding from his rib cage. It was about creating a community even for renters, where you knew who lived next door, and in this way you all kept one another safe and happy and feeling as if you were part of something. The village of Oak Park gave landlords grants to renovate their east-side apartment buildings in the hopes of encouraging more whites to move there. They hired apartment managers to keep their buildings clean, their tenants happy, to encourage more diverse populations to take up residence. By the 1990s, whites had moved to the east side in droves, attracted by the area's beautiful brownstones and vintage apartments with their original woodwork, their claw-foot tubs, their leafy, oak-lined boulevards. It was a testament to cultural and racial diversity. The apartment managers *did hold* Sunday potluck brunches in the courtyards of their buildings where blacks and whites (sometimes, but not always) would share bratwurst and baked beans. They started recycling programs and community services. They built honor-system libraries and reading rooms in the basements of their buildings, filled mostly with romances and old medical textbooks. They planted collective herb gardens and swept their alleyways. And they introduced neighbors to neighbors, friends to friends. They looked out for each other. It wasn't an apartment, Susan always told her clients, it was a cause.

Still, pockets of problems remained, buildings such as the one where Caz lived on Madison and Austin, where muggings weren't infrequent, and a shooting several years back held the corner captive to old reputations. Susan knew more than most how old reputations lingered. Few of the young folks she escorted failed to mention the terrifying proximity of Chicago's west side. Half those who loved an apartment on the east side still ended up moving to Oak Park's west side. Or into parts of Chicago they *imagined* were safer, Lincoln Park, Bucktown, Wicker Park, Lakeview. But Susan McPherson liked to brag how demographers from all over the world came to study the magic formula of Oak Park. You'd find her name, she sometimes laughed, in academic papers from Denmark, Germany, France.

Then September 11 changed everything. Crime was still low, lower than it had ever been, but the statistics didn't reflect the mood of the people. When an Oak Park white man was beaten by three black teenagers who'd come over from the west side during the winter of 2002, the village board began to wonder if the Diversity Assurance program had run its course. Then a series of carjackings by blacks on the west side of Chicago hit the local press, and parts of the Diversity Assurance program were temporarily suspended pending further investigation. Another assault followed, this time by unknown assailants, though the rumor circulated that it was again, *of course*, another group of young, black men from the west side. People suddenly began to feel unsafe in Oak Park. Maybe Diversity Assurance had achieved all the success it ever would.

The white police chief, Brian Mazzoli, wrote several op-ed pieces for the *Oak Park Outlook* in which he decried the rumors of increased crime. He used statistics to prove that despite what anyone thought, crime was actually *down*. Significantly down from what it had been twenty years earlier. Carjackings had dropped by half since 1991, and muggings by two-thirds. The man beaten in the alleyway? That wasn't racially motivated; that was being in the wrong place at the wrong time. "When it comes to the matter of crime," wrote the police chief, "it is most often a matter of bad luck."

Susan McPherson did not mention the controversy to her clients. And Chief Mazzoli's numbers could not contain the angst of the village. The whole country had been attacked, and if trickle-down theories didn't work economically, they certainly worked sociologically, psychologically. Oak Park had caught the disease of the country at large, the post-9/11 pandemic that took over hearts, minds, logic, the reason and compassion of people who, just a day, a week, a month earlier believed themselves free from prejudice. Free from the thoughts of isolationism and insularity and separatism that quickly began to creep into their conversations. Fear took hold and stayed. How fragile it had all become. How untenable. What had taken a generation to build in Oak Park was slowly eroding in a few short years. The landlords pounded their fists in frustration, argued to the village trustees, to the office of village grants, to escorts such as Susan, that they had empty apartments in need of renovation, or renovated apartments in need of renters, that they could not survive without this system of buffers built into the grand experiment that was east Oak Park. In the post–September 11 world, you couldn't keep some people from believing that anyone not standing with you was against you.

So this was the mood by the spring of 2004, the canopy underneath which the mass burglary had transpired. Susan's unshakable belief in the *rightness* of her community seemed, finally, as if it might have been flawed. She didn't want to think that things like Diversity Assurance worked at first, maybe for a generation, but then humans became humans again, falling to their basest selves.

She wondered, in those first few hours after the burglaries, not so much about what was missing from where, not so much

about what she'd *really* lost, but about how she would rise tomorrow morning, walk into the dusty, aging offices of the Oak Park
Community Housing Office, and tell her fresh-faced clients, "Yes,
indeed. No better place than my Oak Park to rest your weary head.
Diversity is the way of the future!" But my street? My home? What
could she say if someone asked her? What might it mean to spend
all these years fighting for something that would only, in the end,
betray you?

Who, she feared someone might finally ask her, who are *your*
neighbors?

Because the truth was, she didn't really know.

# Chapter 8

## 6:23 p.m.

Sofia sat on her knees as she usually did when she spoke to her parents, not because of a desire to prostrate herself, so much as a lack of furniture in their living room. A lot happened on the floor: eating, talking, watching TV, homework, sometimes even sleeping. Her father had called her cousins to come over because he held a staunch belief in the collective. That one family member's tragedy was shared tragedy. After he was finished, he handed the phone to her and didn't need to tell her why. She made the call to the Oak Park police station to inform them that, indeed, she was not missing and arranged to collect her school picture at the front desk. She told the police that her cheerleading practice had run late. She could say anything, she knew, because her parents rarely grasped the context of any conversation. Yet, Sofia, for the most part, didn't lie, didn't fabricate stories. She often wondered why. The things she could get away with! She could have gotten money for fictitious school activities, as she suspected her cousins did. She could have stretched her curfew, redefined critical aspects of her life like other immigrant kids. Yet she did not.

She thought it had something to do with love and something to do with shame. Her entire life she'd watched her parents misunderstand and misinterpret the world around them, and she'd realized that this made her feel protective of them, made her like their parent. The result was a childhood spent shielding her parents from the world, which was ironic given all she knew they'd survived.

Sofia was born in Chicago, but her parents had grown up in Cambodia. Her father's brother, her uncle Nimith, had sponsored their immigration to the United States. Sofia loved her parents' stories from Cambodia, even the ones filled with violence or death or hunger or poverty. The distant relatives who'd died in the genocide—"Pol Pot Time," as her mother called it—even the uncle Sofia never knew who'd been killed on his bicycle delivering bales of lemongrass to the Boeung Kak Market. She especially loved their tales about nature and spirits and palm trees.

Most of the more graphic stories she'd heard came from her three older cousins. They spent their weekends together, lounging on Montrose or Edgewater Beach and eating fish amok on Argyle Street, swapping tales about their relatives.

"You know our grandmother was, like, *crazy*," her cousin Ken told her once.

"Don't say that, Ken," scolded his older brother, Sit.

"I'm just saying, she didn't die in the Pol Pot Time or anything. She died 'cause she was crazy."

"*Shut up, Ken.*"

Their two families met at a Vietnamese restaurant that day ("Not as good as Cambodian food," her mother declared, "but acceptable"), and the kids had a corner booth to themselves. Sofia didn't much care for fish amok—white fish in coconut milk steamed inside a banana leaf—but she loved the way it looked. And she loved coming to the city, to Argyle Street, which was more or less taken up by Vietnamese and Cambodians. The smell of noodle soup permeated the sidewalks, and everything from yellow candles to incense to Kaffir-lime leaves and dried jasmine buds was on offer. It was the closest her family got to home.

On the ride into the city, Sofia had noticed a row of fake palms with bright blue and pink and yellow leaves along the lakefront. The waxy plastic trees felt like an affront to her and made her suspicious of a place that believed if it couldn't have whatever it wanted when it wanted it, a facsimile was perfectly adequate in its stead.

"I just think Sophea should know about her grandma," Ken told Sit.

"What?" she'd asked. "Tell me what, Sit?" Sofia knew next to nothing about her grandmother.

Sit buried his face in a bowl of pho, slurping the noodles loudly enough to make the rest of them go silent. Sit's father glared at him from the next booth.

"Come on, Ken. Why was she crazy?" Sofia asked.

Sit glared at Ken, but didn't shush him this time when he began to talk.

Sofia's grandmother's husband disappeared at the height of the Cambodian genocide, as did her eldest daughter. That left her with two sons, Sofia's father and her uncle Nimith. One day, when she was walking to the creek behind their hut to wash laundry, she spotted a bloated figure in black pajamas. It was not unusual, bodies turning up. All her neighbors had stumbled upon bodies, tried to save themselves from the fates that befell others. The bodies were often not recognizable as bodies, Ken told Sofia. In the water, skin fell off like chunks of steamed fish. The bloated body in the creek had a large, darkened birthmark on the back of its neck. This mark, Ken said, stole Sofia's grandmother's mind.

"Who?" Sofia asked. "Tell me who it was."

"Oum Chhaya," Sit interjected, taking over the story from Ken. "Our father's elder sister."

She'd disappeared long ago, but her body had just washed ashore. Sofia's grandmother lost her mind after that. She began to mumble and wander the village. Once the Khmer Rouge had fallen, she shaved her head in the manner of widows and took to wearing white, the color of death. She slept little. She carried shards of glass in her sarong and would gum the smooth sides when she grew nervous.

When they heard of others making their way to the West, where they would receive food, shelter, and an education from church sponsors, they pulled together every bit of money they could and decided Nimith would be the best option. At seventeen, he could finish his education and make a living sooner. Then he'd send for Dara and their mother. Maybe the West could fix whatever had broken inside her.

Dara was fifteen when Nimith left him to care for their mother alone. He took an apprenticeship at a pharmacy and eventually learned enough to get a job at the bustling Pharmacy La Gare, the busiest and most reliable pharmacy in the city. As the years went on, Nimith would call or write and want to begin planning for his brother's eventual arrival with their mother. It would take money, and many years of filling out paperwork for immigration, and undergoing interviews. Dara put him off, not because he did not have fantasies of what life in America might possibly offer him, but because he could not imagine the logistics of life among foreigners with a mother who had, by then, become equally foreign to him. One life could maintain only enough mystery.

While Dara worked, his mother roamed the city, often spending nights in Hun Sen Park or along the riverfront. He'd find riel in her pockets, but knew she didn't beg. People simply assumed. When he'd find her, she was always compliant, always followed wherever he led her, mumbling to what he assumed was his dead elder sibling. But within a few weeks, she would wander out again, always toward the Sap River, which bisected the city. When Dara met Sary, a cashier in his pharmacy, and married her a year later, Nimith assumed his brother would never come.

One night Sofia's grandmother wandered off and didn't return. Dara hired people to search for her—two neighbors, and the son of one of his fellow pharmacists, and one off-duty policeman. Two months passed until a group of boys bathing in the river saw her body in the reeds, her mouth swollen, her gums and tongue torn to shreds.

Dara called his brother that night. "Okay, Nimith. I'll come now."

Dara never spoke about his mother, or much about Cambodia at all. But Sary would tell Sofia stories of the countryside. How ghosts lived in tall trees, but not palm trees. Palm trees were revered because they had no secrets, hid no bad spirits. Sary missed palm trees the most. The iridescent green of their fronds after a monsoon, how the raindrops looked like diamonds on the leaves. No green she'd found in America could compare. It was a color that made you believe.

"Believe in what?" Sofia had asked her.

"In anything. In gods and beauty. In a soul's peace," Sary had said.

It was one of the few times Sofia saw her mother being her mother. Her mother teaching her a little something about the world, because most of the time Sofia's mother found the world in which she now resided in constant need of explanation. Occasionally, Sofia recognized in herself a vague yearning for parents who were 100 percent parents. Parents who were the directors of her life, not the other way around.

So she lied to the world around her when she needed to—in this case, the police—but never to her parents. And now here they were, on the floor, the three of them sitting in a triangle, while Sofia tried to explain why she had skipped school with Mary Elizabeth. She knew one immediate consequence would be a complete and abrupt cutting of her ties with Mary Elizabeth, though they both were on the cheerleading squad and walked the same route to school and had study period together and shared a lunch period.

"Please," said her father, "please explain it once more."

Sofia was exasperated. Her parents had asked her to go over the concept of skipping school, and she had no real answer. As if, in the telling, she could build an acceptable framework for her misdeed.

"Lots of kids do it," she said. "Skip school from time to time. It's just . . . you know . . . something kids do. It's just fun."

"Fun?"

"Fun."

"You went to the McPherson house?"

"Yes. With Mary Elizabeth. She was skipping school, too." (There was a convenient leaving-out-part about the ecstasy. Sofia did not consider this a lie to her parents. Simply an omission in the service of not overcomplicating the matter.)

Her mother leaned forward. Generally, she allowed Dara to take the lead in such discussions, but she was as lost as her husband in this case. "You have gone to the McPherson house many times," she said.

Sofia nodded.

"This is what I don't understand," said Sary. "If you skip school and then go to a place you always go anyway, how is this fun? You could have waited two hours, followed the rules, and then had the exact same fun. No?"

This was the sticking point, alas. Sofia was backed into a corner.

Luckily, her father provided an out. "There will be consequences at school, then?"

"Yes. Probably. I'll be suspended for a day."

A moment of silence descended on the room while the three of them looked back and forth.

"Suspension," Sofia explained. "It means I'll have to stay home from school for a day. It's kind of like a punishment. From the dean."

Dara shook his head. "The punishment for not going to school is to not go to school?"

"What an odd system," Sary said.

Dara laughed quietly for a moment along with his wife and daughter. "But they have captured the moon," Dara said. It was a common refrain for him, a catchall phrase for anything he didn't quite understand about this adopted home of his. It meant, well, Americans were the first to land on the moon, so they must be doing something right. *But they have captured the moon.* He'd said it the first time when he and Sary had finally decided to leave Cambodia and live in America.

"But they have captured the moon," Sofia repeated.

"Of course, you must not see Mary Elizabeth again," Dara told her.

"I know."

"But do not be unkind to her. She deserves our sympathy."

"I know."

"We can't know what goes on behind the walls of their home."

"Yes, Dad. I know."

The funny thing was, even before this conversation with her parents, even before this "punishment" during the time she was crouching in the bushes listening to her parents misunderstand nearly everything the police were saying, as she felt herself coming down from the ecstasy, she began to feel distant from Mary Elizabeth. Sofia recognized the difference between them in those moments when she pushed the dirt around and thought about how light our tread is on the earth. For Sofia, this afternoon was a one-time experience, an attempt to see what all the fuss was about. But for Mary Elizabeth, this afternoon was, quite possibly, the entrance ramp that led into a whole new glimmering city.

# Chapter 9

————

## 4:13 p.m.

Dan Kowalski watched his wife carefully. She appeared to be holding it together, but he knew appearances could be deceiving, especially in her case. She wore a yellow-flowered bikini top under a Hawaiian flowered sarong. Their Key West hotel room smelled of carpet cleaner. The faux wood grain atop the dresser and end tables irked Dan. You could never tell this from a hotel's website, whether the furniture was made with real wood.

Dan's cell phone rang and Alicia watched him answer. Her eyes were full of tears, though she was not, technically speaking, crying. This bothered him. The neither here nor there of it. Cry or don't cry, but hovering there in between confused him. Did she need him to hug her, or could he go and shower? He flipped open his cell phone. It was Alicia's father, George.

Dan had been on the phone for the past two hours, first with the police, then with the detective assigned to their case, and now with George—who'd driven immediately to the Kowalskis' house.

George started giving Dan a play-by-play: "The police are open-ing all the closet doors. Still dusting for prints. Gah! What a mess! They're taking a lot of photos. Must be a hundred already."

"Can you tell us what's missing?" Dan said.

"The house looks like a tornado hit it," George said.

Dan could hear conversation in the background, the deep voices of a team of policemen.

"The whole street's blocked off. Reporters everywhere."

"What's gone, George? Can you tell?"

Alicia was standing inches away from Dan, trying to hear what her father was saying. Dan leaned back slightly to keep her just out of earshot.

"I'm not sure, Dan. You'll have to make a list for the police. But it's like a bomb went off in here."

"I got that, George."

"We need to call the airlines again," Alicia mouthed.

Dan swatted at the air to shut her up. He could never concen-trate on more than one speaker at a time.

"Listen." George lowered his voice. Chester began barking and Dan could hear George shushing him. "Listen, Dan, Arlene and I are going to clean up as best we can before you two get home."

"We're calling the airline in a minute. We'll get there as soon as we can."

"Yes, yes, I'm just telling you. We'll do our best. It's a real mess here. A real mess."

Alicia reached for the phone, whispered, "Let me talk to him when you're done."

Dan glared in her direction.

"I mean a real mess, Dan. I think it would upset Alicia."

"That sounds great, George." Dan tried to keep his voice upbeat. "We sure appreciate your being there."

"Arlene wants to know where you keep your cleaning supplies." Chester barked again and Dan heard a policeman yell something about locking up the damn dog. George and Arlene had been dog-sitting for Dan and Alicia.

Dan took a stumble step back from Alicia. She threw her arms into the air and mouthed, "What?!"

"Well, that's great that they didn't make it to the basement, George. That's good news. All kinds of things on those shelves, you know?"

"What are you two talking about, Dan?" Alicia said.

Dan shrugged. "Great. Thanks, George."

"Got it," George replied. "Cleaning supplies in the basement—" He stopped, then returned a second later. "The detective needs me, I'm going to have to let you go. But don't worry about a thing, Dan!"

Dan closed his cell phone before Alicia could talk. "He had to go. The police needed him," Dan said quickly, before his wife could protest.

"Whatever. I *told* you I wanted to talk to him."

Dan didn't answer, so Alicia picked up the hotel phone to call the airlines.

Dan and Alicia had come to Key West as part of their annual vacation. Normally, February was the best month to escape Chicago's notorious winter; February held the greatest threat to one's sanity. But Alicia had begun a series of volunteer efforts in the fall, and April was the earliest she felt she could get away. First, she worked Sunday mornings at the Living Room Café, serving homeless people breakfast. Then she began to work two afternoons a week at the Oak Park Economy Shop, sifting through donated kitchenware, CDs, clothes, broken electronics. Half of what was donated ended up in a landfill. Monday mornings she volunteered as a "road-to-recovery driver" for the American Cancer Society, bringing elderly Oak Park residents to their oncology appointments at West Suburban hospital. Then she volunteered with the YMCA's "Kids' Fun Nights," playing kickball and bombardment with preteens after school. Occasionally on the weekends, she convinced Dan to go with her and pick up litter in Thatcher Woods. It was as if she were trying to fix every broken piece of the world. Dan saw this as a willing avoidance of addressing her own weaknesses.

When Dan asked her about this sudden burst of activity, Alicia said she simply needed something to do. She'd never held a full-time job, and even Dan's work as a columnist for the *Oak Park Outlook* was part-time. With their house paid off thanks to her parents, and no children, neither of them felt the pressure of bills and retirement funds, life insurance and college funds, that most middle-class people endured. Dan suspected there was more to Alicia's sudden interest in helping those less fortunate, but he'd long learned from her parents never to push Alicia, never to find out even where her limits were.

Anyway, Alicia was more or less fine now. She'd been fine for years. But she had been an extremely difficult teenager: rebellious, cutting school, ignoring homework. Her parents began to pay her an allowance just to earn a C average.

Then she snapped. The pressure of graduating, of losing her friends, of deciding between a subpar college and a subpar job—but mostly of feeling that she had to decide, right then, what she was going to do with the entire rest of her life—knocked her clear on her ass. The night of graduation, lying in her bed with her whole life stretched out before her, made her feel old. How could such a decision possibly be made in one single summer? No one told her she need not decide the eternity of her life; the possibility of change simply didn't occur to her. The concept of adulthood was so far removed from where she felt she was that she had no idea how to go about making decisions that she was sure would cement her path for the next sixty years.

So she swallowed three-quarters of a bottle of aspirin, a dozen of her mother's estrogen pills, and what everyone believed was half a bottle of brandy. (In truth, she'd spent a month slugging down the brandy and refilling it with a mixture of apple juice and Coke, so the bottle's contents had been diluted.) Clearly, to her, she hadn't actually been trying to kill herself; she'd simply wanted to stop thinking.

Her parents had her committed. She found herself in a psych ward with other girls who were mostly as uncrazy as she was and mostly were stressed-out teenagers not sure how to tackle a non-teenage world.

She loved it in there. She stayed as long as she could, six months total.

She'd met Dan two years after her "stay," as her parents came to call it. A year and a half later, they were married. Her parents were relieved and did whatever they could to keep Dan happy and keep him around. So there were the vacations to Hawaii and Belize, the flatscreen, the Lexus and recently the Prius. There was this trip to Key West and a scheduled Caribbean cruise later in the year. There was the kitchen renovation and the mutual fund and, of course, the very first gift: the house on Ilios Lane.

On the phone with the airlines, Alicia sighed and reached for her Visa card. She briefly looked up at her husband and rolled her eyes, then began to recite the numbers into the phone. When she finished, she covered the mouthpiece and said, "Too bad no one died. We could have saved a hundred and fifty bucks on the change fee."

They were booked on the last flight out of Miami that night.

Alicia hung up the phone softly in its cradle and fell backward onto the taupe duvet. Then she covered her face with her hands and started to cry.

*Finally,* Dan thought, and reached for her.

# Chapter 10

### 7:25 p.m.

Arthur loved to walk at night. The later the better. Tonight, however, with a smattering of news vans still parked outside, Michael McPherson had called a meeting of the neighbors, an *action committee* he'd said, and Arthur was steeling himself to go. He barely knew his neighbors. There was Étienne, the restaurateur next door. And there were the McPhersons and Mary Elizabeth, of course, whom he knew better than anyone else. There were the couple with the barking dog, the immigrant family, the family recently separated with the father left behind. But they were more or less anonymous people to Arthur.

Somewhere in an alley several streets over, he detected a garbage truck and the soft whoosh of a car. He could hear ambient talking, a collective of voices—police officers outside, neighbors, newscasters, cameramen, gawkers.

The police were gone from his house and already a locksmith had installed a shiny, new door lock. He didn't worry that he'd be burglarized again. And he didn't care about most of the stolen items—the old speakers and the handheld voice recorder for auditory notes. The half-drunk bottles of rum and vodka. An answering machine that he hadn't used in years. A handful of CDs and the electronic photo album his sister had made for him several Christmases ago. It was the small stack of Moleskine notebooks fifteen, sixteen years old that he'd kept beside the answering machine on the counter and which represented perhaps five years of speechprint work. He'd always thought of photocopying them, of hiring a transcriptionist in case of a fire. But burglary? Of personal handwritten notebooks? If he were the police, he'd dismiss such an item outright. Who goes into a pawnshop in search of used notebooks? What was the street value for such a personal item? Arthur fought waves of nausea and leaned forward, resting his elbows on his knees. He couldn't even search for them himself, his vision was too poor. They were simply gone.

He sat on his bed, fighting a growing sense of helplessness, waiting, it might seem, until the sanctity of his haven was restored, the one place he felt he could emerge from his own helplessness. This, too, he had to admit, was what had been invaded. Not his home, but his sense of security. He did not want to walk tonight, and he did not want to go to Michael McPherson's meeting because he did not want to face the emptiness of his own downstairs, the bleak square where his notebooks once sat.

Normally, Arthur loved the night. The full silence of it. Cars, birds, sirens, voices, they were all packed up and put away till morning. In all the years he'd lived on Ilios Lane, he'd never had a problem until today. He'd pass the occasional dog walker, or the occasional teenager sneaking home after curfew. But generally Arthur was alone, and he knew the shape of every house, the smell of every garden, every rose and trellis.

He remembered the first night he met Mary Elizabeth McPherson. He was out for a walk, rounding the corner of Taylor Street, when he knocked into her on the sidewalk. She was carrying a half gallon of milk and a Snickers. She recognized Arthur as the recluse who lived across the street and assumed him to be lost. She offered to walk with him.

"I live across the street," she told him. "Across from your house." When he failed to respond, she added, "Michael and Susan's daughter? McPherson? My name's Mary Elizabeth."

It was late, and Arthur felt a reluctant responsibility to walk the girl home. Her hair was a dark nimbus, a single organism that reminded him of the kind of earthy, ordinary girl who has just one small otherworldly quality. Perhaps, he thought, she was scared to be out alone and was too proud to properly request a chaperone, and in this way, each believed one was the other's protector.

"I don't see you out very much." Mary Elizabeth was quiet for a few seconds, then added, "You're like a recluse."

Arthur smiled. Stars poked through the nighttime clouds. "I'm the terrifying man in the movie. The one in the haunted house who scares little children and keeps skulls in his basement?"

"I guess." Mary Elizabeth laughed. "He scares little kids, but he always turns out to be, like, lonely and misunderstood, right? Like Edward Scissorhands?"

They walked on, their rubber-soled shoes in step with each other.

"Don't worry," Mary said. "I don't think you're terrifying. My mom told me you were blind."

Arthur liked the quiet slap of her tennis shoes against the sidewalk. The gentle, rhythmic sound had just the hint of a person, a contour. He hated the hard, abrasive soles of business shoes and cowboy boots on concrete.

"You walk pretty well for someone who's blind. You don't have a dog or one of those tapping sticks or anything." She wanted to ask him, but didn't, if he ever fell off curbs or walked into signposts. She suppressed a laugh at the image.

"Goodness, no! But perhaps that's because I'm not quite entirely blind, you see. Especially at night." He explained hemeralopia to her. By the time he was finished, they'd arrived on the corner of Ilios Lane, just in front of Mary Elizabeth's house. She showed no sign of retreating inside. It must have been after ten, Arthur figured. Far too late for a schoolgirl to be out.

"It's weird when you think about it," Mary Elizabeth said. "How you're blind and also not blind. It's like a superhero power."

Arthur laughed. Her frames of reference seemed limited to movies and cartoons, and he wondered how much the girl read. So few young people read books anymore, it seemed. "How so?"

"Well, you can sometimes see and sometimes not see. I guess it would be more of a power if you could turn it on and off. Like if you're in love and you see your girlfriend with another guy, you can just turn off your eyes so you won't have to see it." She flopped down on the grass in front of him, tossing her milk onto its side. The candy bar had disappeared.

Arthur rubbed his hands together to stave off a chill, unable to bring himself to sit on the grass beside her. Instead, he leaned on her mailbox: 103 Ilios Lane.

"I guess that's pretty stupid," Mary Elizabeth said.

"Not at all. In a way, I suppose it does give me certain, shall we say, power. Not power exactly. But I have perceptions that most people don't."

"Like what?"

"Like what. Well, I've learned to listen to the way people talk and *how* we say what we say."

Mary Elizabeth plucked a handful of grass and began to tear the blades down the middle, discarding one and starting another in that teenage way of absent destruction. "So, like, do I have a weird way of talking?"

"Well, it's difficult for me to listen to you linguistically and socially at the same time. You certainly have your own unique linguistic rhythm. But I couldn't write out the pattern just yet."

"Why would anyone do that? It sounds totally boring." She lay back and rested on her elbows. She wore an oversize flannel shirt and jeans with carnation-pink Chuck Taylors.

"Boring is relative. I'd hardly find a high school social engaging."

"They're not called *socials*." Mary laughed. She waved her fingers through the coolness of the grass surrounding her. "It must be pretty bad, being blind. I mean, it's cool that you have this whole language thing, but still . . . it must suck to be . . . blind. I'd rather lose my taste buds."

Arthur shifted on the mailbox and it creaked. The conversation made him think back to that first year, when he thought his life was over. He tried not to remember that year. He'd been offered prescriptions for how to go on living, as if anyone knew what he was up against. No one, not his sister, not his former colleagues, not his doctors, not a single person in Arthur's life, ever said what this young girl said to him. This stinks.

"I can say this much. I'd never hear the things I hear without having lost the ability to see the things I once saw." Arthur couldn't decide if he sounded wise or just old.

Mary Elizabeth put her head back and looked up toward the sky.

A plane quietly made its way across the horizon. "Still, aren't you mad about it? Mad at God or whatever?"

"In order to be mad at God, one must first believe in God. And if I believed in God, my dear, I'd be questioning a good many other things about the world than just my own burdens."

A silence settled between them and Arthur realized that he did not feel uneasy with her. He heard a scratching sound, a squirrel or a cat on tree bark. He wondered why Mary Elizabeth didn't stand up to leave, why she possibly wanted to sit here talking to him. Surely she had scores of friends her own age, boys to chat with late into the night.

"I have this theory," Arthur said finally, "that the world is divided into two kinds of people. Those who can answer one single question immediately and those who cannot. And those who *can* answer it experience life very differently than those who cannot. It's a very dear price, but I think they get to live a larger life."

Mary Elizabeth stared at him. "Well? What's the question?"

The headlights of a car cruising down Taylor Street illuminated her face for an instant. He yearned to know the color of her eyes. He wondered if Mary would remember him twenty, thirty, forty years from now, when she sent her own daughter out for milk. If she'd remember this tiny moment in their lives. "The question is this." He leaned in just a fraction toward her. "What's the worst thing that ever happened to you?"

He paused for a moment of drama before straightening up again.

"You went blind," Mary Elizabeth shouted in the excitable manner of a game-show contestant. She'd answered in a second.

"Ding, ding," Arthur said, tapping his nose. "I did."

"That's the worst thing that ever happened to you."

"Yes."

She felt the dew from the grass slowly seeping into her jeans and wished she were curled up under the paisley covers of her own bed. Arthur stopped leaning on the mailbox, started to offer her his hand.

"Arthur," she said.

"Yes."

"Is it bad that I can answer for you . . . but not for me?"

## What We've Lost Is Nothing
Candy Kane, blogger

I can't sleep. Perhaps many of you cannot, either. If I'm honest, I don't know whether it's sympathy for the Ilios Lane families who lost so much, or if it's fear that I'm next. That my
friends or family are next. How terrified we are of their tragedy
("But by the grace of God," we say, though who's to say a
couple of them didn't have the grace of God?).

We say they're lucky, don't we—especially the daughter
home alone. No one was injured. It was only "stuff" those
families lost. But I don't think that's true. Our homes are the
haven of a heartless world, are they not? The place we are
most ourselves. What happens when some uninvited person
invites himself in?

Yes, I said *him*. I cannot imagine a woman committing such
a crime. Maybe this is small of me. Guess it's kinda sexist—
and here, in this diverse community, we like to believe we
have moved past all that. But have we? I'm awake here, at
nearly midnight, and I'm just really wondering.

Who were these thieves? What desperation, what desire,
led them to such an act? How many thieves were there? Did
they go to each house together, or have a ratio of thieves-to-
households? One thief to two law-abiders? Were they after
the stuff or the big giant story of it all? Did they target our
community because of who we are? Because of what we
believe? Worst of all to me to think . . . are the thieves now
watching the local news, seeing their victims all upset and
everything, and . . . laughing?

Even the stoic Ilios Lane resident from the news tonight—
I can't remember his name (Mark? Michael? something like
that . . . )—even he might recognize, in time, that what he's
lost is actually quite something.

# Chapter 11

## 7:50 p.m.

Michael and Susan McPherson had gone from house to house in the hours after the robbery and invited the neighbors to a meeting at their home. Their street was still blocked off with police tape. As Michael and Susan walked, he put his arm around her. He felt the flash of cameras, the eyes of a dozen reporters following them from one door to the next. Every neighbor they'd spoken with had agreed to come by.

Michael McPherson had barely talked to Mary Elizabeth since she'd admitted to playing hooky and taking ecstasy. She refused to reveal whom she had been with.

"I'm already grounded for a month," she'd said, laughing. "What're you going to do? Ground me for like a year if I don't tell you? Ground me till college?"

In a stroke of dumb luck, Mary may well have scared the faceless bandits away before they could steal more. And there were worse places she could have gone while cutting class. Michael didn't like what she'd done, certainly, but he was relieved she'd come home instead of wandering to the house of someone he didn't know, or taking the train in to some seedy section of the city. Now that the burglary had happened in this same space, how could Michael McPherson—amid the chaos—convince Mary that this was still her safe haven?

He had to wonder, had they really lost *nothing*, as he'd said to the media? Or had they lost something so enormous there existed no name for it?

Michael was having trouble reconciling the impotence he felt over failing to keep his family safe with the impotence he felt over failing to coax the full truth from his daughter. She refused to identify whom she had done ecstasy with. The way he saw it, she owed it to him to tell him everything. This was the hierarchy of parent-child relationships. One didn't need another reason.

"Look, Dad," Mary had said, "I totally get why you want me to tell you, but I promised her, and you've always told me I should be loyal. You said loyalty is the hardest thing to get back from people once you've betrayed them."

"Loyalty to your *family*," he'd said.

Michael wished he were better with words. He didn't know how to handle Mary's insurrection. The great secret of parents, he realized, was just how powerless they really were.

The day Mary Elizabeth had been born, he remembered how Susan had cried; and he'd forced himself to cry with her.

"I know," he'd said to Susan, smiling, hugging her.

Susan shook her head.

He sat back, then, stopped hugging her, and balanced on the edge of her hospital bed, thinking, *Hormones*. They'd been through it once already, with Thomas, three years earlier. In tears one minute and hysterical laughter the next.

"I'm crying," she said, "because I can't think of a single place in the world that I can make safe enough for her."

Now Mary Elizabeth was practically an adult, and the world seemed a more dangerous place. Michael remembered something that Susan had once said, when both the kids were small. How one of the scariest days for a parent wasn't when your kids got their driver's license or left home for college. It was when you realized their sense of logic and reason matched yours.

"You never specified *family* loyalty," Mary had said. "You only said loyalty."

Michael focused his eyes on her, tried to make his face stern enough to intimidate her into confessing. "Well, that loyalty includes a responsibility to tell the truth."

"I *have* told the truth. Not telling you the name isn't lying. It's just not telling you the name. You can't just invent what you think truth is."

"Watch your tone, young lady."

"Yeah, okay, so if Mom went to the store and bought milk, eggs, and bread, and you asked what she bought and she said, 'Milk and bread,' would she be lying because she totally left out the eggs?"

"Don't be ridiculous, Mary."

"Seriously, Dad. I'm seeking your parental *wisdom* here. Would she? 'Cause the rules are a little unclear."

Susan came into the dining room and led Michael out. It was best to let it go for now, she convinced him. They could dole out a punishment later. Susan had been in his office halfheartedly cleaning fingerprint dust. It found its way everywhere, onto tall shelves, into crevices, between the planks of the hardwood floor; places that hadn't been touched in years and years.

"There are bigger things to worry about right now," she reminded him.

Michael always felt Susan was too easy on the kids—Mary Elizabeth and Thomas, who was now at the University of Illinois in Champaign. Michael would deal with the Mary situation once this neighborhood fiasco had died down. It was up to the McPherson family to show a united front.

When Michael and Susan stopped at the Cambodians' house, the father had had to call his daughter, Sofia, to come translate. Michael explained slowly, but beyond the door, as he invited them to the meeting, he could see an older teenage boy that he recognized from other visits. Michael was not introduced. He'd heard that the boy and his two brothers lived somewhere in the city, but they came every few days, their arrivals announced with blaring rap music out the open windows—even in winter—of a rusting Pontiac. The boy was wearing a stained tank top with an unbuttoned flannel shirt and a bandanna around his forehead; he served something cloudy in a glass—cider? Scotch?—to Sofia's mother, who sat on the floor, her back against the couch. She took the glass and nodded a weary thanks.

"So you'll come with your parents?" Susan asked Sofia, making sure she'd be there to translate. "Maybe about eight?"

Sofia nodded.

Michael saw the boy scowl and look in their direction, then quickly turn away. His jeans were torn at both knees, two of the belt loops dangling by mere threads.

"That your brother?" Michael gestured toward the boy. He knew that Sofia didn't have any siblings.

"Cousin."

"Cousin, yes," Michael said. Susan gently pulled at him to leave. "Is he in high school, too, then? Somewhere around here?"

The boy turned for a moment and gave Michael a deliberate stare. Then he disappeared farther into the living room.

"Michael?" Susan said, pulling harder.

Michael craned his neck searching for the boy, but couldn't see him. "You were in school today, then, right?" he called loudly.

Susan gasped, yanked on her husband's arm.

"We'll see you tonight, Mr. McPherson," Sofia said. Michael was sure he saw fear in her eyes just before she shut the door.


Now, Michael stood before the bathroom mirror thinking about what he'd say when the neighbors came. He cleared his throat, tilted his head back, and began to floss. He had a constellation of shaving bumps on his neck. *What we've lost is nothing . . . compared to what we'll lose if we don't unite.* That was good. He'd try to remember that. *. . . Unite or we'll lose. . . .* He jotted it down on a notepad by the sink. *What we need is a task force.*

After all, Michael's entire professional mandate involved connections. His company, Lowry Brothers, made modular steel bridges. They weren't beautiful bridges by any stretch, but they were resilient in times of chaos. Natural disasters, infrastructure improvements, war . . . those were the moments that called for the modular steel bridge. Michael reasoned that the invention of the modular had been akin to the invention of plastic or Ziploc bags or the microwave oven. It made people's lives so seamlessly easier, they had hardly noticed. The modular bridge was still utilitarian, yes, but this very element, Michael believed, was most relevant to their situation.

He dabbed a quarter-size dollop of Brylcreem into his cropped, wiry hair. The McPherson hair, Mary hated it. "It's like inheriting debt, instead of some rich aunt's estate," she'd once complained on a particularly humid day. Then she rolled her eyes—how *do* teenagers become so adept at that skill?—and left the room. He'd never admitted to her how much he hated it, too.

"Your hair is part of your identity," he'd yelled. "It makes you a McPherson. You should be proud of it!"

Mary had circled back to his room. Her look was toxic. When was it that children took flight from their parents? Michael suspected it was far earlier than anyone ever cared to admit, five, six years old.

Mary, it seemed to him, had been born taking flight.

"But, Dad," she'd said, "what if you're exactly the person I don't want to be like?"

He washed the Brylcreem off his hands, made a final adjustment to his tie. The doorbell rang and he heard Susan's steps across the linoleum downstairs. The neighbors had begun to arrive. He wondered if Sofia would bring her cousin, and where he'd been all day.

# Chapter 12

## 8:00–9:54 p.m.

Dara and Sary sat straight-backed and hip-to-hip on a puffy suede love seat. Sary's toes barely reached the floor. Their daughter, Sofia, sat at their feet on the floor, resting against an arm of the chair. Americans had such big furniture, like clouds. It swallowed you. Fingerprint dust floated in the air, glittering in the gentle glow of floor lamps. It seemed as if everything were softer in America: towels, toilet paper, sofas, grass, motorcycle seats, beds, clothing, sponges, hair, cattle, people. Except the voices. Americans spoke, she thought, as if in competition with a wall of blaring speakers; even all these years later, it seemed to her their primary mode of conversation was the yell. When Sary had first moved to Oak Park, she was unnerved by the quiet of the streets. So few people outside.

In Phnom Penh, the noise was everywhere. You were never alone. But Americans thrived on solitary lives, it seemed to her. They chose to be alone, all the middle-aged, unmarried people, the young girls who put off marriage indefinitely. She couldn't understand what existed inside someone who could live that way, live without others.

"I believe it would make Detective Wasserman's job a whole lot easier if we formed a communication channel," Michael McPherson announced. "The point man, so to speak. He won't have to update all of us all the time if, say, he updates me and then I update all of you."

Several heads nodded in agreement.

This was the first time Dara and Sary had been in the McPhersons' house, or any of their neighbors' homes. A faint floral scent was in the air, with a dusty overlay, Sary thought. The room seemed too full. Maybe that was the key to understanding how Americans lived; they filled their homes with furniture, rather than people. In Cambodia, it was just the opposite.

Not understanding much of the proceedings and with Sofia serving as a lackluster translator, Sary took to counting the family pictures in the living room. *Moi, pbee, pbai, pbooun, bpram* . . . There were ten, she thought . . . maybe eleven or twelve. She couldn't quite tell with Arthur Gardenia's head in the way. It seemed strange to have so many pictures all in one room yet none showing the family in formal attire. One shot captured Mary jumping in the air, her legs splayed in a split, her arms spread toward the sky in a V. Sary found herself embarrassed for Mary; she couldn't understand how Mary's parents had allowed her in such a pose. Sofia had assured Sary and Dara that cheerleading was a normal American-girl thing to do. But given what Sary now knew about her daughter's whereabouts that afternoon, she was beginning to wonder if Sofia was as honest as she and Dara had always assumed.

Sary studied the other photos. In one Mary was sitting beside her mother *in the grass*. Why the grass? Didn't they soil their clothing? Sary wondered. A large photo next to it showed Michael and

Susan on a boat wearing sunglasses, their hair blowing wildly in the wind. Michael was dressed in shorts, and Sary could even make out the hair on his legs. Everyone who came into the McPherson house would see them at their worst . . . hair disheveled, full of silly grins and skimpy, soiled clothes.

*"Mama."* Sofia was touching Sary's calf and said in Khmer, "Mr. McPherson wants to make a list of everything that was stolen from our houses."

"Why?" Dara asked.

"We have paper here," Susan said, offering ballpoint pens to Helen Pappalardo and Sofia. Michael leaned down and whispered to Susan, glancing once toward Arthur. "Or, I can just write it all down here," Susan said, holding up a notebook.

Everyone kept their shoes on, Sary noticed, even Susan and Michael. It had taken Dara more than a year to convince Sary that she mustn't take off her shoes when visiting American homes. Sary wiggled her toes. They felt constricted. So unsanitary. All the dirt from the outside world coming to the inside. Yet, American homes were mysteriously clean and free of this dirt.

"We'll make a copy for all of you and you can carry it around. Say you're at a garage sale, you might come across something, and you'll have the list to cross-check," Michael said to the group. "My golf clubs were taken. They'd be the sort of thing you might come across."

"A garage sale, Dad?" Mary said.

Susan shushed her daughter, mumbled something encouraging about garage-sale season approaching.

Michael cleared his throat. "Were you able to explain to your parents?" he asked Sofia. "Just in case they don't understand. We want transparency here."

"Definitely, yes, Mr. McPherson. I told them."

"Tell him my hand phone was taken," Sary whispered to Sofia. Sary wasn't sure why she was whispering. Something about the moment seemed to call for it

"My mother's cell phone was stolen," Sofia told the group.

Michael McPherson nodded sagely to Susan, who wrote it down in the spiral notebook on her lap. She sat in the other overstuffed, beige suede chair, her legs crossed like a yogi. At the top of the page, she'd written *Stolen Items*. Under *Cambodian Family*, she wrote *cell phone*.

"Okay," said Michael. "And?"

"And what?" Sofia asked.

"What else?" He glanced quickly, around the room. Sofia's cousin, of course, had not come.

"Oh, just her cell phone. That's it."

Helen Pappalardo, in the small foursquare house beside the McPhersons', let out a tiny gasp. Aldrin Rutherford, Craftsman bungalow between the Kowalskis and Étienne Lenoir, who'd had bicycles and power tools stolen, among other items, suddenly perked up.

Michael took his hand out of his pants pocket, where he'd been diddling with a pocketknife on a tiny keychain, weaving it through his fingers. "Your mother's phone? That's all they took?"

Sofia nodded. So did Dara, though he wasn't entirely sure what he was nodding for.

"They don't have anything to steal, Dad," Mary said.

Sofia turned sharply toward her. "Shut up. We do so!"

"Well, not really, you don't," Mary said sheepishly. "Like, no offense. You're lucky!"

"What do you know?" Sofia shot back. "We have lots of stuff. We have loads of money in the bank. Loads! You don't even know!"

Dara touched his daughter's shoulder. He may not have understood her words, but he certainly understood her tone of voice and body language, and he frowned on such public displays. Sary reddened.

"Girls!" Michael McPherson yelled, making all of them jump. "This is not the time and place."

"But, Dad, I was just saying maybe they were, like, lucky in a way to be poor."

"We're not poor," Sofia said. Her parents had told her recently that they had enough money to send her to a university that wasn't even a state school. If she did well in high school, she could go to just about any college she wanted.

Mary leaned toward her. "It's okay that you're poor."

"We're not poor!"

Both Sofia's parents worked at FedEx, the 7:00 a.m. to 3:30 p.m. shift. They worked all the American holidays (they also worked the Cambodian holidays, of course), and they never turned down overtime. They put boxes on conveyor belts and took boxes off conveyor belts and saved every penny they possibly could.

"You're sort of poor," Mary said, wanting her friend to understand that it was okay, that she didn't think anything differently of Sofia.

"That's enough, girls!" Michael McPherson said, but he realized in that moment that he was staring in the face of his daughter's infamous accomplice, a certain Sofia Oum. He should have known, given who her relatives appeared to be. What other secrets, he wondered, did that quiet girl have?

# Chapter 13

———

## 8:00–9:54 p.m.

As Arthur sat on the McPhersons' couch, his photochromatic lenses cut into the bridge of his nose, a tiny line of sweat forming in the indentation. The lenses felt heavy and claustrophobic over his eyes, and he found it difficult to concentrate on what Michael McPherson was saying. Arthur had long believed deep down—though no doctors had confirmed it—that he would someday go completely blind. He didn't know how he had come to this knowledge, but he'd grown to accept it. In a strange way, his disability was not a bad one to have . . . he could don his glasses and to some degree see in black-and-white whenever he wanted to. But total blindness. Blindness without any hope of reversal? That was something different altogether. He decided that if he lived his life now, when he could still sometimes see, then maybe when the day finally came, he wouldn't feel such misery. If he took the pain, the despondency, in tiny medicinal doses, then he was placing a bet on his own emotional resilience. Keeping at bay the magnificent sorrow that threatened him.

When the college offered him disability pay, he had no choice but to take it immediately. He stopped driving. He hired people to help him maintain his life.

It had been his intention to hire Mary to come and clean his house, give her a little pocket money. She'd be far less expensive than his cleaning service. But after a few weeks, he'd discovered that Mary had a most extraordinary voice. Soft, young, calming in a way that he couldn't quite ever remember in any other voices from his life. A soft vibrato emanated from the back of her throat as she spoke, a shaky undertone of vulnerability, the eternal teenage search for one's place in the world. So he began to ask her to read to him, and then he began to tape-record her reading to him.

They read upstairs, in his office, he in his worn leather chair, while she sat at his desk, the small, green library lamp aimed directly at the book so it wouldn't hurt his eyes. Arthur hoped she'd forget he was there, sometimes, and get lost in the words as he did.

*"There is a housing project standing now where the house in which we grew up once stood,"* she read not long ago—part of a weeks-long Baldwin kick he'd put her on, *"and one of those stunted city trees is snarling where our doorway used to be. This is on the rehabilitated side of the avenue. The other side of the avenue—for progress takes time— has not been rehabilitated yet and it looks exactly like it looked in the days when we sat with our noses pressed against the windowpane, longing to be allowed to go 'across the street.'"*

She'd looked up and laughed for a minute, asked Arthur when it had been written.

"Early sixties, late fifties," Arthur'd said. "I can't quite remember."

"It's so funny, about all this historical stuff."

To Arthur, of course, it wasn't history. It was life, it was his youth, and it was beginning to feel like yesterday, as is so often the case with aging. The further away we get in years, the closer it marches in memory.

"What's funny?" he asked her, sitting up, but covering his eyes with his palm. She switched off the light so that they sat in darkness—an act that had become a habit for her. They spoke, so often now, in darkness.

"It's like this dude could have written it today. About Austin Boulevard."

"What do you know about Austin?"

"Are you kidding me, Arthur? My mom never shuts up about Austin Boulevard." Her chair squeaked, the roller wheels skidding on the floor's plastic protector as she pushed her seat into and out of the desk—a habit that Arthur tolerated.

Mary was used to talking in the darkness, though she knew if she ever told her friends that she spent her free time sitting in the dark with an old man, no one would understand. It *was* odd, she knew. But it was comfortable, too. As if she were alone, but not alone, and though she didn't have the words to describe it, she recognized the rarity of those afternoons all the same. At first she'd thought she was just doing a good deed, like the kind teenage girl in the movies who befriends the lonely old man, but after a few weeks, Mary wasn't sure that it wasn't the other way round, the kind old man befriending the lonely teenager. Ultimately she just really liked hanging out at Arthur's house, where she could ask questions without feeling stupid, and where she could curse without being told off, and she could even move things around downstairs because he'd never know the difference, and so she came to feel quite at home, sometimes more at home in *his* house than in her own.

"My mom talks about the lady who started the Housing Office like she's freaking Gandhi," Mary said. "She had death threats and all that from the Ku Klux Klan. I think her kid maybe had a bodyguard to walk to school and stuff." Mary herself walked to school. She wondered what it would be like to have to walk between two giant musclemen just so you'd be safe. What about all the other kids? Would the bodyguards have to sit in class, too? Would they have to go to the bathroom with you? Mary wondered if the kid had been popular or outcast, celebrated or shunned.

"It's funny," Mary said. "I wonder how that family would answer your question, Arthur. About the worst thing that ever happened to them?"

Arthur murmured a kind of *hmmmm*. He'd never thought much about the historical dimensions of his theory, people for whom life—he naturally assumed—was far more difficult than in the present.

"I mean, that lady who started the Housing Office? She'd probably say that the worst thing that ever happened to her was like being almost murdered, or having her family almost murdered. I mean, apart from *actually* being murdered, that's pretty bad."

"Yes."

"So she could have given you an answer in like a second, right? But she did it anyway, sent her kid to the same school with the bodyguard, and kept working on opening the Housing Office. She could have moved away. Or at least stopped, and the worst thing to happen to her would be over instantly and her kid would have been safe."

"We can assume."

"It's weird."

"What?"

"She just kept on doing it."

Arthur smiled.

"I wonder if I'd do that, Arthur? Keep going even with all the danger, even if it could kill me? Or kill the people I loved?"

Arthur wanted to answer her, wanted to give her a short, sharp sentence that would stay with her for always. But nothing came to mind. This was what happened in real life. Words failed you in the moment. People failed you. The world failed you.

Mary tugged the chain and the lamp came back on. *". . . These two,"* she read, *"I imagine, could tell a long tale if they would (perhaps they would be glad to if they could), having watched so many, for so long, struggling in the fishhooks, the barbed wire, of this avenue. . . ."*

At the McPhersons' meeting, Helen Pappalardo—in bright pedal pushers and a dark sweatshirt from Northern Illinois University, her alma mater—sat next to Arthur. She'd been jotting down the missing items as they were listed:

| | |
|---|---|
| Motorola cell phone | GE answering machine |
| Xbox | paperweight globe |
| Dell laptop | Griffin voice recorder |
| IBM laptop | BlackBerry (2) |
| Panasonic DVD player | checkbook (US bank) |
| Griffin speakers | Moleskine notebooks |
| golf clubs | Hewlett-Packard printer |
| jewelry box | Epson printer |
| pen set | Epson scanner |
| hand-crank radio | Canon digital camera (2) |
| Bosch headphones | Canon video recorder |
| Samsung DVD player | bicycles (2) |
| Canon all-in-one printer | lawn edger |
| silver dollar coins in bank | laser pointer |
| electric drill | iPods (multiple) |
| television | liquor (liquor???) |

"Look, this is obviously a difficult time for all of us," Michael said. "The vulnerability, the fear. I know I'm scared. For my family. For those I love. I believe now is one of those moments where life really tests you. When you become one of those people in the stories we've all seen. You know the ones. Where what you think can *never* happen to you suddenly does. And we have to stick together here in this. Be a united front."

Michael let the thought dangle in the air for a moment. It felt like the end of the meeting.

Dara nodded and stood, said a halting "Thank you" in quiet English.

"Well, then," Arthur began, but then he wasn't sure what else to say. The meeting was clearly over. Lists had been made, suggestions for action, but the stinging quiet of the moment said what none of them could quite articulate: there was nothing to be done. They had been violated, invaded, they had suffered losses of a material nature that did not feel material at all, somehow. Why was everyone saying how lucky they were when they felt the exact opposite of lucky? Lucky would be to have not been burgled at all, to have not been forced into this uncomfortable ad hoc alliance. Soon, they would return to the normal obligations of life: work, school, errands and chores, the making of meals and the filling of gas tanks, the filing of papers and washing of sheets. All of it happening with perhaps the only sign that anything at all was amiss was an unusual quiet, a stillness in the way they'd move, in the way they'd answer their phones or walk down the corridors of their fluorescent-lit offices. "Before we go, I think the question ought to be asked," Arthur said.

Michael's head jerked back in surprise. Besides listing what had been taken from his house, Arthur hadn't spoken at all. "What question? I don't think we overlooked anything."

"Has anyone . . ." Arthur struggled to get the words out, to get them just right. "Is there a reason someone would do this? Have we any known enemies?"

The room went silent. Dara touched his daughter's elbow to translate. No one met anyone else's gaze.

"Let's not—" Michael started to say.

"He means did any of us, like, really super piss off someone?" Mary said.

Susan shot her daughter an angry look.

"We know what he meant, Mary," Michael spit out. "There's no need to editorialize." He breathed in deeply, tried to think of what to say. "I'm not sure this is the time or place . . ."

"It seems to me the perfect time. The perfect place," Arthur said. "We might as well be honest. We're in this together. Our fates tied to one another, you might say."

Aldrin Rutherford had an angry ex-wife, but no one suspected her.

Michael looked toward Sary and Dara. "Maybe if there's someone we *know* who's capable of something like this? I'm not suggesting we cast aspersions on one another, but paths can take unlikely turns, run across all kinds."

No one looked up at Michael.

"Paja Coen lost a big contract recently—I think it was for Wrigley's," said Helen, referring to the brand manager who lived on the top floor of the two-flat, above Dara and Sary. She was returning from New York later that night. She'd moved to the street just a few months earlier. "I ran into her in the alley last week and she was pretty upset."

"Dad, you didn't get that promotion you were expecting last

month, remember?" Mary said. "You had that big fight with your boss?"

"That's enough, Mary." Michael held as much control in his voice as he could.

". . . since we're doing the whole confessional." Mary smiled.

"This isn't the kind of thing Arthur's asking about," Michael said.

"This is really for the police to figure out," Susan said. "What's important is that we're here for each other."

Aldrin Rutherford had been standing during most of the meeting, one elbow resting on the mantel above the fireplace. He gestured toward Sofia and Mary. "How about you kids? Any bad seeds in your circle of friends? You were cutting school today, weren't you, Mary?"

"This is enough!" Susan slammed the notebook on the coffee table and stood up. "This isn't helping. None of us deserved this. I don't care what's happened in our lives. We all have our challenges, but this line of inquiry won't get us anywhere."

"Susan—" Michael began.

"I think we're done here," she said.

Slowly Arthur rose, then the Cambodians; Aldrin Rutherford walked around the living room toward the door, and then Helen Pappalardo burst out crying. Arthur instinctively recoiled. Susan took a step and knelt before her.

"My house looks like it's been bombed," Helen said. "Bombed. Not burgled. I didn't know . . . Everything's been *touched*. I have bread crumbs all over the kitchen. Bread crumbs? Why do burglars need my bread crumbs?"

"Why did they need my notebooks?" Arthur said quietly. But no one heard him.

It was exactly what they all needed, a refocusing of their energies toward something, *somewhere*, other than their own fear, their own suspicion.

"I'll help you clean it up. Mary and I will help you," Susan said, gesturing toward her daughter.

"I'll take Arthur home," Michael offered.

"Please, let me," said Aldrin Rutherford.

"I can certainly find my own way home," Arthur said.

Sofia translated for Dara and Sary, who stood, half-smiling at their neighbors, all of whom had sprung into a kind of stilted action, galvanized by the public display of what they each felt privately.

# Chapter 14

――――

## 9:50 p.m.

On the flight from Miami to Chicago, Dan Kowalski had attempted to make a list to coordinate his upcoming investigation, while Alicia dozed beside him, the Xanax making her snore gently. Perhaps *investigation* was too large a word . . . his own, as he'd call it, *poking around*. He'd follow the police on their leads, but he needed to look up the crime stats of his neighborhood. How many of those crimes were solved? How many had turned violent? As both a known local media voice *and* now a victim, surely he could get a level of access like no one else. Maybe his story would surpass just a recounting of the investigation, maybe it could say something about all of them, the progressive politics of Oak Park as it abutted this new crime wave (could he call it a crime wave? Could that be fact-checked?). Maybe he could even look beyond the *Oak Park Outlook* and go to the *Chicago Tribune*. Of course he would start with the police. He knew a fair number of them from his Village Life and Letters column.

He had to wonder—though he'd never say it aloud—where had all his neighbors been? Not that he was blaming his fellow victims. But the Cambodians, were they even legal? Did they even speak English? He wasn't a great proponent of hard-line assimilation—live and let live in the US of A—but perhaps just a small starter course of sorts wouldn't hurt? There was no blame here, but for all he knew, they were living among fugitives.

From O'Hare, Dan and Alicia sat anxiously in the backseat of the taxi. They were nearly home now, waiting at the light at the off-kilter intersection of Harlem and Chicago Avenues. "I hate this intersection. In a town built on the grid system, how do you mess that up?" he asked Alicia, as they waited for the light to change.

"You ask me that every single time, Dan."

"Yes. Because I still don't have the answer."

She glanced out the window. A tiny woman, hunched over and still wearing a winter coat in the spring weather, filled her gas tank at the station on the corner.

"I mean, seriously. I'm just saying, how hard could it have been?"

"Every. Single. Time." Alicia said very, very quietly.

Dan thought of the flatscreen television—George had already told them it was gone. Along with his Xbox and his set of beer coolers from Bali. Alicia's parents had given them the television on their tenth wedding anniversary, two years earlier. He'd resented it at first. Were they suggesting Alicia and Dan couldn't afford to buy one themselves? But, as usual, Dan had been charmed by Alicia's father, who'd joked that it was a reward for enduring a decade under the same roof as Alicia. The *Reed* women, George had said, laughing, placing an unspoken verdict on his own wife's maternal line, as if he and his son-in-law were doing the world a *favor* by taking Arlene and Alicia and the mothers and grandmothers who preceded them

(Ada and Beatrice and Irma, et cetera) off the matrimonial market. Dan had laughed, nodded knowingly, then felt a mild twinge of guilt for not standing up for his wife. But even Alicia admitted that she was, in her words, "just this side of crazy." It hadn't taken Dan long to thoroughly enjoy the new television, which had a sharp, luminous picture. Almost like a cinema display, Dan learned. High-definition. And cinema quality came at a price.

Unable to sleep on the plane, he'd already begun a column about the burglary, conscripting the words of his neighbor, Michael McPherson, after he heard them on the news. What we've lost is nothing, Dan began, but more important, what those thieves don't know is who they're really dealing with here. We are not an easily intimidated people. We are more than neighbors. We are friends. We are community. We are people who band together in adversity. What's happened to our little street is a tragedy, but it's a tragedy of… That's where he got stuck. A tragedy of opportunity? The sentence carried too much drag. Maybe he'd write about the takeaways, the lessons parents could impart. Oak Parkers loved to talk about lessons for children. Not that he and Alicia had any. But children were good. Children resonated.

The taxi rounded Taylor Street, and Dan began to make a mental list of his contacts at Village Hall. Suddenly he realized Alicia had been talking to him, and he had no idea what she'd said.

"I'm not sure," he said, hoping the generic response would suffice.

"Oh my God, Dan?!" Alicia said. The light turned green and the taxi lurched forward. "How can you be so cavalier?"

Dan noticed a vein in Alicia's forehead begin to pulse, which happened whenever her blood pressure rose.

"I mean, if the old lock didn't keep them out, how can a new lock keep them out? It's totally stupid. Maybe this was just a precursor, a kind of warning."

He noticed she'd begun to shake. "Burglars never hit the same house twice," he blurted. He hoped this sounded less the obvious fabrication it was and more the comfort he'd been shooting for.

"You don't know that, Dan. You don't know." Her voice rose, she turned toward him and her eyes had a kind of wildness.

He wondered how long she'd been talking to him before he tuned in. He wished he were a better listener, a better husband. He'd never been good in emergencies. He froze rather than acted. He'd climbed a tree with a friend once as a kid, maybe they were six or seven, and the kid fell out of the tree as might have been predicted, and he broke his wrist and lay on the ground writhing while Dan sat in the tree staring down, frozen into a kind of stupor. A neighbor, finally, came out and saw the boy and called an ambulance.

"Alicia, calm down."

"What if this was something, I don't know, something to see if they could pull it off? What if there's an even bigger plan sometime in the future? I know they won't come back tonight, but what about next month? Next year? How can we know?"

The taxi was nearing their street and Dan needed to direct the driver. "Alicia"—Dan put his hand on her thigh—"don't borrow problems from the future and put them in the present.—Left here, please."

She shoved his hand off her leg. "Are you fucking kidding me? Did you *really* just say that to me?"

One of Alicia's shrinks once suggested this to Dan, that in the absence of current troubles, Alicia borrowed them from the future. The line had stuck with Dan.

When they arrived at the entrance to Ilios Lane, they were surprised to see yellow police tape spanning the entire width of the road. Several news vans were parked along Taylor Street along the side of the McPhersons' house. The bigness of it all stunned them into a momentary truce.

"We'll have to go to the alleyway," Dan told the driver. "To the back door."

"You live on this street?" The driver perked up in his seat. It was the first he'd spoken to Dan and Alicia. "That's some bad luck, friend."

# Chapter 15

## 10:05 p.m.

É tienne left his car at the restaurant and walked the mile back home to Ilios Lane. As he approached, he could see the bright lights of television news crews still parked on the street, their spotlights like oversize, garish stars.

After the police left, he'd spent a long time cleaning the restaurant's kitchen. The shallots went into the garbage. The brass cleaner came out from the dry-goods closet and he began to shine his two large copper sauté pans. He'd found them in an antiques store years ago in the tiny mountain town of Jerome, Arizona. The idea of culinary continuity, twenty-first-century food prepared in nineteenth-century pans, thrilled him. His own favorite cookbook had also come from the nineteenth century: Jules Gouffé's *Royal Cookery Book* (*Le Livre de Cuisine*). Gouffé was the first to combine what he called "Domestic" and "High-Class Cookery," which appealed to Étienne's sense of egalitarianism. The book had woodcuts that repulsed most diners: a rabbit on a spit, severed calves' feet in a mock embrace around its head, the head of a wild boar with thick whiskers and snout hair. But Étienne loved how the pictures today seemed mildly subversive.

After several hours of cleaning, he found himself turning to his favorite recipe—one he'd never offered on his menu. He warmed equal amounts of flour and butter in a saucepan until it was a smooth paste, then mixed it with minced beef in a stainless-steel bowl, adding beef broth, salt, and pepper. He cooked the mixture lightly for a few seconds, then took it off the heat, sprinkled in fresh parsley, thyme, and chives, a smidgen more of broth and one egg. Voilà!

The hamburger. *Exalted.*

Étienne ate two, not bothering with buns (he hated how they always fell apart under the stress of what he believed was the perfect burger). After he'd cleaned up, he tossed his apron in a small tub of dirty linens and closed up the kitchen.

Étienne could not pinpoint exactly where his love of France had originated. He was, according to his father, one-quarter French. He knew the arrondissements and the metro lines; he'd spent some time studying Guillard, the designer of the art nouveau metro stations in much of Paris. And the food had been his educational inspiration: mascarpone, crème fraîche, moules-frites, chèvre chaud, coq au vin—he valued the basics. He loved how these things were both routine and extraordinary. And the country itself, so warm, so washed-out, colors that bled softly into one another. When he closed his eyes and thought of France, he envisioned pale lavender, pink, gold . . . colors that kept and comforted you. Not the drab browns and grays of his Midwestern existence, winters where the colors disappeared under dirty snow, summers where the houses, so stately in size and architectural detail, were diminished by the blandness of their palettes.

On Erie Street, Étienne walked perpendicular to Ilios Lane, passing Arthur Gardenia's house on the corner—his own was beside Arthur's. He turned left up Taylor and walked through the Ramseys' yard through the alley and to his own back gate (he'd done this same trail earlier in the day when he'd discovered the wild mess of his burgled house. He'd jotted a quick note of what was missing and made his way back to the restaurant). The dark grass was damp from sprinklers, and Étienne could feel his tennis shoes taking in water. He emerged into the alley beside their garage, peeking left to make sure no news crews had set up shop. Then he dashed across the alley and in several large steps covered the length of his own weed-choked backyard and up the four wooden steps to his back door. Glass shards from his lavender bouquet crunched under his feet, dropped and scattered by the burglars on the way out. Inside the house, he retrieved the flashlight that he kept just inside the doorway. All his neighbors still believed he was on vacation in Paris. If he turned on the house lights, he'd cast suspicion.

Carefully, he bent and untied his wet shoes, wedging them off at the heels and leaving them by the threshold. He wasn't in the house three minutes before he heard an insistent knocking at his front door. He ignored it, but the knocking continued. He gingerly took off his wet socks and laid them atop his shoes, then rolled up his jeans to just above his ankles, sliding into a pair of slippers stationed at the back door. He could feel himself stepping on things in the dark—dirt, glass—the floor was slick with fingerprint dust. He accidentally kicked a plastic Tupperware tub and it skittered across the floor. Cabinets stood open, papers strewn about, a ceramic bowl in pieces in the doorway. Étienne's heart thumped. In the past, he'd spent the week in darkness to hide from his neighbors his not having gone anywhere; now, the burglary meant his home contained hazards he'd never before had to contend with in the dark. With the brokenness surrounding him, the chaos of his home, he considered giving up the charade. Meanwhile, the knocking grew louder. He poured himself a small glass of water from the filtered pitcher he kept on his countertop and snuck a glance through the side window. He recognized one of the detectives standing outside. Briefly, he toyed with ignoring them, but then thought better of it. They had already questioned him at the restaurant. They knew he was home. He had no choice but to swing open the door.

"Hello again!" he said in the same overly exuberant tone he'd used earlier that day.

Before the detectives could respond, Étienne spotted Michael McPherson emerging from his home—kitty-corner to Étienne's—and making his way toward the news crews, his face serious, stern. Other neighbors quickly followed, including Susan McPherson, trailed by Mary Elizabeth, then the Cambodian family, and Aldrin Rutherford and Arthur Gardenia, whose houses sandwiched Étienne's. Practically everyone on Ilios Lane, it seemed, except him. Michael McPherson, Étienne realized, looked exactly as he wished himself to look—confident and calm, yet serious and reliable.

Michael glanced across the street and stopped when he saw Étienne standing on his front porch. Étienne. Not in Paris. The news crews turned to see what'd gotten Michael's attention.

"Mr. Lenoir," Detective Wasserman said, extending his hand. "I believe you've met my colleague."

Étienne nodded, smiling and also not smiling, his eyes trained on Michael's.

"We wondered if you could answer a question for us?"

The news cameras raced over and their sharp lights suddenly began to shine on him.

"Of course," said Étienne, conciliatory, shrinking. Suddenly he bent forward into a slow dive, the taste of hamburger rising from his throat. Étienne nearly vomited.

The following day the news stories would lead with this tidbit. Étienne Lenoir, who was supposed to have been on vacation in France, and who had never gone. Not this time, not ever. For Étienne, a deep and abiding shame came to replace whatever feelings he'd had over the loss of his things—not because he'd been so publicly caught in his years-long lie, but because the publicity of it made him realize he'd never had the courage to go in the first place. If the burglaries hadn't ever happened, he'd have kept up the façade of France forever.

"According to the National Passport Center records," Detective Wasserman said to Étienne, raising his eyebrows, pretending to consult his notebook, "you have never received nor even applied for a passport."

Part Two

———

# Wednesday, April 7, 2004

# Chapter 16

————

## 8:55 a.m.

C az had promised to sit with Mary at lunch. It was enough to make Mary feel overheated, short of breath. He'd sidled past her desk at the end of their composition class, in which they'd spent forty-five minutes comparing the narrator in Zora Neale Hurston's *Their Eyes Were Watching God* to that in Maxine Hong Kingston's *Woman Warrior*.

"Pissed-off chicks," Dave DiMartini had whispered to Caz, who whispered it to Mary, who giggled.

"Hey," Caz'd said after class. "See you at lunch."

It was less asking and more telling, but Mary didn't mind. The teachers had all been nice to her, telling her she could hand in homework late, inquiring about her family, about how she was doing. When they heard her father remark to reporters about her illness, Mary's unexcused absence from school the day before suddenly disappeared. She could get used to this kind of attention. Her homeroom teacher reminded her of the counseling service available to all students and offered to write her a pass. The counselor, a man in his midforties, seemed like the kind of person who would keep a brood of cats in the house.

Sofia had always been popular, the whole Asian thing. Some of the girls accused the boys of having "yellow fever." But Mary Elizabeth had always felt herself more of a fringe character, marginally acknowledged by the freaks, the geeks, the preppies, the poshies, the burnouts and hipsters, the jocks, the nerds, the chills, the gays, but not particularly welcomed by any of them. To her, the fault obviously lay with her hair. Her parents wouldn't let her dye it, even though her mother, Susan, had dyed her own hair blond for as long as Mary could remember. In any case, it wasn't so much the color as the shape; it moved as a singular force, like a barrister's wig from an English crime drama. Her mother called it "unbreakable." As in Samson. Providing Mary with some kind of mysterious strength, which she thought was supremely stupid. But now, both she *and* her inglorious coif had been invited to lunch by Caz.

She spent the next hour trying to figure out how to merge her own initials with Caz's. Mary Elizabeth McPherson and Christopher Alexander Zaininger. MEM and CAZ. Mary realized they both had middle names that began with vowels, and she suddenly felt there was something to that, something she'd somehow failed to see in the past. She toyed with finding Sofia in her biology class and telling her about lunch, but then worried Sofia would somehow wrangle her way to their lunch table and Mary's one chance with Caz would be ruined.

She drew a heart with a purple gel pen on the inside cover of her notebook and filled it with:

CAZ-n-MEM 4-ever

CAZMEM

MEMCAZ

CM.AE.ZM

C + M = TLA!

She wondered if he brought his own lunch or ordered from the counter. She wondered if she should order from the counter as she usually did or just nibble on the granola bars she'd brought from home. But granola bars were boring, the nerd's candy bar. If she ordered at the counter, should she get pizza—the suggestion being that she was cool, just one of the guys, a down-to-earth girl—or salad, suggesting that she was elegant and mature. Salad offered sophistication, while pizza said tomboy. She decided on salad and a cookie, elegance with a little impulsive deviance thrown in.

Today, she felt, could really be the start of something, some whole new life, the opportunity to reinvent herself to a public who had barely noticed her before. And what had she lost in the burglaries? Nearly everything taken from her family's home had been her father's. Karma indeed! she thought. Hell, she even wriggled out of cutting class. Maybe she should run for student government? Maybe she should take up an instrument such as the drums? Maybe she should use her newfound celebrity for a good cause? Better cheerleading uniforms? Shorter class periods? Homelessness? Where trouble and intolerance had loomed just a day earlier, opportunity now seemed to present itself. This moment, she recognized, must be seized.

She remembered one student when she was in eighth grade who'd suddenly been whisked out of class by two men in dark suits and sunglasses, never to return. Turned out, his father worked for the embassy of Uruguay, or some other -guay, and someone had tried to assassinate him that morning. The boy's entire family had been collected and put on a plane back home for their protection. It was all so incredibly romantic, Mary remembered. The student's status rose immediately to the top tiers of social legend. Stories began circulating that he had quietly and secretly—heroically, even—intervened in fights, saved girls from roofie-spiked drinks, stood up to vindictive teachers. He'd become a moral compass for classroom injustice.

There was a downside, too, though. At home Mary's father and mother had a series of squabbles the night before that lasted well past midnight and promised to continue for some time, and her father was particularly frenetic.

"That Francophile freak!" he'd shouted, slamming the door behind him after he'd spoken to the reporters loitering around the McPhersons' front lawn. "I never trusted him. Never."

"Helen's got a real mess at her house," Susan said, straightening the cushions in the living room, plumping them back up to their original airiness. "We tidied up a bit, but I should go back tomorrow. It's just a *scene.* We really got off lucky when you look at her place."

"Why the fuck would he lie? I mean what for? To *us*?"

"Language, Michael!" Susan's face had a sheen of sweat across it.

"Yeah," Mary whispered. "Don't want your fucking language to fuck me up."

Susan stopped plumping and looked at her daughter for a moment. Mary felt a spike in her stomach. Her mother, dorky though she may have been, was also Mary's loyal advocate most of the time; disappointing her father elicited no particular feeling in Mary since it happened with such frequency, but her mom was another matter. After a second, Susan redoubled her efforts on the pillows, then moved on to stack coasters. Mary exhaled and sat on the stairs leading to their bedrooms.

Michael paced. "He's just snaky, that guy. Too stupid to really pull something like this off, but still. He's just . . . fucking weak."

"Michael! The language!"

He stopped pacing and seemed to notice Mary for the first time.

"Who are you talking about, anyway?" Susan asked.

Mary had a sinking feeling that a fight was about to erupt. She wished she had retreated to her room the moment she walked in the door with her mother. Over at Helen's, her mom mostly tried to get Helen to stop crying, while Mary swept up broken plates and picked up shirts and dresses and hangers and threw them in a pile in the corner of Helen's bedroom. It wasn't exactly cleaning so much as redistributing the mess.

"Étienne, the idiot," Michael said. He rubbed his eyes with the balls of his hands. "The guy with the restaurant."

"Étienne our friend and neighbor?" Susan said.

"He may be your friend, but he's no friend of mine. And he's no friend of this family."

Susan put down the coasters.

"He's not in France. He's home, across the street, talking to Wasserman on his front porch."

"Maybe he flew home when he heard the news."

"You can't fly home that quickly from Paris." Michael McPherson glanced at his daughter. He stood on the tile in the foyer. "The look on his face," Michael said, quieter now. "You should have seen it, Susan. It was guilty, guilty, guilty."

"Oh, he's just an insecure guy. We should eat at his restaurant more. Support our neighbors."

"He cooks with rats!"

"He doesn't cook with rats!" Susan picked up a cushion that she'd already plumped once and began to beat it wildly.

"And you." Her father suddenly pointed at Mary. "Don't think I don't know!"

Mary, taken aback to have suddenly been yanked into the drama, didn't say anything.

"I know exactly what you're up to." Two steps and he was smack in front of her. "Your secret friend. Don't you think for a minute that I don't know. You think I never tried to pull the wool over my parents' eyes? You think I wasn't a teenager myself, young lady?"

Mary, despite herself, reddened, trained her eyes on the floral wallpaper border that ran the circumference of their living and dining rooms.

"Who do you think it is?" Susan asked, glad for a change of topic. Mary, she reasoned, had actually done something wrong; Étienne, on the other hand, was being unfairly accused by her husband simply because he had a few quirks—not that Michael would ever admit that, she knew.

"Oh, I know who it is." His finger wagged in Mary's direction. He'd left the foyer and was standing in the living room now. "I know exactly who it is. It's that little Chinese girl down the street."

"Cambodian, Dad. God!"

"They *are* Cambodian, Michael."

"It doesn't fucking—"

"Michael!"

He took a deep breath, balled his fists, then flexed his hands.

"It doesn't *matter* what they are. You think you can protect her identity, but you're as transparent as a window, my dear."

"Nice," Mary snapped. "So now you're a poet. Whatever, Dad. Sofia's cool."

There was a moment, when you were in trouble, where it didn't much matter anymore how much shit you added to your rap sheet. She turned and ran up the stairs to her bedroom. How could she keep her parents from telling on Sofia? Now she'd look like she'd ratted out her friend. Why couldn't her father just keep anything to himself? She didn't mind being punished; she knew she'd done something wrong. But Sofia really was innocent. The whole thing had been Mary's idea.

Michael had shouted after her, "Don't think you can hide out in your room, Mary Elizabeth McPherson. This isn't over!"

Mary flopped diagonally across her bed, straining to hear her parents' conversation.

"Now her family," Susan was saying . . . Mary could just make out the words through the heating vent in the floor.

"France . . . America . . . bullshit . . . ," her father said.

"Michael, please! Étienne may embody some oddities—"

"Oddities? Susan, he's a nutcase."

"—but Étienne certainly is not capable of grand-scale robbery." Several bright lights suddenly went dark outside their living-room window. News crews packing it up.

Michael ran his hand absently over his forehead. "I tell you one thing, that little Sofia isn't as innocent as she makes out either. And her cousin! He couldn't even look me in the eye when we were there."

"Jesus, Michael, you all but accused him!"

Upstairs in her bedroom, Mary turned over in her bed. Her parents were wrong. Sofia *was* as innocent as she made out. Half the boys in school followed her around with wagging tongues and she didn't even notice. Mary hoped her father would keep it to himself. Her only consolation lay in that he'd have to go through Sofia herself to tell her parents. Mary was almost sure he wouldn't go to the trouble. As for Sofia's cousin, Mary had no idea what her dad might do.

# Chapter 17

## 10:15 a.m.

The Kowalskis returned home the previous night to a house wholly in order, not a speck of dust anywhere, not a piece of furniture an inch out of place. Alicia's parents had cleaned up everything and were waiting up for them when they returned. Except for the blank spaces of what had been taken, you'd never have known anything was amiss. Her father handed her two shiny silver keys, for the new back-door lock. "The burglars used a screwdriver to get in," her father told her. "I don't know how the police determined this, but they did. A screwdriver!" He seemed both baffled and momentarily impressed by this feat. Alicia's mother jumped in and hugged her daughter, rubbing her back, letting her know that the police had everything they needed—they'd dusted for prints, looked for evidence, and Arlene had cleaned up every last trace of the mess.

Alicia wondered what it had looked like. The chaos and disorder of invasion. Dan thanked her parents profusely, but Alicia stayed silent. She was awed not by what they'd lost, and not by what was happening on Ilios Lane, but by how completely her parents could mask it all in a sheen of normalcy. The only hint of something amiss, indeed, was just how very clean it all was. Alicia never kept her house this spotless. She found herself wanting the chaos, wanting the mess. It was *her* mess, after all, wasn't it? Or was it? The house, the things in the house . . . it had all come from her parents. Perhaps it was only proper that they be the ones to clean it all up. Alicia looked first at her mother, then her father, before she allowed Dan to lead her up the stairs and into bed for the night.

Then, she dozed briefly, awoke, tried unsuccessfully to read herself to sleep, downed a shot of lemon vodka, and drifted off for half an hour before Dan's snoring suddenly spurred her awake again. Finally, at four in the morning, she got up and swallowed a mouthful of NyQuil, which knocked her out cold—at least until her father came in to say good-bye. She felt his hand on the side of her face, but she could not force her mind awake, could not process any of what he said to her. She felt Chester jump up on the bed and curl up in the bend of her legs. When her father bent to kiss her, she was pretty sure she murmured a thank-you, but then fell immediately back to sleep, even before her father had made it to the bottom of the stairs.

She was awakened by her doorbell. She opened one eye and looked at the clock—10:15 a.m. The doorbell rang again, and she noted that Chester was not wildly barking, which meant Dan must have taken him out for a walk. Alicia would have to call their dog walker, let her know they were back. They shared her with Aldrin Rutherford next door, who had a little shit-kicker dog, white and fluffy and stupid. Or at least, he'd *had* a dog until his wife took the kids and the dog and moved out of the house. Alicia knew she and

Dan didn't really need a dog walker, but she told herself it was a way to contribute to the local economy.

Alicia stood in a fleece robe, her hair flattened on one side, still in the sarong she'd slept in under the robe. She tried to blink away the harsh daylight.

The man in front of her wore a golf shirt and khakis. His teeth were a severe white and he carried a laptop bag over one shoulder. Holding out a business card, he introduced himself as Mark O'Brien, from some alarm-system company. "All of us at ADT want you to know how very sorry we are about what happened to your family yesterday, These kinds of things, targeting innocent people, we wished they never happened."

Alicia nodded, heard a thump that she suspected was a bird flying into a window, but she couldn't locate the origin of the sound. "Who are you again?"

"Mark O'Brien. ADT." When she didn't respond, he added, "Residential security systems."

She was having trouble thinking straight through her NyQuil haze and wished Dan would come home. Why had he abandoned her on this morning of all mornings?

"If I could have just a moment of your time. We make special allowances for people in your situation."

"My situation?"

He shifted the laptop bag to the other shoulder. "Recent victims. It's our way of . . . shall we say, easing the blow of the burglaries, trying to get you back a little peace of mind."

Alicia felt the instant urge to hug him. She heard "peace of mind" as a kind of beacon, and she moved aside and gestured for him to come in. Before she shut the door, she caught a glimpse of the McPherson yard. A lone reporter, lounging on the grass beside a Volvo station wagon, a notebook closed beside him. He appeared to be reading an oversize book, holding a bright yellow highlighter in his hand. Was he a student? Alicia wondered. Some journalism major hoping for a scoop?

Thirty minutes later and still dazed, she'd signed a contract for a brand-new home-security system with door and window sensors, motion detectors, one SafePlace Pro 2000 Touchpad, a smart-voice wireless feature, a carbon monoxide detector, a silent alarm, and six window decals and a yard sign. Installation was 20 percent off; monthly monitoring would cost them just under $600 a year, with 10 percent off the first year because of her "recent victim" status. Alicia glossed over the particulars, but it didn't matter. All she heard, over and over, was "peace of mind." When he left, she climbed back up the stairs and fell into bed and thought how Dan had still not returned, but even that didn't matter anymore. She had *peace of mind.*

In fact, Dan wasn't far. He'd stopped at the McPhersons' to talk to the reporter, a journalism student named Paul Patterson, while Chester panted beside him. He missed entirely the stranger emerging from his house.

# Chapter 18

### 9:35 a.m.

It was morning, and Arthur's sister had appeared at his doorstep. Barbara, who insisted on being called Bobbi (which had always sounded strangely elastic to Arthur in a most unfeminine way), visited perhaps monthly, if that, despite living a half hour away in a suburb called Downers Grove. Why the residents didn't band together to create a name just a hint more appealing baffled him. Uppers Grove? Marginally Happy Grove? How had such a name stuck? To make matters worse, she'd married an Englishman with the unfortunate last name of Blandford. She sounded like a bit player from a golden age soap opera. A community-theater star. Bobbi Blandford of Downers Grove.

She spent her days doing mammograms. He couldn't imagine how she did this all day long, year after year, hiking one sagging breast at a time atop a plastic tray. He had no real experience with breasts himself, but Bobbi had once compared the aging woman's bosom to raw chicken. *Not in a bad way,* she'd said. *It is what it is.* Arthur moaned and quickly changed the subject.

Certainly, Arthur saw the importance of her work. No one could argue that. But the monotony of such a task! He couldn't imagine. Still, she was a believer. When summer came around, her weekends filled with charity walkathons and fund-raising for breast-cancer research.

She'd arrived at his doorstep weighed down by heaps of dark-blue cotton sheets. "They'll do until we can sort out curtains for you," she told him.

"Bobbi, you cannot come in here and demand how I'll have things in my own home." Then he immediately regretted saying it. Hadn't the police all but blamed him yesterday for his own burglary? Hadn't the lack of curtains substantiated a measure of his complicity in the matter? For once, his sister was right.

She didn't answer, but Arthur knew that by morning's end he'd be downstairs helping his sister hang the sheets. For starters, Bobbi was five feet tall. Without a ladder, or Arthur's help, she had little hope of a sheet's actually catching on a rod.

"What brings you here so early anyway?" Early mornings were inconvenient, not only for the terrible light, but because Arthur had become, over the years, nocturnal. He rarely rose before noon, and now here she was in a midmorning frenzy.

"Do you know how many burglaries we have in Downers Grove every week, Arthur? Do you?"

"What's that got to do with anything?"

"Well, do you?"

He sat down, elbows on knees, face in his hands. He could feel a migraine coming on. "I assume your inquiry's rhetorical."

"The point is that you have to *lock your doors*, Arthur. The point is that you have to live with the appearance of a normal person. You have to use curtains. You have to turn lights on and off. You have to know what's in your house and who's in your house!"

Arthur and Bobbi had had this discussion in many forms. She'd long wanted him to have a live-in "companion," as she'd called it. A maid/cook/cleaner/nurse all in one. But Arthur felt fully capable of taking care of himself. He operated at night. He wore his glasses. He worked. Yet his way of living offered no reasonable defense to Bobbi. To her it was a life of hardship that he'd endured alone far too long.

"You have nothing to prove," she told him over and over. Nothing to prove to anyone. Arthur wasn't at all sure he agreed with her.

As she put down the sheets, she gasped in a sort of horror. It made Arthur jump. "The dictation machine! Oh, no, Arthur. They took your dictation machine? Oh, dear Lord."

Bobbi had bought him the machine some years ago for verbal notes. In his list for the police, Arthur hadn't even written it down. Hadn't so much as noticed its absence.

"Insurance should cover that," Bobbi said. "Have you checked? Have you even spoken with your insurance agent?"

Of course, he hadn't.

Arthur rose from his seat in the living room and walked upstairs. Bobbi followed, dropping the issue of the dictation machine temporarily. He settled into the auburn leather chair in his office, whose fabric was worn down on the arms and the seat cushion was indented and welcomed his form perfectly. His headphones lay at his feet. He hadn't listened to a thing since the police had left his house the day before. He envisioned his notebooks in

some Dumpster, buried under rotting lettuce and Styrofoam packing peanuts and thought he felt an actual skip in his heartbeat.
He could not bear to have the headphones on, to remind him of
so many years of lost work. A dim night-light glowed from the
wall, but the room was otherwise dark. Still, Arthur found himself
squinting slightly at his sister as if the circumference of her human
force was too much for him.

The phone rang. Bobbi picked up and launched into a conversation as if the call had indeed been meant for her. Arthur felt as if
he were being "handled." He found he had to quell the urge to pull
the phone cord from the wall altogether. Bobbi hadn't said a thing
about the lost notebooks.

"That was the police. They offered to come and get you and take
you to the station for your fingerprints."

"I'll go later myself. I don't need the escort." At the end of the
meeting at the McPherson house the night before, Michael had suggested a few of them go to the police station together and Arthur
had agreed.

"That's what I said. I told them I'd take you myself."

"Bobbi, I don't need an escort *from anyone*." He couldn't decide
who bothered him more—his sister or Michael McPherson. At the
moment, his neighbor had a minor lead.

"You don't even know their hours."

"It's a bloody police station, Bobbi. *It doesn't close.*"

Outside, Arthur heard a dog barking, and it suddenly occurred
to him that he hadn't heard his neighbors' dog in quite some time.
At the McPhersons' last night, he'd learned that his neighbors' names
were Dan and Alicia Kowalski, and that they were on vacation in
the Florida Keys. Up until that point, he'd known them as the own-
ers of the large black dog named Chester. Chester's barking kept

Arthur awake. Arthur had never much liked dogs, and even less so as his hemeralopia progressed. They were unpredictable, occasionally deadly. And they offended his sense of olfactory decorum. He knew immediately when he'd entered a house with a dog. It was a musty, dank smell. Dog. A smell that Arthur associated with moldy dairy. Clearly, Chester had returned to the home front.

Arthur tried to ignore the insistent barking as Bobbi began to thumb through his mail, zeroing in on his unpaid property-tax bill, which was now a month overdue. "A month! Arthur! My God."

Arthur had no real excuse for this oversight. He'd received the bill in time. He had the money in his account, but he generally paid his property taxes late simply because he couldn't abide the idea that so many of his own tax dollars paid for area schools when he'd never had children himself. He understood the point, that the tax burden was shared equally, that he utilized resources that school-children perhaps didn't and vice versa, but something about the school in particular irked him, something about his never being given the opportunity to have children. He told himself he was far better off than those poor families such as the McPhersons who'd dig their own graves of debt getting their kids through college. But he wasn't sure this was true. After all, children had given him his life back, had given him something to work for again. The voices of children.

"Listen, Arthur." Bobbi had come round to face him, and now she was bent over before him, her hands on his knees. "You're not going to like this, but just hear me out."

"No, Bobbi."

"You don't even know what I'm going to say."

"I will not have a live-in, Bobbi. We've discussed it and I won't talk about it again."

"Stephen and I talked it over. Just hear me out." She had a smile in her voice, a glow almost. He couldn't see it, but he could hear it. Perhaps she was going to tell him she was a grandmother. She'd waited years for one of her three children to have a child, but so far no luck. Arthur wished someone would shut up the damn dog.

"We've decided to redo our basement. Gut it, the works. Stephen's at home right now going through boxes, seeing what we can get rid of. Just *organizing* it, you know? And we've already called an architect. We don't want something halfway, something just done on the surface. We want a fabulous new apartment down there. Something that'll really dazzle."

"That's wonderful, Bobbi. Sounds like a good project." Why wouldn't she get her hands off his knees? Why was she so . . . hovery?

"Kitchen, bedroom, full bathroom, dining area . . . we're hoping to use the whole footprint of the house if we can." She was almost giddy now, encouraged by Arthur's approval of the idea. "We might even be able to get two bedrooms out of it."

He wondered if this was the beginning of her retirement plan, rehab the house to make a little rental income. Perhaps she'd work up the curiosity to travel a bit now?

"And we want your input on the whole thing, Arthur. Design. Colors. Lighting. Everything."

"What on earth for? I haven't any interest in that sort of thing."

"Oh, but you should."

"Do you hear that dog? It's my neighbor's dog. Thing drives me batty."

"We'll do it any way you want it, the design I mean. Whatever suits you."

"Have I got a window open up here? It does seem unusually loud." He looked around, but nothing seemed different. His office window had long been blocked by a bookcase, filled to overflowing.

Bobbi stopped for a minute and looked around. "I think the windows are closed. Anyway, what do you think?"

"It's a fine idea."

"It *is*?"

"Well, yes, Bobbi. You and Stephen can do whatever you like. It's your house."

"But about you, I mean. You'll do it?"

"Do what?" Arthur felt his stomach begin to churn. Bobbi stood up and stretched her legs. She was wearing knit trousers and a gray College of DuPage sweatshirt that had to have come from his days teaching there.

"Live there. In the new basement. With us. You'll do it, Arthur?"

Arthur noticed, in that moment, that Chester had gone quiet.

# Chapter 19

## 8:36 a.m.

Michael rose early and called Detective Wasserman at eight thirty. Under the circumstances, Michael felt the sheer volume of homes involved ought to elicit some useful evidence, maybe even a lead or two. Who knew what could turn up overnight?

"Look, Mr. McPherson," Wasserman said, "I know it's frustrating. It seems like it ought to be easy, but what we're dealing with here—scale aside—is pretty typical stuff."

Michael asked how that could possibly be so. How could a whole truckload of stuff just vanish?

"Daytime robberies, for one. They're much more common than night. People work. Criminals know it, and unfortunately I don't have to tell you thieves don't tend to hold nine-to-five jobs like the rest of us." Burglars didn't often carry weapons—they were, in Wasserman's experience, a nervous bunch whose lives were generally not going well, and home invasions were often just a crime of opportunity. Michael's house was a case in point. Thieves probably got into the office, started grabbing stuff, heard Mary, and dashed out. Given how much of each house was *undisturbed*, Ilios Lane was a relatively quick hit, despite the sheer number of residences involved.

"Look," Wasserman said, "all these things you're thinking: barking dogs, vans parked on the street. They're pretty ordinary during the day. You hear a dog barking like crazy in the dead of night, you see a van with dark windows parked in the middle of the alley at night, they'd mean something to you. But during the day, people operate under the assumption that they're safe. I'll tell you something. You know what keeps people safe from break-ins? Safer than all the sophisticated alarm systems and fake yard signs? Tire swings keep people safe. Playhouses. Tricycles in the yard. Signs of little kids. A house with little kids is a house with people in it, going in and out all day. You want to increase your safety on Ilios Lane? Hang a couple of tire swings. Build a tree house with your neighbors."

"You know, I'm sure I've seen some west-side kids hanging around here. City kids, I mean. Young men."

"There isn't a border, Mr. McPherson. So unless you have something a little more solid—"

"Suspicious, I mean. I see a lot of suspicious people. There's some young gangbanger kids, the nephews of the Cambodian family, you might want to check out. One of them looked at me *very* suspiciously yesterday. Really made my skin crawl." Michael noticed the greasy pizza box from last night's dinner still on the counter, two slices gone hard. He had to stop himself from reaching for a slice. He heard a thumping over the phone, as if Wasserman was pounding on a stapler.

"Mr. McPherson"—Michael thought he detected impatience in the detective's voice—"I promise you we are on top of this. I have a whole team devoted to your street, and we're going to use all the resources at our disposal to figure out who did this and why. Just let us do our job."

Michael rubbed his forehead and closed his eyes for a minute. Upstairs, he could hear Susan turn off the shower. Mary had already left for school. "These neighbors, we've formed a kind of group, you know. A collective."

"I've heard. That's good. You need to support each other."

Michael ground his teeth for a second. "I need to be able to tell my neighbors something. Media's camped out in front of my house and they're charging at me every time I walk out the door." This was not, technically speaking, true. When Michael looked out his bedroom window, only one reporter was still lingering.

"Keep it simple, Mr. McPherson. Short and sweet."

"Can you at least update me about the case? Even something minor?"

"I can update you about *your* case. Confidentiality laws don't entitle you to hear about your neighbors' cases."

Michael could feel his heart pounding, his blood heating up. "You know, Detective," Michael said, taking a different tack, "I'm not sure if I told you what I do for a living. I sell bridges. Modular bridges."

"Listen, Mr. McPherson—"

"They use them at Ground Zero. Compact modulars. You can put them up in a day, then break 'em down and take 'em with you. They're ugly as hell, but they're exactly what you want in times of chaos. Minnesota? Remember that bridge? That was what you call a *critical bridge failure*. Critical. We assume infrastructure stays structurally sound forever."

"Mr. McPherson, I do apologize, but—"

"What I'm saying, Detective Wasserman, is that I'm your bridge here. To my neighbors, to this community. We've had a critical failure, and we need—*you need*—a compact modular."

"Mr. McPherson? I hear you." The detective went silent a moment while someone spoke to him in his office. Michael couldn't make out what was said. "I promise you, I'll give you an update when there's one to give. Don't forget you all need to come in here and do your elimination prints."

"I'll get us all together," Michael promised. "We'll all come in at once so you don't get interrupted all day. This afternoon, we'll be there."

He hung up and leaned against the kitchen counter. The first twenty-four hours of an investigation were critical, and he wanted to keep the pressure on, let the department know there was more at stake than just stuff—it was the sense of safety in their whole community. Behind him, the smell of a burning pot of coffee began to waft through the kitchen, and he heard Susan turn on the blow-dryer upstairs. He poured himself the dregs. Through the window he could see a cluster of tulips emerging near the alley. He'd never been a gardener himself. Maybe this summer he'd get out there, plant a bit, do some weeding. He wondered if Wasserman had really listened to him at all.

# Chapter 20

——

## 1:20 p.m.

S usan did a double take behind the wheel of her gold Honda Accord. She thought she saw Michael's Ford Focus in the driveway as she drove past Ilios Lane. Why wasn't Michael at work? His commissions had gotten so small that he hadn't received a bonus in five years, and Susan had had to go full-time at the Oak Park Community Housing Office. The month before, he was passed over for promotion to a guy who'd been with Lowry Brothers only three years. There was talk of layoffs, but then the talk flittered away, and Michael, chastened, continued in the same job with the same title and territory he'd had for years.

"Ilios Lane!" the client in Susan's car yelled. "I didn't know we were so close!"

Susan had just shown her an apartment on Austin and Augusta. "Well, the next property is a good four, five blocks away still."

"I mean, you must be able to practically see Ilios Lane from the apartment, no?"

"No."

"It seems like you could. Like you should be able to see it." The girl was looking at Susan suspiciously, the diamond in her nose sending strobe flashes across the dashboard. The two had just finished looking at a mint-condition, rehabbed one-bedroom on Austin Boulevard *with* parking, and Susan was annoyed that the young woman had not immediately recognized this as a rare find.

"No," Susan said, a little more firmly than she should have. "Really, you can't." Susan knew what always sealed the deal for her clients was her own life. "I've lived on the east side for sixteen years," she'd tell them. "I raised my kids here," she'd add, even though her own street did not have a single black family and never had in the years she'd lived there.

They used to work, these aphorisms of hers. The family, the kids on the east side. But things had been tough lately. There were the assaults by the three black boys who'd come over from the west side, there were the muggings, first in the bank parking lot on Madison, and then in the alleyway behind Ace Hardware. And now these burglaries on her very street, in her very *house*. Already, she'd had two clients today and the burglaries had concerned them both.

Now this twentysomething girl, with the pierced nose. The kind of funky young adult who'd have moved into the east side without a second thought back in the nineties. Today, driving through the neighborhood, she was vacillating, eyeing Ilios Lane in the passenger side mirror as it fell behind them.

Susan had fallen into her job at the Housing Office largely by accident. Almost to the day after she graduated college she met Michael at a Jessie and the Jawbreakers concert at the Hideout. They waited eight years to marry, waited so long that it seemed in equal proportions both inevitable and entirely unlikely. Yet a month into their marriage, she found herself pregnant, and when Thomas was born, she'd had to quit grad school and her job as a social worker's assistant to care for him. From that moment, she recognized in her own life a cliché she'd always worked hard to avoid. She vowed to return to school, but of course never did. After a few years with Tommy, just when a return to grad school seemed possible, she got pregnant with Mary and kissed away another four years. Eventually she found work at the Housing Office as an escort, taking people around the town, showing the highlights: the Lake Theatre and Barbara's Bookstore, the little diners and gift stores, Petersen's Ice Cream parlor and Erik's Deli. Lately, it had gotten harder and harder with all the chain stores moving in—the Gap and Borders and Trader Joe's. But mostly her job was to show them apartments on the east side, encourage them to be part of Oak Park's diversity, be part of the wonder of this unusual village.

Susan had loved her job. She believed in the program and loved meeting all the different new people who came to look at the apartments. In the dozen years she'd been at the Housing Office, she'd seen tenants become lifelong friends, seen a few meet each other and marry and have children. Dan Kowalski, her neighbor, had been an early tenant on Austin Boulevard, until he married Alicia and moved to Ilios Lane. She'd shown the Cambodians the downstairs apartment in the two-flat just two doors down from her and they'd lived there for years now.

Michael tolerated her work, but didn't think what she was doing was all that innovative or would ultimately change much of anything.

"Human nature," he'd tell her, "wants to be with its own."

"You're wrong," she'd insisted. "We are changing things. We *have* changed them."

"Just wait," he'd scoff. He'd nod sarcastically. "Just wait. You'll see."

But she'd use her own life to refute him. In college she'd dated a black classmate of hers named Harley, who would go on to be a brilliant sociologist at Northwestern University, but back when they were nineteen, his world was a revelation to Susan. He'd grown up in Milwaukee, a black among whites. He was more comfortable, he told her once, in a room full of whites rather than blacks because he'd grown up around white people, and this, he believed, was the defining sadness of his life. It left him feeling groundless, floating above everyone else, standing at doorways knocking, his whole life, knocking. "It's what I'll always do," he'd said. "I'll always be knocking at doors. I'll never be inside anywhere."

"Not mine," she'd told him. "My door's open."

He'd smelled like warm tea and coconut. They dated for six months and he told her stories about being on the bus and having all the seats taken except the one beside him. He'd tell her of walking through campus at night and hearing the footsteps of the young women in front of him speed up. He'd tell her things she'd later read in books by Richard Wright and the Steele brothers, the clichés in which white fear manifests itself. She'd listen to Harley talk about his life, and then, later, she'd read about that same kind of life, that same experience, in every African-American narrative put to paper, and it would make her want to break off the high heels of the women who scurried more quickly before him, pour water down the gas tanks of taxis who refused to stop for him.

The afternoon he finally ended it with her, she cut him off, said, "This is the part where you tell me it's not me, it's you, right?"

"It's not so small," he told her, "as to be about me."

She wanted to ask if it was about her then, if he was too ashamed to say so, if it was *he* who couldn't get past the idea of *her*. She didn't understand the barriers weren't about her, about any one person. He had taken on the philosophies of the young and idealistic, those who, for the first time perhaps, were suddenly able to place themselves in the larger framework of the world, people beyond the homes they grew up in, the parents and neighborhoods who'd raised them. For Harley, Susan thought, it seemed as if this idea hadn't freed him, as it had her, but had further imprisoned him.

"This is not solvable by us," he told Susan. "I'm sorry. I can't be with someone I have to explain my world to every day."

"That's not fair!" she cried. She'd stopped just short of begging.

"You're right. Not fair to either of us."

She thought she had begun to understand now, the exhaustion of it all, being with someone like her. Even someone with good intentions, even someone with an open mind, with all the right beliefs, still lacked the tangible, corrosive evidence of experience. That gap was impossible to fill.

Her husband, Michael, had always told her the whole Oak Park program was racist, trying to get white people to live among black people. He believed in free markets, even in the field of sociology, that you rehab the buildings, raise the rent, and see who comes. Stay out of nature and you'll see how nature really works. Look at our own damn street if you need evidence.

Now, some small part of her feared Michael might have been right. September 11th Syndrome, they called it at the Housing Office. People were skeptical in the same way they'd been skeptical in the early and mid-eighties. They were scared. The fear brought out their worst tendencies, tiny kernels of bigotry and racism. It wasn't just white people who began to voice these fears. It was anyone with a middle-class income. Indians from Delhi, Chinese from

Shanghai and Hong Kong. The only universal in all of this was that everyone's fear found the same targets: poor blacks. If they were poor and they were black, then they were sure to live in crime-infested neighborhoods no matter how much the gardens were kept up, no matter how full the recycling bins were. Susan was not too big to admit that she was scared. Scared for the program, scared for the neighborhoods she'd worked so hard to transform, and scared—she had to admit—for her family. For herself.

Later, back in her office, she pulled a lease for the girl with the pierced nose. She'd found a place on Oak Park Avenue, the top floor of a six-floor flat where the five other apartments housed thirty-somethings with urban sensibilities and decent salaries. And white skin. The girl was coming back in the morning to give her deposit and sign the lease. Susan couldn't help but feel slightly deflated.

Her boss, Evan, came in to chat. Evan was hardly a boss. He was one of her closest friends. He and his wife, Viv, often came to Michael and Susan's for dinner parties or vice versa. The families' children went to school together. They ran into each other at Unity Temple occasionally, though Susan was admittedly a halfhearted Unitarian—more interested in the community than the message. They'd known each other twelve years, since Susan's first day on the job. She turned around in her metal folding chair. The entire office was reminiscent of a church basement, tiled floor and cheap, secondhand furniture, leaky ceilings.

Evan told her he was surprised she came to work. Said they'd all have understood if she'd wanted to stay home. "Is there anything you need, Suze?"

Susan sighed, shrugged. "A stereo."

He laughed. They sat together for a moment without talking, the kind of silence that might have been awkward with lesser friends.

"Really. If you need some time . . ."

"I'm fine, Evan. It's a burglary, not a death."

He pursed his lips and nodded, his eyes glancing out the store-front window as the elevated train passed their office.

"What?" she said.

"What?"

"You're doing that thing with your cheek. You're here for *something*. I know that look."

He laughed, picked up a blue lead pencil from the table, and began to roll it between his thumb and forefinger. "It's just that the robberies—"

"Burglaries," she corrected.

"Burglaries?"

"We all had a semantic lesson from the detective yesterday."

"Well, you know, it's only been a day. Maybe you want to take some time? Take a little vacation."

"Work is good for my constitution," she said, smiling.

Evan put down the pencil and leaned toward her. "Things have been tough around here, Susan. You know that. I don't have to tell you that. All of you escorts have it rough."

"What is it, Evan?"

He drummed his fingertips on the table. "The burglaries have come up today."

"I know. My clients asked about them, too."

"They've come up a lot, actually. The clients, the other escorts. Everyone's talking about what happened. Everyone just feels awful."

Suddenly, she began to understand what he was saying. She felt her heart begin to sag. "Twelve years, Evan. I've been here twelve years!"

He waved his hands at her to stop. "It's not that. You'll always have a place here. *Always*. I want to stress that, Susan. You will *always* be like family to every one of us."

She was aware, only now, that no other escorts were in the room. Evan must have planned this moment, this talk. They must've all been in on it. She felt captive in that wide-open space.

"We just think with things the way they are, it might be good for you to take some time off. To take care of things."

"What things? There's nothing to take care of, Evan. You want me to take care of *things*?" She felt her voice rising, wondered if clients in the front waiting room could hear her. "You want me to go shopping or something? Because that would take care of *things*. Shopping would be the only fucking *thing* I could do in this situation."

"You'll still be on the payroll," he offered in such a quiet voice, Susan had to strain to hear him.

Her body seemed warm. Was she overheating? Was the thermostat turned up? "The payroll? You think I work here for the payroll, Evan? For the lucrative benefits package?"

"Calm down, Susan."

"You calm down!"

He took off his glasses and rubbed his eyes for a moment. "Susan, it's very difficult for everyone here. And with the burglaries, the other escorts think it might be good to try and lay low for a while. You know, everyone sees you on the news, and . . ."

"The news? It's my newfound celebrity status? Jesus, Evan. I'm here. I'm still here. I live this program. I *am* this program. What better advertising do you need than a victim who's still a believer?"

**Listserv: Oak Park Moms**

**Messages in This Digest (13 Messages)**

**Messages**

**1a. Re: POLICE ALL OVER ILIOS LANE?????**
Posted by: "Hilary500" hkulauzov@ibkbinc.com Hilary Kulauzovick
Wed Apr 7, 2004 7:45 a.m. (CST)

Every home robbed, apparently! Police have no description of guilty party, and not released any leads. They have established a tip hotline. Just a reminder to everyone to keep yourselves safe. Even Oak Park isn't a haven, especially so close to the west side (not that I'm profiling. Just saying reality of our geography). Best crime prevention tip I ever heard was to know your neighbors, ie: who belongs in the area and who doesn't. Hilary Kulauzovick

On Apr 6, 2004, at 3:45 p.m. "Deb_ST" deb_ST@yahoo.com wrote:

---

>Anyone know what's happening on Ilios Lane? Just drove past on Erie St and there's police everywhere! Cars, police tape, etc. etc. Very scary! Please give info asap . . .

>

>

>

**Reply to sender | Reply to group | Reply via web post | Messages in this topic (2)**

## 1b. Re: POLICE ALL OVER ILIOS LANE?????
Posted by: "Al_n_Bev" Al_n_Bev@aol.com Al Thomas
Wed Apr 7, 2004 7:45 a.m. (CST)

Unfortunate occurrence on Ilios Lane yesterday afternoon, was mass burglaries of every household. Rumors are going to float around. My parents cabin in northern MI was robbed a couple years back and they ended up selling the place. Felt too insecure there, especially my mom, who never wanted to be alone there again. We have to remember that were living in an urban place with all the dangers and threats that anyone has who lives in a city. Oak Park likes to think it's diverse and free from crime but who are we kidding? No place in the world is free from crime. Look out for your neighbors and your family. Be safe, Al and Beverly Thomas.

**Reply to sender | Reply to group | Reply via web post | Messages in this topic (2)**

## 2. Free train table and Legos TAKEN!
Posted by: "blabbingmums" blabbingmums11@hotmail.com
blabbingmums
Wed Apr 7, 2004 7:50 a.m. (CST)

The free train table and Legos have been claimed. Thank you.
http://blabbingmums1@blogspot.com

**Reply to sender | Reply to group | Reply via web post |**
**Messages in this topic (1)**

### 3. Participate in a study aimed at improving memory and cognition
Posted by: "cognitive studies" cogstud@uic.edu Dr. Indira
Mehmet
Wed Apr 7, 2004 8:00 a.m. (CST)

Are you interested in improving your memory?
If you answered "yes" then researchers at the University of
Chicago are looking for you. The Behavior, Cognition and
Memory Lab is currently conducting a study examining
"Think It Through: Train the Brain." The current study
involves computer games and memory recognition tasks.
Participants will spend 30 minutes per day, 6 days per week, for
8 weeks engaging in games. Participants can do these games
at home on their own computer via the internet. Cognitive
recognition tasks and tests will be completed at the University
of Chicago, Hyde Park campus before and after the 8 week
sequence. If you are healthy, aged 18-60, and an English
speaker you may eligible to participate.
For more information CONTACT:
Dr. Indira Mehmet
cogstud@uic.edu
(773) 555-7274

**Reply to sender | Reply to group | Reply via web post |**
**Messages in this topic (1)**

### 4. Parking Problems AGAIN on OP Streets
Posted by: "Alice Jenkins" AliceJenkins44@edevcorp.net Alice
Jenkins
Wed Apr 7, 2004 8:10 a.m. (CST)

Called in my boyfriend's car to the parking Nazis last night,
and AGAIN this morning there was a ticket. This is the
third time this year this has happened to him. I'm sick of this
parking crap. FIVE nights a year per license plate is ridiculous!

Does anyone have any advice at all? I can't bring my son to sleep at his place in the city as that would require me to drive all the way back to get my son to school by 8:15 a.m. and it's just not practical. Nor is allowing my boyfriend to stay over at my house only five nights in a calendar year reasonable. Does anyone else have this problem? Should I build a driveway through the front yard of my apartment building? This might ultimately make me leave Oak Park if there isn't a solution! AliceJenkins44@edevcorp.net

**Reply to sender | Reply to group | Reply via web post | Messages in this topic (1)**

### 5. Volunteers needed for OP Library annual book sale . . .
Posted by: "George Miscowitz" George_Miscowitz@aol.com
Wed Apr 7, 2004 8:10 a.m. (CST)

This year's Oak Park Library Books sale, held annually in July, is looking for volunteers to sort the donations we're already receiving. Come to an information session on Monday, April 12 from 7-8pm. Volunteer hours are flexible. This is a great way to introduce yourself to the community!
Contact: George Miscowitz, OP Book Sale President, George_Miscowitz@aol.com, 708-524-0097

**Reply to sender | Reply to group | Reply via web post | Messages in this topic (1)**

### 6a. Re: Mass robberies on Ilios Lane!!
Posted by: "Ellen" elancaster7211@resourcesdev.org Ellen Lancaster
Wed Apr 7, 2004 8:20 a.m. (CST)

Oak Park is no safe haven, and those who take pride in living in a diverse community should think about why such a thing is something to be proud of at all? Is it not a form of racism to be "proud" of living among minorities? If I were a minority, this would not sit well with me at all—in fact, I'd be likely to

run screaming from Oak Park. Should we not be recognized by who we are, not what we are? So we live near the west side. Fine. There will likely be crime associated with such a geography, an urban setting where the forces of poverty and its ills are constantly beckoning. I'm proud to have friends who are diverse, but NOT because of that diversity. Rather, because those friendships are fulfilling to my life.
Sincerely,
Ellen Lancaster

On Apr 6, 2004, at 6:30 p.m. (CST) Stevenson/Blair sbfamilyop@yahoo.com wrote:

---

>>>Police chief is asking all to be on the lookout for suspicious behavior, or dumped goods in alleyways, etc. seems there aren't any leads yet, but just a reminder to keep doors locked, and make sure alarm systems are up to date. No one injured, but v. scary. Will post more as I learn more.
>Robert Stevenson/Mandy Blair
>Washington Blvd.
>
>
>

**Reply to sender | Reply to group | Reply via web post | Messages in this topic (6)**

### 6b. Re: Mass robberies on Ilios Lane!!
Posted by: "MMV" MMVanderbilt@aaconsulting.com
Melinda Vandenberg
Wed Apr 7, 2004 9:02 a.m. (CST)

Police have no leads on Ilios Lane? Really? How about they do a little looking east of Austin? I know that's not a popular view here in Oak Park, and I appreciate your view Ellen, but do we really think someone from, say, Hinsdale popped over to help himself to the vast surplus of electronic gadgets that Ilios Lane residences offered? Come on. I like a diverse population

as much as anyone here, but we're kidding ourselves if we don't think this was perpetrated by at least SOME west siders.
On Apr 7, 2004, at 8:20 a.m. "Ellen" elancaster7211@resourcesdev.org wrote:

---

>>>Should we not be recognized by who we are, not what we are? So we live near the west side. Fine. There will likely be crime associated with such a geography, an urban setting where the forces of poverty and its ills are constantly beckoning. I'm proud to have friends who are diverse, but NOT because of that diversity. Rather, because those friendships are fulfilling to my life.
Sincerely,
Ellen Lancaster
>
>

**Reply to sender | Reply to group | Reply via web post | Messages in this topic (6)**

### 6c. Re: Mass robberies on Ilios Lane!!
Posted by: "S_Perez" S_Perez@unity.org
Wed Apr 7, 2004 9:05 a.m. (CST)

I think we need to separate what happened on Ilios Lane from how we feel about diversity assurance. As a minority, I am thrilled that someone from the majority culture allows this debate, and welcomes a variety of people and views. That's the magic of Oak Park. But as a minority, I feel equally that my status should be defined either by my opportunities or my failings; there is a rather subtle bigotry I hear when diversity assurance is discussed around Oak Park and I would prefer not be spoken for. Allow me to speak myself. Ilios Lane, it has to be pointed out, has little or no diversity by Oak Park standards. Is this the fault of those residents? Certainly not. Do they care? I have no idea, but I can tell you that I don't care. We're an affluent area. An area that, quite honestly,

welcomes minorities who fit certain economic standards. What
Oak Parker would take issue with living beside an African-
American doctor or lawyer, after all? But what about a family
of four displaced from the west side, headed by a single mother
and living off WIC and Section 8 and other social programs?
The answer to that question, to me, offers a bigger truth.

**Reply to sender | Reply to group | Reply via web post |
Messages in this topic (6)**

### 6d. Re: Mass robberies on Ilios Lane!!

Posted by: "ErinsWorld1" erinsworld@yahoo.com Erin
Ballantine
Wed Apr 7, 2004 10:15 a.m. (CST)

S_Perez, what you say makes a lot of sense, and I agree with
much of it. I've always been skeptical of diversity assurance
(and affirmative action). But it's also imperative to remember
the historical, institutional and socio-economic racism that
Diversity Assurance was born out of. In an ideal world, no one
would be judged by anything other than ability, but we don't
live in an ideal world. I do not believe for a minute—even in
today's climate—that were a white and a black with the same
education and background up for the same job that it would
go to the black ON MERIT as opposed to EOE. Had equal
opportunity and affirmative action and diversity assurance
never existed, we would still almost certainly be living in an
age of blatant and even mandated discrimination. I'm not
sure I see the wrong of having diversity as an open, and oft-
discussed objective for all of us.
On Apr 7, 2004, at 9:05 a.m. "S_Perez" S_Perez@unity.org
wrote:

---

>>I think we need to separate what happened on Ilios Lane
from how we feel about diversity assurance. As a minority, I
am thrilled that someone from the majority culture allows this
debate, and welcomes a variety of people and views.

Reply to sender | Reply to group | Reply via web post |
Messages in this topic (6)

## 6e. Re: Mass robberies on Ilios Lane!!

Posted by: "C. Hughley" cynthiahughley172@yahoo.com
Cynthia Hughley
Wed Apr 7, 2004 11:00 a.m. (CST)

Before I married and had children, I managed property in
upstate New York. Lots of myths exist around household
safety and burglaries and thought I'd share some of what I
learned:

a. Fences don't work as well at keeping people out as they do
   at keeping people hidden.
b. Burglaries happen MOST often during the day, while people
   are at work, rather than in the dead of night.
c. Having signs of children outside the house—swings, toys,
   etc.—often signals a daytime presence in the home and can
   be more effective than alarm systems.
d. Burglars WILL strike homes despite dogs and alarm systems.
e. In multi-unit buildings, the top floor is just as likely as the
   ground floor to be targeted (fewer witnesses on top floors!).

Be safe!
—Cynthia

Reply to sender | Reply to group | Reply via web post |
Messages in this topic (6)

## 6f. Re: Mass robberies on Ilios Lane!!

Posted by: "Pamela S. Merriman" PSMerriman@aol.com
PSMerriman
Wed Apr 7, 2004 11:16 a.m. (CST)

Diversity Assurance is an Oak Park Fair Housing Ordinance
aimed at establishing racial diversity in multi-unit buildings.
The program began in 1984, and grew out of a village diversity
policy established in 1973. In part, the policy was meant to

combat drug and gang violence that bled over into Oak Park from Chicago's west side. Do we know whether what happened on Ilios Lane came from west siders? Certainly, we don't, not yet. But is it likely? Certainly, it is, I believe. There seems to be an equating of racial consciousness with "racism" as a general social ill. But is recognizing another race any different than recognizing, say, hair or eye color? I speak here not of the belief that any of us are better than another, but from the seeming belief that any recognition of difference—even in celebration or jubilation—is "racist." But herein lies my question: does the recognition and consciousness of multiple races equal racism? Is that not simply what diversity assurance is attempting to answer? I would like to believe that we live in a post-diversity assurance society. Oh, how I would like to believe that. What is a valid point to me is the idea of taking pride in our diversity. Perhaps an attempt at no distinction— racially, or programmatically—ought to be the aim. In any case, my heart goes out to the Ilios Lane residents who surely feel this debate is very distant from the profound vulnerability and fear they must be experiencing. As we debate the merits of our community's programs, let's not forget where the current debate emerged from. . . .

Best,

Pam Merriman

On Apr 7, 2004, at 10:15 a.m. "ErinsWorld1" erinsworld@ yahoo.com wrote:

---

S_Perez, what you say makes a lot of sense, and I agree with much of it. I've always been skeptical of diversity assurance (and affirmative action). But it's also imperative to remember the historical, institutional and socio-economic racism that Diversity Assurance was born out of.

On Apr 7, 2004, at 9:05 a.m. "S_Perez" S_Perez@unity.org wrote:

---

I think we need to separate what happened on Ilios Lane from how we feel about diversity assurance. As a minority, I am thrilled that someone from the majority culture allows this debate, and welcomes a variety of people and views.

**Reply to sender | Reply to group | Reply via web post |**
**Messages in this topic (6)**

7. **This week's Iraq War protest MOVED . . .**
   Posted by: "Pauline Shuman" paulinescauses60@yahoo.com
   Pauline Shuman
   Wed Apr 7, 2004 11:39 a.m. (CST)

PLEASE NOTE: This week's protest against the illegal Iraq War will begin at Unity Temple at 9:00 a.m. sharp on Saturday, April 10. Please attend if you can, and if you believe the Bush Administration has broken international law with this invasion. All are welcome!
For further information, contact:
Paulinescauses60@yahoo.com
708-555-6447

**Reply to sender | Reply to group | Reply via web post |**
**Messages in this topic (1)**

# Chapter 21

## 12:10 p.m.

Mary took her finger and thumb and broke off a minuscule piece of cookie. She'd eaten two bites of salad before the thought occurred to her that something terrible, something *green*, might well lodge itself betwixt her teeth and ruin, *absolutely ruin*, her chances with Caz, who sat next to her on the white, plastic bench in the lunchroom, his hip touching hers. She was utterly frozen in place. His hip. Her hip. Her underwear went soft and wet the minute he sat himself casually down, not *across* from her, not *inches* away from her, but so close that his hip touched hers. Her entire body zinged from her toes up. How could she have held herself together through composition and social studies with Caz sitting just two desks behind her all this time? With his hips so alive, so *charged*. She was grateful that she hadn't, until this moment, known of his electric hips, though she felt a vague but growing fear that she would never again be able to concentrate on the *Mistakes Made During* the Vietnam War and the *Miscarriage of Justice That Was*

Watergate and the *Tactical Long-Term Brilliance of* the Marshall Plan, knowing that Caz and his hips were just two rows back.

"Salad and cookie," Caz was saying, "is like totally yin-yang, ya know? Like the balance of all things. Like how one keeps the other one in a kind of circle—no, like a hug or something, right? Like it all equals zero, nothing and everything."

Caz was blazed on a fatty of pure Hawaiian gold. Mary had an inkling about this, though she wasn't paying much attention to what was coming out of his mouth with his hip being *so* near hers. She had no idea what he was talking about, except a vague admiration for her choice of foodstuff.

"Nothing and everything," she agreed. "Yin-yang."

They went silent and Mary's mind buzzed trying to think of how to fill the void. She nibbled a chocolate chip. Caz did not play sports. He was not interested in cheerleading. He did not join clubs or participate in extracurricular activities, and he had a reputation for having purportedly passed only one class: small-engine repair. She could ask him about ecstasy, but even that as a diversion was so new to her she knew almost nothing about it, except how warm it made you feel and how much fuchsia buzzed around the periphery. He'd slept with dozens of girls, if one was to believe the stories, and so to be able to hold on to Caz for as long as a month, as Jenny Nellinger had, was a feat of intrepid and heroic proportions. Jenny'd been popular ever since, her 32B cups canonized in photocopied, black-and-white pictures on lockers all over the school. Not like Cindy Hamilton, caught at a house party with his dick in her mouth and her top around her waist, camera phones flashing like paparazzi, and she'd eventually had to get the administration *and* her parents involved in keeping the pictures from endless e-mail loops. She was thirteen years old then, and two years later she tried to kill herself. Mary, like everyone else who hadn't been there at the time, agreed that Cindy was a stupid slut who had it coming to her by wearing braless tank tops and short shorts and screwing loads of guys all the time starting when she was eleven years old, because otherwise why had she allowed so many pictures that night? Eight, ten, twelve camera phones captured the moment—Caz's head thrown back, eyes closed and grinning, and Cindy kneeling in front of him on her knees, her eyes closed, too. Caz had said he was doing her a favor, letting her blow him. She'd begged him, he said, and Mary, like everyone else, had said it was kindhearted of him when you really thought about it, to take an unpopular—smelly!—girl such as Cindy and let her have a piece of him.

Mary did not want to remind him of any other girl at that moment, especially Cindy, who (it had to be pointed out) had never once sat in the lunchroom with him before the eyes of everyone. When Mary thought about it, she could only remember Jenny sitting near Caz at lunch. Not one other girl. Until now. Until Mary herself.

But the silence was killing her.

"So here's a question," Mary chirped finally. "You have to answer the first thing that comes to mind."

He looked at her sideways, nodded in slow motion.

"What's the worst thing that ever happened to you?"

He stopped chewing his pizza. Mary instantly wished she'd asked something else, something about music. Yes. That would have been the subject. Hadn't she heard a rumor somewhere that he played the drums? She turned her head away and picked between her teeth with a fingernail.

"What the fuck kind of question is that?"

Mary blushed. Suddenly, Arthur's theory began to feel flimsy and inconsequential. She remembered her father telling her once that the key to sales wasn't what you said, it was the confidence with which you said it. She tried to keep her voice steady. "Can you answer?"

"I can. But why the fuck does anyone want to talk about the worst thing that ever happened to them?"

Mary stared at him. His eyes were glassy and his long hair smelled like smoke and cheap shampoo. That was the key to Caz, she thought, the answer to that question, getting him to confess, to reveal himself. He may not have answered her, certainly; didn't boys keep everything inside? Wasn't that what she'd heard? But knowing there was a secret there at all was something. Even Jenny Nellinger probably didn't know that. It was enough depth for one lunch period, Mary recognized. Don't get all philosophical on him. Guys didn't like it when girls were too smart. When they were too emotional. Keep it light. Keep it silly. She pushed her cookie away from her.

Caz broke the silence. "So you were, like, totally home when that dude broke into your house? Like, he could've seen you, right?"

"No one knows if it was a man or not." Coy. That's how she'd play it.

Caz laughed. "Burglars aren't chicks. They're dudes."

"Chicks can be burglars," Mary said, aware of this being her first attempt at the vernacular use of the term *chicks* in conversation.

"Name me one chick burglar. Just one."

"You name me one dude burglar." Mary wondered if he believed the burglaries were the worst thing to ever happen to her. She supposed they were, though all the stolen items belonged to her parents, and if the burglaries hadn't happened, she'd never have been sitting here, right beside Caz's hip with the whole lunchroom watching. So it'd be a hard point to argue. Helen Pappalardo had it bad, Mary thought. Helen was freaked-out, and her house had been turned into a disaster zone.

Caz laughed hard, harder than her retort had earned, and she snapped back to the moment, to her hip touching his. "Right on," he said. "But Al Capone was a dude."

Mary was aware of being watched. The whole lunchroom, she felt, was collectively *watching* and *trying not to watch* as Caz and Mary Elizabeth McPherson sat hip-to-hip laughing. Mary hoped people were noticing her *not* eat. And noticing how it was Caz laughing, rather than her. Translation: Mary Elizabeth McPherson was the source, as opposed to the brunt, of jokes currently amusing Caz Zaininger. This moment, she thought, could change *everything* for her.

"Bonnie and Clyde," Mary said. "Bonnie was a chick." Then she added quietly, "A girl."

She felt something in the small of her back: Caz's hand. He leaned toward her ear and whispered, "I didn't know you were so cool." His voice was low, sensual, a voice she'd never before heard come out of him. An *intimate* voice.

She felt the hairs on her neck stand up. She could not respond. She could not move. Her only sensation, beyond the quiet buzz of his voice and the heated cloth below his hand, was the smell of ketchup and hot dogs that persisted in their school cafeteria.

"Dude," he whispered to her, "you're making me so hot I could stick you right now."

Caz was a year older than Mary and was known for his epic parties, the various apartments he'd lived in over the years crammed to capacity with beer and bodies, and thus he'd long had a rather limitless supply of available girls. His experiences had started young and remained bountiful. He lived with his father, who was a truck driver and therefore only home every few days. Caz had more or less fended for himself since he was ten years old. It took Mary a moment to understand what he meant. A terribly antiseptic word for *it* flitted through her brain ... *i n t e r c o u r s e.* Her body went imperceptibly slack for a moment and she slumped back toward Caz's hand just the tiniest little bit. No one saw it.

But Caz felt it.

And he caught her.

# Chapter 22

———

## 11:40 a.m.

Dara and Sary sat next to each other in the fluorescent-lit break room at FedEx. Of the residents of Ilios Lane, they were the only ones besides Susan to have gone to work as usual the day after the burglaries. Sary had again asked her eldest nephew from uptown to come over with his two younger brothers and stay with Sofia. It hadn't occurred to her to call the landlord. It was the house *she* lived in, the house *she* had failed to protect. Responsibility, she believed, lay with her and Dara. Though she could not speak for the rest of her neighbors, she knew exactly why they had been victimized, which was subsequently why she and Dara sat knee-to-knee in the break room having a quiet, imperceptible-to-the-outsider argument.

"We cannot do it," Dara was telling Sary. "*I* cannot do it."

"You must," she fumed. "You must build it."

Dara was frustrated. Sary refused to let go of her beliefs. Beliefs that to Dara seemed ancestral, outdated.

"Neaktu had no home," Sary said. "He *must* have a home. Think of your family. Your daughter. We have failed to keep her safe."

Dara felt a growing agitation between his shoulder blades. How many times would she say this? *Neaktu had no home. Neaktu had no home.* Dara wasn't even sure he believed in Neaktu anymore. He tried a new tactic. "Neaktu does not come to America. He stays only in Cambodia."

Sary scoffed at him. "Don't be a fool! Spirits are not contained by our land boundaries. We *must* build him a home or it will be worse next time. Think of it, Dara. Think of Sophea home alone while we are at work. She is vulnerable. She is unsafe."

This thought, Dara had to admit, chilled him. His only child, alone, while Neaktu the destroyer hovered around her. The real trouble, Dara knew but could not admit to Sary, lay with him. He feared he could not build the kind of spirit house that a protector such as Neaktu would find beautiful and welcoming.

In Cambodia, men learned to make such spirit houses from their fathers and grandfathers. They were made of wood or cement, with horns on the roof and seven-headed naga snakes atop hand-carved walls. The roof had intricate, singular tiles laid one after the other. The windowsills and doorways had Sanskrit or Pali prayers carved into them, the languages of ancient Buddhism. In Cambodia, he'd been a pharmacist. Even the pharmacy had a small spirit house for Neaktu, to keep the sickness in their customers outside the shop. Without a beautiful house to entice him, Neaktu would never stay outside where he belonged. He would enter Dara and Sary's house, anyone's house, unless he was given a home of his own with offerings of fruit and money and incense, things to keep him satiated in the spirit world.

In America, no one had spirit houses and yet people were, for the most part, safe. Even when there were car crashes, Dara knew that Americans believed them to be accidents, rather than from the guiding hand of an angry ancestor. He wanted to believe the way the Americans believed. He wanted to believe his life was wholly under his control. But he'd grown up being told otherwise, believing that spirits were around him all the time, in the tops of trees and the doorways of unprotected homes, in intersections and in lakes and in rivers and in buildings. In cacti and flowers, in rice and wind. The spirits controlled the human world, and the humans had to tend to the needs of those who'd passed into the spirit world. Perhaps Sary was right. Perhaps Neaktu had visited them, taken just a cell phone, just a token, as a cautionary word, a sign to let them know he was unhappy. Be careful. Be cautious. Be mindful. Be warned.

A coworker nicknamed Grimace walked into the break room and sat at a Formica-topped table just down from theirs. He kept to himself, mostly, but had nodded when he'd walked in. His face carried scars from an earlier life Dara and Sary knew nothing about, scars that had earned him his nickname. He popped open a bag of Doritos. In the quiet room, the sound was oversize. Beige lockers spanning the length of the wall behind Grimace created a tedious backdrop, reminiscent of a kind of industrial incarceration. Grimace pulled a magazine from his back pocket and began to read. Dara saw blond women draped over motorcycles.

Sary stood to let Dara know their break was over. Her face was tight, furious and sad at once. He'd only seen her that way before when they first learned Dara wouldn't be allowed to work as a pharmacist in America without redoing school. They didn't have the money for him to redo school, and even if they had, both Dara and

Sary knew it would go toward Sophea's schooling, not her father's. But that angry, sad face had been *for* Dara then, wanting to fight for him, wanting to take on his own disappointment, his own dream of something different and better in a new place. This time was different. This time, Sary's expression was directed *toward* Dara. In his lower back and in his knees, he felt the fatigue of standing too long, the weight of what he knew he had to do. For his daughter. For his wife.

"Okay," he told Sary. "I'll try to build something."

# Chapter 23

----

## 2:16 p.m.

After she left the Housing Office, Susan sat in her driveway. She knew Michael was at home, and something kept her from wanting to face him. What was it, exactly? His overzealous grasp for power and control? He'd always been that way, someone for whom leadership had been elusive. He'd been passed over as management material his whole career, more times than Susan could count. And even before then, he'd been an average student, an average baseball player, an average runner. In her darker moments, she'd accuse him of being an average father.

She hated this about him, his averageness. He'd been the antidote to Harley, uncomplicated in the ways Harley was complicated. Michael had been dependable. He'd been *there*. The problem, she told herself back then, was that dating someone like Harley, who carried a kind of magnetism and darkness inside him, would sap all her energy, eventually (the irony today was not lost on her, that she herself had required so much of *his* energy). She'd be better off with a Michael McPherson. But she knew now that the very qualities of what made him average cast the burden for everything else onto her. She now saw the eight years they'd waited to marry as a sign she'd overlooked. If you wait so long, there's a reason. Now, nineteen years and two children later, she knew the truth. It hadn't been a fullness of commitment; it had been apathy. Only in moments like this, moments when Michael's yearning to lead, when the disappointments he carried about himself were so blatantly and embarrassingly on display to her, was she reminded of whom she'd really married, whom she'd spent—maybe even wasted—half her life with.

The burglaries weren't *his* fault. Her being temporarily laid off wasn't *his* fault. Yet somehow these two events seemed linked to a husband she was eternally, darkly, deeply disappointed in. Which made the weakness, ultimately, hers. After all, she was the one who'd said yes.


Michael was inside the house, sitting at the dining-room table, paper in front of him, pen in hand. Sting wafted from the kitchen radio. Michael's intention was to write a list of every possible thing he could do, and every possible lead he could offer the police. He'd begun by trying to think of anyone who might have access to their homes, anyone who might know, or be able to gauge, their comings and goings. So far, he had:

| | |
|---|---|
| FedEx/UPS deliveryman | Telephone companies |
| Postman | Utility companies |
| Internet companies (?) | Taxi drivers |
| Dog walkers | Hoodlums |
| Gardeners | Gangs |

| Babysitters | Handymen |
| House sitters | Airline reservation agents |
| Maids | CIA |
| Travel agents | FBI |

Then, in tiny script at the bottom of the page, he wrote:

Etienne?
Cambodian gang?

He was just about to write a list of questions when he felt a hand on his shoulder and flew into a momentary spasm.

"What are you doing here?" It may have come out more harshly than he'd intended.

"I could ask you the same." Susan wandered into the kitchen and filled a glass with water from the door of the fridge. She noticed last night's pizza box still on the counter and felt a surge of rage. He couldn't even toss out an empty pizza box?

"Larry thought it might be a good idea to take a little time," he said, referring to his boss. "To get on top of this thing."

*On top of this thing*. Susan cringed at the description. She knew Larry wouldn't have said such a thing, wouldn't have offered time off. The man was monosyllabic, had the personality of a cinder-block wall. Michael must have asked. He must have presented himself as de facto leader of the Ilios unfortunates. Must have convinced Larry that he was the abiding foundation for the collective trauma of Ilios.

He had called in sick once when he was sure the electric meter was being misread and they were being overcharged. He watched the meter's numbers every fifteen minutes, created an Excel spreadsheet, typed an angry letter to the electric company, and, at the end of a twenty-four-hour period, realized the bills had been right all along. It wasn't that Michael was or wasn't a fighter, Susan often thought; it was that he wasn't able to pick his battles, which made him less a man formed by justice—as he believed himself to be— and more a man formed by anger.

She wondered how much time off Larry had given him. She even wondered whether Michael was telling the truth at all.

"No clients today?" Michael was asking her.

She gulped down too much water at once and choked half of it out all over the counter. Michael either did not hear, or did not acknowledge her momentary coughing. "There were clients all right," she said after a moment. "But Evan thought it might be a good idea for me to take some time off, too."

"Why?" Michael shouted as if she were two houses down. She hated this about him. The strength of his vocal cords even in his normal speaking voice.

"Apparently, I'm a bad advertisement for east Oak Park at the moment. My face in the news."

"You haven't even spoken to the reporters." Michael was taken aback for a moment. *He* had been the point of contact. *His* face was all over the news. Susan had merely stood beside him.

"Well, what can I tell you, Michael? Evan asked me to take a little time off until things die down."

"You sound pissed."

"I *am* pissed!" She walked back into the dining room and stood behind a chair across from him. "I mean, what better advertise-ment than someone who's been through this kind of thing and *still* believes in the diversity mission, right?"

Michael shook his head. He knew it wasn't her fault, but he couldn't help but think she'd somehow thwarted his plan to take action, even if the precise nature of that action eluded him. And this ridiculous idea of diversity. People were people, and someday she'd have to learn that difficult lesson.

"Anyway . . . " She rubbed her eyelids. "I guess if you're home, we won't have another break-in."

Michael slammed his pen on the table. "What in the hell is that supposed to mean?"

Susan shook her head. "I'm sorry. I don't know where that came from. I was being funny."

"No, I don't think you were, Susan." He felt the urge to stand up, his muscles tensing.

"I'm sorry, Michael. I really didn't mean it." She'd meant the chances of a second burglary with a second family member home had to be about nil. Though hadn't she also meant to hurt Michael just a bit, to poke fun at the idea that he could protect any of them from anything? That he could in any way offer help to the police? His ridiculous list?

Susan's eyes were mildly bloodshot and she needed some Chap Stick. Michael wondered if she'd been crying, "cracking," as Mary called it. The two of them had made it their inside joke, but the first time Mary had said it, he'd been there, too, and all three of them had laughed and laughed. Now, it was as if he'd never been in the room. Did they even *remember* him there?

"Are you saying the burglaries are somehow *my* fault?"

"Michael, of course not. I'm just . . . " She stole a quick glance at him and then backed up toward the kitchen again. "It was the stress talking. I'm sorry." She set her glass in the sink and took a deep breath. "I'm going for a run."

"Okay, fine, but then we need to do those elimination prints for the police. I've asked some of the other neighbors to head over there together later." He was only half talking to her. He stared at his list, trying to remember what he'd intended to do, before she'd thrown him offtrack, practically *accused* him of the burglaries. As far as he was concerned, she couldn't leave the house fast enough.

"Why?"

"Why what?"

"Why do the neighbors need to go together? What's the point?" She was picking a fight, she could feel it in herself and yet she was powerless to stop.

Michael did stand up this time—and marched into the kitchen. "Because we are a community, Susan. Because we are all in this together."

"Fine, Michael. You want to appoint yourself our grand leader, that's just fine."

"What in the hell has gotten into you? You of all people recognize *community*, don't you?" He said the word *community* as if it were toxic. "Neighbors with neighbors. We're all we've got in this thing."

Susan held up her hand in what she hoped looked like a truce. But Michael shouted after her as she left, "The police are pretty *busy* in case you haven't noticed. Wasserman has a pretty full *caseload* in case you hadn't noticed. If we all go together, we'll save them some time, Susan . . ."

She knew she was being a bitch. What disturbed her was her complete absence of remorse.


Susan's runs followed no particular route, though most often she ran west, a fact she'd never once thought about until now. West. Never east. Never toward the ghetto, never even along Austin Boulevard, that arbitrary razor's edge where safe and unsafe collided in a kind of perceived dark energy. She spent her days trying to convince people that the east side was safe, that the gangs of black teenagers hanging along the cement front porches of brick two-flats and multi-units meant no harm. That the blaring rap music, the laughter of inside jokes, was simply teenagers engaging in teenagedom. Yet, she herself, a Believer in the Cause, in the experiment, in the laboratory that was Oak Park, had never before run east.

Perhaps this was what had really happened at work that morning, perhaps she'd only mouthed the words all along—*equality, diversity. Assurance.* Perhaps her coworkers had picked up on some kernel of insincerity in her, some element of hypocrisy far below the surface—so far that she herself was unaware of it. She lived on the east side, yes. In a lovely, two-story foursquare, painted the butternut squash and olive green of a Midwestern fall, on what until yesterday had been a quiet, safe cul-de-sac three full blocks west of Austin. How far, she wondered for the very first time, how far exactly, to the social and prejudicial millimeter, was Three Blocks?

Susan stretched her calves on the curb. She pulled each leg up to grab hold of her ankle and stretch her quads. If she kept her run relatively short, she'd make it home before Mary returned from school. She rolled her shoulders, reached up toward the clouds, and then down to put her palms on the sidewalk. She stretched and stretched.

Then she ran east.

# Chapter 24

---

## 2:38 p.m.

Sofia and Mary Elizabeth sat across from each other in the library during their study hour. Mary Elizabeth had her biology book open to a page on mitosis. *When cells divide into two daughter cells, each with the same number and type of chromosome as the parent . . .* She wondered if somewhere deep inside it the cell felt pain. Her thoughts circled back to Charles Darwin again, and she searched through the dusty aisles until she found a section of books about him. Mostly, she found the same pictures of him over and over. Darwin in profile, his bushy beard reminding her of a sea sponge. Occasionally he faced forward, and then she could see his gaze, over-size brow shadowing his asymmetrical eyes. He looked sad, in every picture. It wasn't simply that a photograph seemed never to capture him smiling; it was that he looked downtrodden, as if the idea that so many people disbelieved him had left him shattered. After fifteen minutes, she gave up her search for a smiling Darwin, but that look in his eyes stayed with her. It reminded her a bit of Arthur Gardenia.

When she got back to the table where Sofia sat before half a dozen books about palm trees, Mary knew she had *so much* to catch up on with her. Starting with her dad's knowing they had done ecstasy together and ending with Caz and his promise to meet her after school. Both her parents would be at work, so she and Caz would have the house to themselves until at least five thirty. She could hardly concentrate. Two luxurious hours, maybe a bit more. She had a momentary vision of them, together, in her parents' bubble bath, Caz slowly washing her hair. Her kinky, curly, terribly embarrassing hair. He would hold it in his hands and it would be shiny and straight and fall in a cottony wave to her shoulder blades. She felt her thighs tingle whenever she thought of it. Caz. In her house. She tried to remember how she'd left her room. Messy? Tidy? Was anything embarrassing on display? A book maybe? Or bad music? Would he ridicule her framed portrait of Man o' War, or would he understand a girl's infatuation with horses? (She ought to take the picture down, she thought. Maybe the whole horse thing ought to be over at her age.) What about the color—mostly purple, though lately she'd gotten into black and had even begun working on her mother to let her paint one wall black. She knew if she got her mother on board, her father would be forced to go along. She told her mother that a black wall was a sign of her individualism.

She began to wonder what Caz's lips would feel like. Soft? Chapped? She'd been kissed once, in eighth grade, by Jeremy Weiner, but they hadn't done tongues, and later she found out he'd been put up to it for five bucks from Joshua, Caleb, and Cameron, his three best friends. They'd called themselves—and still did—the Gang of Four. Her shame lasted the rest of the year. She'd wanted to switch schools, but she could think of no compelling argument that would convince her parents. She'd never told them about the kiss. If there was one thing she couldn't talk to her parents about—and indeed, there were far more than one—it was boys. Sex. Even kissing was out of bounds. She had carried her shame alone, that her one true kiss had required payment (the logical train of thought followed that this was, perhaps, not technically a "true" kiss, but this was even more painful for Mary Elizabeth to admit to herself).

On this day, though, fifteen-year-old Mary Elizabeth McPherson still had the illustrious hope of youth, and her hope was that Caz could change everything. She had no misconceptions about becoming his girlfriend. She doubted she'd be that lucky. But maybe she could hold on to him for a couple of weeks. Or even just the rest of *this* week. Long enough for a few key people in school to see her with him. That's all it would take to turn everything around for her. Her hip still burned where he'd touched it with his own at lunch. In public. In front of everyone.

Sofia was not interested in sitting with Mary Elizabeth, especially after the accusation of her family's supposed poverty the night before, but they'd chosen their seats the first day, and now they were stuck with their seating arrangement. She knew Mary Elizabeth would talk to her about Caz, about how they sat so close to each other during lunch. Everyone saw it. You could hardly *not* see it. Caz was practically on top of her, and her face blushing the entire lunch period. Plus she hadn't eaten a thing. Caz had scarfed his lunch. If Mary Elizabeth had eaten just half of what was in front of her, her fellow classmates might have believed what they were seeing, might have believed that she had some sort of control in her new dealings with Caz. But, alas, the full plate revealed her insecurity.

Sofia pretended to concentrate on her book, *An Encyclopedia of Cultivated Palms.* She had a report due on palm trees by the end of the week—an assignment that she could practically write off the top of her head. She'd been in love with palm trees for all of her life. She used to listen to her mother talk about the palm trees of Cambodia, how green they were, almost iridescent green, an obscene green. Sary talked about the noise of the monsoons, how sometimes you couldn't hear the person right next to you, how the rain scared her when she was young. But for Sofia, it was the greens of the palm trees she pictured, the endless variety. The tall, tall coconut palms, or the thick-trunked oil palms. There were more than six hundred varieties of climbing palms alone. For Sofia, palm trees had a familiar foreignness to them, she didn't live among them and never had, yet palm trees were in every picture, every story she'd ever heard, from her parents' other lives. Once, she read about a rare palm tree called a sangapilla, which had the most beautiful scent in the world. But the closer you got to it, the more the scent disappeared. Sofia loved the idea of something being so lovely from afar, something so determined to be alone and wonderful in the world, something so convinced of its own worth, that its beauty was self-contained.

"We were totally touching," Mary Elizabeth said in a loud whisper. "Like, totally. Not a little bit, not an accident, but almost our whole legs."

Sofia suddenly wondered how long Mary Elizabeth had been talking to her, how much she'd missed.

"I mean, it's a sign, right? He likes me, right?"

Sofia lifted her eyebrows. "You know my family's not really poor."

Mary Elizabeth leaned back in her seat and raised her eyebrows.

"I'm just saying," Sofia whispered. "The meeting last night? We're not poor."

Mary fished out a highlighter from an old makeup-pouch-cum-pencil-case on the table beside her. "Okay, fine. I get it." Sofia could tell her friend was unconvinced. "Anyway, it *is* a sign, right? About Caz?"

Sofia had about as much experience as her friend when it came to boys, despite being the object of affection for so many. "I guess so."

"But he wouldn't have touched my hip like that with his, right? I mean, it was *totally* obvious."

"Yeah. Totally." Sofia put her finger on a paragraph about the Ceylon date palm so she wouldn't lose her place.

"So what should I do?"

The Ceylon date palm was not a popular palm. Sharp spines and lacerating leaf edges made it difficult to handle, and it was notoriously picky about water and heat. It hated cold. Hated overwatering. Hated underwatering. It was bushy and disorganized and Sofia loved it for all these reasons.

Mary was impatient, leaning so far toward Sofia her chest was on the table. "Should I do it?"

"What?"

"It. You know. *It*. With Caz." Mary's face was lit up, a pale blush starting from her neck, rising up to her forehead. "If I get a chance."

Sofia did not care what Mary Elizabeth did or did not do with Caz. To her, he seemed unwashed and uninteresting. Mary had suggested Sofia's family were a bunch of poor immigrants, and Sofia had simply grown tired of the stereotype. She was sick of hearing hypocritical Americans like Mary—whose families bought every damn new thing advertised, but sold their souls into a lifetime of debt to provide a college education—talk to Sofia's parents as if *they* were the irresponsible ones simply because they had been born in the wrong place at the wrong time. So far as Sofia was concerned, Mary Elizabeth McPherson could have sex with Caz Zaininger and get herpes and crabs and pregnant all at the same time.

"You can't pass up the chance with Caz, Mary. It might not come again, and then what would he tell people about you? You don't want to be a prude, right?"

Mary Elizabeth smiled, put her hand on Sofia's. "Thanks. *If* I get the chance."

Sofia looked down at her book, pulled her hand out from under Mary's, and tried to ignore the sick feeling blossoming in her belly.

# Chapter 25

## 1:50 p.m.

Alicia was always split right down the middle about seeing her parents, and she never quite knew why. They never pressured her about grandchildren, or her lack of a career, or anything really. She'd always felt herself lucky in this way. She knew other grown women whose parents hounded them about everything. Alicia experienced none of this. But then maybe this lack of pressure signaled something worse: apathy. When she'd announced her engagement to Dan Kowalski after dating for just six months, they were thrilled. They threw a lavish engagement party at the Naperville Country Club and invited two hundred guests—some of whom Alicia couldn't remember having ever met before. She was so young, and so caught up with being a *cause célèbre*, she never once stopped to question the proceedings; her father held up a glass of champagne and toasted to *her*, to her future, to her choice, to all hope everywhere.

But why, she wanted to ask him?

What have I done to deserve the applause of strangers and friends?

She took the corner of her sarong and wiped the sleep from her eyes, then went downstairs for food—her parents had stocked the fridge with berries, milk, yogurt, and croissants, as if she and Dan were going to throw a brunch. She'd fallen asleep again after the ADT salesman had left and had only just woken for the second time that day. She couldn't remember when she'd last washed her hair, and she really *had* to change out of her ridiculous sarong. It had deep wrinkles around the waist and odd lumps where the fabric had gotten stretched, creased, bunched. She could hear Dan downstairs talking to Chester: "Good boy, bring that here. Good boy!"

Finally, the NyQuil fog seemed to be dissipating; she had a vague recollection of signing a contract, a vague memory of the fight with Dan in the taxi the night before.

The telephone interrupted her. "Sweetheart!" her father said in a voice that was overly cheerful, full of trepidation as if he feared actually speaking with his daughter. Alicia had a sense that her parents lived inside a double canopy of fear—fear that Alicia would return to the psychiatric treatment facility where she'd spent so much time twelve years earlier, and fear that Alicia would somehow destroy her marriage simply by being Alicia and return to live at home again. Alicia had once overheard her mother say to her father that she'd raised Alicia from birth to eighteen—*through her most challenging years*, was how Arlene put it—and now it was George's turn to take the lead. As if Alicia were not an adult, more than a decade deep into her own independent life. All they wanted, they told Alicia, was for her to be happy. Alicia translated that to mean she had to keep Dan happy, and Dan would likewise keep Alicia happy, and in this way the world would go on without complication. So what if George and Arlene helped this happiness along a bit by giving gifts every now and again? A television here, a set of copper cooking pans there. Perhaps the occasional piece of furniture. The dog. And of course there was the house itself. But George and Arlene told each other that young married "kids" such as Dan and Alicia had it rough these days. Who could afford to buy a starter home? What *was* a starter home anymore anyway?

And Alicia and Dan, for their part, always accepted.

Alicia told her father she was fine. Dan had gone out into the yard with Chester and a tennis ball.

"Your mother and I thought we should come over later. Bring you all dinner."

"Dad, there's no need. Really."

"I understand that, darling. But family ought to be together at a time like this."

She walked to the bathroom and tried to pee quietly enough that her father wouldn't hear. She didn't flush. She could hear Chester suddenly start to bark like mad outside.

"We have to go to the police station in a while," Alicia said, "and I really don't know how long that's going to take or what else they might need, Dad. It's really okay. We're really okay."

"Alicia, there's no need to pretend with us. It's a *very* traumatic thing you've gone through. *Very.*" She recognized her father's tone of voice as the same one he used with young girls selling Girl Scout cookies. Firm, but fair.

"I'm not pretending, Dad. I just don't know our schedule."

"Well, we'll bring dinner and you all just come when you can. We can let ourselves in." They had a key, of course. They'd always had a key.

"Dad . . ."

"Your mother's insisting."

From the living-room window, Alicia could see that Dan and Chester were in the front yard with that damn prepubescent reporter she'd seen earlier. One of his Doc Martens, she noted, appeared to be untied, and she had a sudden image of him tripping, cracking his forehead on the pavement. Chester was on his hind legs; Dan gripped the collar in a strong hold, so the dog barked weakly as his front paws clawed at the air. Alicia noticed a slight bulge on Chester. He always gained weight at her parents' house. Too few walks with too many treats. The young man opened, then closed, then opened again the viewfinder on his handheld video camera.

Then she saw her husband's face, the welcoming smile beamed directly toward the reporter. In Alicia's experience—not that she had much of a history with crime or media—it was best to keep to yourself.

"Dad, do whatever you want, I have to go." She clicked off the phone and watched her husband for a minute, holding Chester still in one hand, and gesturing across the whole of the street with the other.

She thought again of the contract. What had she signed, exactly? She tossed the phone onto the sofa and dashed to the dining room, saw the paper on the table, the installation scheduled for the following day. She'd written a check. For how much? She had no idea now. And where had Dan been? Walking Chester? She was sure he hadn't even bothered to call Lauren, their dog walker. Alicia needed to call the alarm system people. She needed to call Lauren. She needed to call and tell her parents to *please, please* not come for dinner. If everyone could give her a minute to calm down, to breathe, she knew things would be okay.

She started with the path of least resistance, dialing Lauren's number first. It rang and rang as she wandered into the kitchen, ate some blueberries out of the plastic container with the fridge door open. Finally, a recorded voice came on the line to say the number was no longer in use. It hadn't occurred to Alicia that they did not know Lauren's last name or where she lived or anything at all besides that she'd been a dependable dog walker for all of five weeks. And now, it seemed, she'd vanished.

# Chapter 26

## 3:15 p.m.

É tienne sat in the interview room at the Oak Park police station, stomach growling because he'd missed lunch and now it was late in the afternoon. He'd come in to do his elimination prints and found himself . . . what? He wasn't sure. Arrested? Accused? In trouble?

The object of attention, certainly.

Why was he so awkward? he wondered. Why wasn't he like others who so seamlessly worked their way in and out of conversations? People who could, for example, simply thank a bank teller after a transaction? A quick thank-you? He'd tried it. So many times he'd tried it, but there he'd be, thanking some woman behind the counter at Bank One and he'd realize how stiff his posture had gotten, how he'd look just past her face, perhaps at the clock behind her, and he'd know by her facial expression, by her impatience, that however he was attempting to do it was abnormal. A beat behind in the music of life. Why, he thought, couldn't he say things worth listening to? Things like those of his neighbor Michael McPherson, who said the most beautiful phrase Étienne had heard in a long, long time: *What we've lost is nothing*. To someone who'd never had much to begin with, such as Étienne, the items he'd involuntarily parted with were only half the pain. The other half was knowing he'd never be the kind of person to say, on a whim, in a moment of crisis, *What we've lost is nothing*.

Étienne had loved the idea of having a restaurant ever since he was a small boy. It both propelled him into the world of socializing and hid him at once. If he couldn't ever talk comfortably *around* people, then perhaps people would speak *of* him, of his food, of his heady, complex culinary creations. In his parents' home, he'd lose himself in food, in slicing vegetables, shucking corn, snipping off the tips of green beans. He pitted cherries and used an oyster fork to flick watermelon seeds from individual slices. As a boy, his mother gave him these jobs, he knew, because they were her least favorite. But he loved them. The rhythm, the expectation. There were no surprises. When you pulled husks off an ear of corn, there'd be corn underneath. Maybe a worm. But that was about the extent of the unexpected. Étienne craved the habitual. His mother was an unremarkable cook, but to Étienne—Edward, still, in those days—food allowed him what conversation could not: the chance to interact with the world from a safe distance.

There had been so few people in his life, for *all* of his life, that the change from Edward to Étienne had gone undisputed. But now, under the glare of fluorescence both literally and figuratively, Étienne's shame was boundless, his restaurant perverse. How *could* he not have seen the truth of things? Night after night, the lack of patrons, the bland food he tried so hard to enliven. Some nights, he didn't even bother turning on the restaurant's lights. Customers came, but rarely returned. He had no regulars. He'd never once had every table full simultaneously—and there were only a dozen tables to begin with.

The obvious redemption, Étienne realized, would be to *become* that thing he dreamed of—to go to France, to learn to cook, to learn the language, to learn his way around the tiny cobblestone streets and the menus of the greatest restaurants. But his was not that kind of story. Étienne knew he would not end up standing at the river Seine during a glittering, amber sunset, where a woman in a striped cotton shirt and strappy flats stepped gracefully toward him.

The sudden jolt of the soundproof door startled Étienne.

"Sorry, there . . . ," Detective Wasserman mumbled.

Étienne blinked.

"So, we've got your fingerprints." Wasserman sat down across from Étienne. "We're still working on the rest of the . . . victims, and . . ." The detective tapped a small stack of papers into alignment, then leafed through them absently.

"Can I . . . can I do anything else?" Étienne ventured. "For you?"

The detective glanced toward a mirror that Étienne guessed had officers on the other side. He imagined them laughing, snickering at him. There was nowhere to look, so he tried to look nowhere.

Wasserman leaned forward, spoke quietly. "Listen, Mr. . . ."

"Yes. Étienne. Please."

"Étienne." Wasserman made the slightest glance toward the window, and back. "Yes. Mr. Lenoir. Listen, you're not a suspect." The detective waved his arms out for a moment, encompassing an absent crowd. "We don't expect to . . . ah . . . What I mean is, we aren't holding you here. But what we can't figure . . ."

He expected Étienne to jump in here. But Étienne was unlike most people, who feel the need to fill conversation voids. Étienne lived mostly in the space of silence.

The detective cleared his throat and leaned back. He was a nice man, Étienne thought. Not tough. Not off-putting. Gentle, in a way.

"I guess we're all just wondering Mr. Lenoir, why all the lies?"

"Lies?" Étienne straightened up at the word. "Lies?"

"You know, the trips to Paris. The fake name. Sneaking around. I mean, you haven't done anything wrong. So why the lies?" Detective Wasserman looked earnestly at Étienne's face, deeply, and perhaps even with a tiny fragment of sorrow. "We're just curious."

Wasserman waited.

Étienne's eyes shot round the room, took in the table, paper, detective, walls, chairs, mirror. Mirror, chairs, walls, detective, paper, table. He rubbed his hands along his thighs once or twice. "I hadn't thought of them as lies."

## What We've Lost Is Nothing
Candy Kane, blogger

**Reader Comments**
**6 Comments—Add Your Comment**
**(Comment Policy)**

Dr. J. S. Alexander
*Posted: Wednesday, April 7, 2004 6:59 a.m.*

It is worth pointing out that Ilios and Troy are believed to
be synonymous names for the famed city of Homer's *Iliad*,
though I doubt very much Oak Park's *Ilios* thieves were aware
of such connections. Perhaps one might look toward fate as
our primary human failing, by which I mean we are *doomed*
to ours no matter the circumstances, and certainly no matter
our own behavior. At least I have always thought so. I have
long wondered how such a name appears in a town otherwise
populated by Taylors and Divisions and Austins and other
such commonalities. I empathize with you, Ms. Kane, not
because of your insomnia as you might assume, but because
of the eternal displacement the unfortunate events of our
own *Ilios* have thrust into our otherwise (relatively) idyllic
existences—as if we needed reminders of our own fragilities!
Take heart that what has happened here is not unique, indeed
is hardly worth our fretting at all, sadly. Though I do wonder,
as I sit preparing for my day, if we are not just a bit like those
gods of Homer's, pondering in the weak light of dawn the
unfortunate tragedy that is, ultimately, humanity.

Jon Salgado
*Posted: Wednesday, April 7, 2004 8:04 a.m.*

I think giving the perpetrators ANY kind of air time, in our
thoughts, in our blogs, in the media, anything is exactly what
gives them thrills. Don't give them the satisfaction, Candy!
I'm with the Ilios Lane resident who says what they've lost is
nothing. He's right. No one can take away the important stuff,
right?

---

Andrea from Oak Park
*Posted: Wednesday, April 7, 2004 9:56 a.m.*

Candy . . . I feel your pain. I couldn't sleep last night either!
That's what it means to be part of a community, part of a family,
part of anything that is meaningful in our lives. I wish you
courage AND a restful night tonight!

---

A Townshend
*Posted: Wednesday, April 7, 2004 10:04 a.m.*

To: Jon . . . I agree. Don't give those damn criminals a split
second of your brain power. But it's also naive to think a crime
of this scale, even without serious casualties, won't leave us
just feeling a little less secure in our lives. We need to find
strength in ourselves, find the tools we each need to endure
these kinds of events. I recently finished self-defense training
certification and though I pray I'll never need it, it sure makes
me feel secure knowing I have it. (I highly recommend it, by
the way!)

---

Smith from Oak Park
*Posted: Wednesday, April 7, 11:42 a.m.*

Come on, people! All this whining! It's the tenth anniversary of
the Rwandan genocide in case anyone would like to ponder
REAL problems in the world. Teddy Kennedy called the war

in Iraq "Bush's Vietnam" (an apt description in my view). U.S. casualties in Iraq are skyrocketing, and it appears that the potential medical miracle of stem cell research is about to be halted. Let's just try to keep a little perspective while we ponder those burglaries over on Ilios Lane.

---

PRS774@yahoo.com
*Posted: Wednesday, April 7, 2:13 p.m.*

To: JSAlexander
You're a fucking blowhard. Bet you'd feel differently if your house were on Ilios Lane. Or your family's. Why don't you go bury yourself in some library somewhere . . . give the rest of us a break from your bleating sophistry! (Yeah. I can read a dictionary, too.)

---

# Chapter 27

———

## 2:57 p.m.

S usan had begun running east, but then, a block from Austin, on Humphrey she subconsciously veered north. It so startled her that she'd stopped running abruptly and looked around. She was still in Oak Park. *East,* she thought. *I meant to run east.* She stood just south of Iowa Street, on a road with budding oak trees and foursquare houses painted in gentle earth tones, a couple of brick two-flats, and Craftsman bungalows. A few pieces of litter skittered across the lawn in front of her. The afternoon traffic on Austin had begun to pick up and she heard an angry driver lay on his horn. A thick layer of gray enveloped the sun, and the days weren't yet long enough to feel that summer was truly on its way. Susan bent down to double-tie her shoelaces. Why had she suddenly veered north?

At Iowa she decided she would take a new route back east. She turned right and came abruptly to a dead end. She backtracked on Iowa, then to Humphrey, and left through the alley that ran east. She passed over Austin Boulevard, made her way to Chicago

Avenue and then to Central Avenue, where the tidied lawns of Oak Park gave way to glass shards and weeds blooming on the cement, boarded-up windows, sagging porch roofs made of corrugated metal, and graffiti walls. She passed vacant lots and the Austin branch of the Chicago Public Library and the YMCA and could feel her heart at work, her legs and arms warmed up and energized. She passed a rusty bike rack lying on its side and Mt. Calvary Church and the Fraternité Notre Dame Soup Kitchen, which she hadn't known existed until now. The space looked clean, and for a fraction of a second she even pictured herself volunteering there some weekend. Maybe with Mary. The next song came on her iPod just as traffic was changing, so she began to run faster, turning down Race Avenue, which seemed a ridiculous street name for the west side of Chicago, and she almost wanted to laugh. Then abruptly Race Avenue came to a dead end at North Pine, and she turned right and came to Levin Park, abutting the el tracks. Music streamed from rusting cars parked in a baseball diamond with no bases. Black boys in baggy pants and Starter jackets leaned against a few of the cars. One dribbled a basketball.

Susan felt a rock form in her stomach, her fists beginning to clench. The boys were doing their thing, minding their business. Keep moving, she told herself. Ignore them. Pretend you belong. The boys spotted her and she heard their conversation go silent.

The hoots and hollers built up slowly at first. The boys were fourteen, fifteen, sixteen. Keep going, she breathed. They began to move toward her, laughing, high-fiving each other, punching each other's fists, feeding off her nervousness.

She remembered a story she'd read once. A young girl was running alongside the woods when two wolves emerged from the shadows. The girl ran as if their presence meant nothing, though she was scared out of her fucking mind. The wolves ran alongside her in a pack for a while, until finally one of the wolves peeled off, and then a few minutes later the other one, and the girl had come to see the ridiculousness of her fear, that nature would take care of you if you let it sometimes, the moment now seeming more of a miracle to her.

So Susan ran, and a few of the boys, laughing and hollering, began to run alongside her, but she said nothing, just kept running, even though she was already past the distance and time she normally went, and she was breathing deep, filling her lungs, but never feeling she had quite enough air. And then she thought she felt something, the tiniest brush against her ass. A feather. A leaf. A hand.

She nearly stopped.

She should have stopped.

Was it the wind? A piece of litter tossed around by a sudden gust? A shard of glass gone airborne under her feet? Was it the wing of a low-flying, lost bird? Or was it one of them? Those young boys, laughing, following? In the story, the wolves eventually grew bored and left, and she felt warm tears beginning to form in her eyes, but she *would not* cry. She would hold it all in, ask more of her heart than it had ever before given. The boys would go, eventually. They would tire. They would peel off, one at a time. She could outrun them. She would not respond, would not acknowledge, would not give them the satisfaction they craved.

She ran.

And they kept right up with her.

# Chapter 28

## 3:40 p.m.

Sofia's report on palm trees wasn't going well. Her parents were due home at any moment, and her cousins from Lawrence Avenue had shown up earlier than she expected. She liked her cousins, but she knew they were intimidating to look at, with their white tank tops, low-slung, ripped jeans, and folded bandannas that flopped over one eye. Imitation hoodlums. Their family carried scars of a recent past, expected more of their children because they'd come from so much less. She and her cousins hadn't learned about the Cambodian genocide from their families or their textbooks; they carried it in their blood, from the genetic pain passed down to them, the aberration of a generation's madness. She wore the uniform of this new world, too, just like her cousins, only hers was a short skirt and letter vest, roll-top white socks and pom-poms. She jumped, she cheered, she tumbled, while her cousins leered and loitered and lingered from gritty Chicago streets. Deep in their hearts, they—all four of them—carried the weight of history and expectation.

Her three cousins—Sit, Lin, and Ken—rolled up in a rusting, white Pontiac, windows down, speakers pumping "We Don't Give a Fuck" by Fabolous. In the front seat, Sit drove, with Lin beside him and Ken in the back, a ranking determined by age, and they bobbed their heads in time to the heavy beat.

Sofia thought about the traveler's palm, a tall, fan-shaped plant whose mythical reputation, like so many other myths, exaggerated the truth. *Ravenala madagascariensis* (country of origin: Madagascar; referred climate: tropical). Surprisingly, she'd learned it wasn't technically a palm or a tree. Tall, elegant, and enough of a hard-ass to survive monsoons and hurricanes, the traveler's palm was (like its distant cousin the banana tree, which also wasn't a tree) an herb. To dendrophils such as Sofia who demanded exactitude: an erect herb. The mystery of it appealed to her, how it had managed to mask its true identity, everyone assuming it was one thing when it had been something completely different all along.

*People believed,* she typed for her research paper, *that no matter which direction the palm was planted, the tree would orient itself so that its fan tips pointed east and west. It would twist and bend and do whatever it had to do to lead lost travelers back to where they'd come from, or farther toward where they wanted to go.*

The challenge of palm trees was learning their secrets. They needed little human intervention, and pruning commonly killed them. They weren't good for climbing either, not like the whorish oak with its many branches. Sofia loved the *Washingtonia*, tall and erect, featured in so many Southern California television shows, but its coconuts, if dropped from high enough, became weapons.

Sofia's cousins always stopped by unannounced. There was never a reason for their drop-ins, not like with her American friends, who scheduled visits with aunts and uncles and cousins around holidays and birthdays, never arriving spontaneously. Something about the sophistication of having a schedule, an order to one's calendar, appealed to Sofia. In her house, she'd often wake up on a Saturday morning and find her cousins in her living room, camped out in front of old reruns of *Tom and Jerry*. Sofia closed her notebook and went outside to greet them.

Sit had jumped up onto the roof of the car and was lying back, watching the gray clouds lumber across the sky. No trees were in front of Sofia's house. Lin and Ken leaned against the car; Ken was tossing a bottle of Coke into the air, then catching it, preparing to see how far the fizz might fly if it burst open. They snacked on gas-station cupcakes.

"There is nothing, not one damn thing, that tops the Sno Ball," Lin said. The most verbal of the three, he'd argue a point he didn't believe in just to see if he could win.

The same lone reporter Sofia had seen camped out earlier ran over to them and began to bombard her with questions.

"Yo, you don't want to talk to her." Sit lifted just his head from the roof of the car to speak.

The reporter introduced himself as Paul Patterson. He didn't look much older than Sit.

Sit propped himself up on his elbows. "Yo, I *said*, you *do not* want to talk to her. You hearing me?"

"Just one question?" Paul Patterson asked. His hair was tousled, and his nose had a smattering of pimples, but Sofia thought he was just the tiniest bit cute.

She shrugged. "I'm a minor. You don't want to talk to me."

Paul Patterson wandered back to his Volvo station wagon, dejected.

Lin turned to Sofia. "What do you think, Fee, Sno Balls or HoHos?"

"I don't know, Lin. Who cares?" Her parents never let her eat the kind of food available for purchase in gas stations.

"But just say," Ken said, as the Coke bottle landed squarely in his palm with a thwack. "One or the other."

"I have a lot of work to do."

"You *always* have a lot of work to do," Lin teased, but she knew he worked just as hard. He'd won a partial merit scholarship to the University of Virginia next fall, where he was hoping to be premed. In his freshman year of high school, he'd won an essay competition through the Cambodian Cultural Organization of Chicago that earned him a free trip to Cambodia, where he met distant relatives for the first time. He was shocked that the capital still had unpaved roads.

Of the three brothers, he was the only one fluent in Khmer. He had always been the one closest to Sofia, more like a brother than a cousin, and though he didn't know it, she hoped to follow in his footsteps someday, premed maybe, or some sort of conservation work. She didn't know the particulars yet, but she knew it would involve the salvation of man or nature.

"I've got a paper due at the end of the week," she said.

Sit jumped down from the roof of the car, from his cloud meditation, and leaned down to give her a hug. "You okay, Fee? You freaked-out?"

"I'm fine, Sit." She pushed him away. "They only took Mom's cell phone."

"It's not the shit, Fee. I'm saying, you need our help? You need us to do anything?"

She laughed then. "What are you going to do? Go find the burglars yourselves? Go hunt them down and, what? Make them choose between HoHos and Sno Balls?"

The four of them turned to see Michael McPherson emerge, determined, from his front door, pursed lips, eyes like rockets. He held a cell phone in one hand, keys in the other. Paul Patterson ran toward him. When Michael saw Sofia and her cousins, he had a small hiccup in his stride. He shot them the slightest of glances and turned toward Paul Patterson. Sofia cringed, wondered if Mary had confessed to her father about their afternoon cutting school. It seemed impossible that it had only been a day earlier. When she'd left school to walk home, Mary was still there, standing in the parking lot, waiting for Caz. She'd rushed on the off chance Mary Elizabeth and Caz wanted to catch up with her.

"We're here to protect you," Ken said to Sofia. He was still so small, about five foot two, that the thought of him protecting *her* made her laugh out loud. Ken was like Lin, had a mind eternally awake, questioning, reasoning, expanding, but a posture at odds with how he lived. She knew he'd gotten one B in his life, and his parents grounded him for half a summer. Two kids on bicycles rode past the entrance to Ilios Lane, slowly down Taylor Street, to look in. Sofia thought she recognized them from school. Across from the McPherson house, Arthur Gardenia emerged in dark glasses from his front door, flanked by Sofia's neighbors above and beside her house. Sofia wondered if Mary Elizabeth and Caz had managed to miss her father; she couldn't quite imagine how such an introduction might go, and she hoped for Mary's sake she'd dawdled long enough on the walk home to avoid such a scene. But Mary must have timed it right, Sofia realized. Mr. McPherson would never leave his daughter at home alone with a boy who looked like Caz.

"Man, what *is* that guy's problem?" Sit said, gesturing with his head toward Michael. No one answered him. No one knew what Michael's problem was, but it didn't matter; Sit hadn't expected an answer. Michael McPherson's gaze did not move from them. Nor did Sit's, from Michael.

"So, Sofia, what palm tree are you writing about this time?" Lin poked her in the ribs.

She rolled her eyes.

She'd been the object of ridicule on more than one occasion for her interest in palm trees. "Why not a tree you can actually see around here?" Lin had once asked her. "A tree you can climb? Fuck, we'll even build you a little tree house if you want. An oak. A chestnut. A maple."

But she couldn't explain that the not seeing them was part of the appeal. It was the only plant she knew that had to kill itself to survive, that had, at its core, perfect balance, darkness and light. "Every new leaf that grows on a mature palm," she'd once explained, "comes from the death of another."

# Chapter 29

## 3:40 p.m.

D ara and Sary stopped at the hardware store on the way home. Dara held a crumpled list in his hand, written on the back of a receipt: planks of wood, a saw, maroon and ocher paint, a hammer, and nails. He had no idea how to go about building a spirit house. The ones from Phnom Penh were mostly made of molded cement. He knew he'd never be able to shape the curved horns of the roof, and he hoped Sary would be happy with whatever his effort eventually looked like. Sary had told him Sofia would help, would look on the computer for designs. There was nothing that couldn't be found on the computer these days, Sary assured him.

At Home Depot, he and Sary wandered under the fluorescent lights, not knowing where to look. The light strained his eyes, his lower back aching from standing and lifting and bending all day and from walking on hard cement floors. His feet had never gotten used to anything but flip-flops. His toes were crammed into black-soled dress shoes that tapered at the front, but only cost $5 from the

Oak Park Economy Shop. Sary walked behind him a step or two, soundlessly.

They passed a display of outdoor furniture and barbecue grills the size of love seats, then a wall of wrapped-up hoses and garden tools. They turned down an aisle that was largely aluminum pipes with tiny drawers of unfamiliar gadgets. They wandered the aisle of sinks and toilets, on towering displays as if poised for invasion, and went through the paint displays. Finally they walked down an aisle where Dara spotted a self-assembly birdhouse. It was bare wood, intricate, with several notches and levels, and immediate relief spread over him. It was small for a spirit house, but would Sary notice? Even the biggest spirit houses in Cambodia tended not to be more than a square yard. The one they'd had in their living room in Phnom Penh had sat on the floor in the corner, just over a foot tall, with an altar just big enough to burn a few incense sticks and offer a little fruit. Dara looked at Sary and raised his eyebrows, gestured toward the birdhouse with a look he hoped said *compromise*.

"No," Sary said.

"Be reasonable." The kit weighed less than three pounds, and Dara held it in a blue box before her. "I can paint it so it's beautiful. We'll keep the front panel off so Neaktu will have a wider berth." Dara liked the price tag, too: $16. But he didn't mention this to Sary.

"It's too small." Less than half a meter. "Neaktu would be insulted by something so small."

Dara put the kit back on the shelf. A woman with a ponytail and fraying, paint-splattered jeans skirted past them, narrowly missing Dara's head with a garden hoe protruding from her shopping cart. Even she, it seemed to him, was probably more capable than he of building something.

Sary stepped closer to him so that they were almost touching. He could see something in her eyes, a panic that he hadn't noticed before. "We have upset the ancestors, Dara. That's why this happened. They are angry with us for ignoring them once we came to America. So angry they have made everyone around us pay."

Her voice was shaky. She was truly terrified and he had overlooked this. "Sary." He put his hands on her upper arms to calm her, but she shrugged him away.

"The aunties, the uncles . . . and they are right. They are angry and they are right. What have we done since we came? Who have we become?"

"We have not forgotten them, but we are in a different place, among different people. We work. We must adapt."

She'd heard the line for a decade. "We *have* adapted! Look at Sophea. Look how she behaves, like an American girl, doing as she wishes with no thoughts of her family, of what's expected of her."

"She missed *one day* of school, Sary."

"Not missed, Dara. She left. She broke the rules *on the very day a thief came to our home. To all of our homes.* This is our caution, Dara."

He felt heat rising off her, surrounding them, and he realized he hadn't made the connection before Sary pointed it out to him. He felt dizzy. A worker in an orange smock walked past them pushing a wheeled ladder. The two moved so they were flush against the birdhouses. Maybe Sary was right. Maybe they had angered their ancestors. He'd thought they were okay, making their way in Chicago up to the temple on Lawrence Avenue for Pchum Ben every year. They offered fruit and money to the ancestors, but it wasn't the fruit of their homeland. It was apples rather than dragon fruit, pears rather than mangosteen. American dollars rather than Cambodian riel.

He looked down at his wife, with her questioning eyes. She seemed never to lose her faith, even here in a place where ancestors took only three generations to be forgotten. "Okay. Okay, Sary. We must have the monks come to place the house in its proper position." He smelled sawdust and metal as he spoke, heard announcements on the store's PA system in a language he would never fully understand.

Sary nodded. She did not gloat. She simply offered her husband a silent thanks.

Dara pulled another birdhouse from the shelf, a "winter chalet" from a company with a French name. It had latticework around the edges of the roof and trim around the windows. Fake flowers bloomed from tiny window boxes. Built to resemble a "New England cottage," the birdhouse stood nearly a meter high. Would the ancestors see this as a halfhearted attempt at pacification? Would they think this new and Western design welcoming? Or would they be offended at its true purpose—an oasis for avian refuge?

But Sary smiled at the picture on the box. "Don't worry." She placed her hand gently on Dara's forearm for a moment. "They'll have to love it. It's much more beautiful than our own house."

Dara smiled back at her.

# Chapter 30

## 3:51 p.m.

In her kitchen, with her bookbag still at her feet, Mary Elizabeth shivered as Caz kissed her ear. She could feel dampness from his tongue around her temple, and suddenly he was lifting her shirt up, up, up and over her head. It so surprised her she didn't know what to say, and she had to stifle a giggle for reasons she did not at all understand. Goose bumps erupted on her skin. Giggling, she thought, was exactly the wrong response to anything in this moment (which only compelled her to want to giggle more, which only made it harder to hold it in). Caz ran his hands atop her bra until her nipples were hard candies. "Nice," he said, kissing her neck. But then she began to think about her parents, about time and space and how they hadn't yet made it to her bedroom. What if her parents came home early? What if the clock in the dining room clucking away every minute had gone haywire while she was at school? Her lips felt swollen, a haze of dry crust settling on them when Caz moved on to her neck. She was embarrassed by her flesh-colored bra, not even an inch of tantalizing lace (her mother never let her shop at Victoria's Secret, where Mary Elizabeth yearned to buy an overpriced, brightly colored, complicated lace bra that would, perhaps, just peek out slightly from her shirt. She'd buy dark purple and wear it under white T-shirts, under tank tops, under button-down shirts that would accidentally on purpose reveal a deep hint of freckled flesh as she bent over her lunchroom tray).

This moment with Caz was both exactly like and not at all like the scene she'd imagined. For starters, they were standing just inside the plate-glass door where the dining room and the kitchen met, as opposed to her bedroom. Caz's hands were like hard, little rods, rubbing her, kneading her. She felt the back of her legs tingle. Caz pulled up first one side of her bra and then the other, so that her breasts bounced out, but the clasps remained tight around her back. She crossed her arms in front of her, but Caz brushed them away, gently took her by the wrists, and pulled her arms behind her back, then held them together loosely with one hand. She felt a stickiness in her underwear, the uncomfortable touch of wet cotton, and found herself wishing she could run to the bathroom, wipe herself clean in the—God forbid—likely possibility that Caz's hand would wander down there. What would he think if he felt such sticky liquid? Would he think she hadn't bathed? Would he think she was dirty? She was pretty sure such a move by him would constitute third base, which seemed respectable enough without evolving into tramp territory. But then what if that wasn't enough? Or if it were too much?

Suddenly, his mouth was on her nipple, his tongue licking around it, his teeth gently gnawing at the hard flesh. He groaned. She watched his mouth with a sense of detachment. She was aware that breasts were part of this whole scenario, but she was surprised that she could barely feel what he was doing, as if the nerve endings in her nipples were inoperative. The clock ticked the minutes past, more quickly than it seemed sixty seconds could hold. She figured she should probably moan or breathe heavily as so often happened in movies. Did girls do this at certain points, or just throughout? She wished she'd paid more attention.

Caz pulled one of her arms free and rubbed her hand over his crotch. "Nice," he said. "Right?"

She didn't answer. Health class loomed in front of her, the teacher, Mr. Allen, going through the biological mechanics of sex—"the body's physical plot" he'd called it—and when he got to the point of entry, Jon Silverman had from the back of the room shouted, "Go in the back door!"

The class erupted.

Mr. Allen was unfazed, prepared as he always was for *one* in every class (students fancy themselves so blissfully imaginative, he'd said at a faculty luncheon). Jon Silverman, thereby, became the chosen one. "Thank you for your *creative* input."

Jon Silverman laughed. "You're welcome. Sir."

"And now, if you wouldn't mind explaining the rest of the act of sexual intercourse for the class . . ." Mr. Allen held out a stick of white chalk. "Do feel free to use the board."

Caz undid his button-fly jeans and pulled down the waist of his underwear and she felt it on her stomach, pressing into her skin. What was it? she wondered. The foreskin. Yes. It had to be. Her eyes were squeezed shut; she wouldn't look down, had never actually seen one in person. Guys had called it a rod. But it didn't feel at all like that pushing into Mary's belly. Rods were thin and sharp. This felt more like . . . what was it? Mary couldn't quite place it. More like . . . an uncooked potato, peeled. Caz still held her hand, directed it toward his penis, then squeezed her hand around it. She tried to pull away, gently. Too gently. He didn't notice. He groaned.

"It's for you," he whispered.

"After the penis gets hard," said Jon Silverman, "the dude sticks it into the chick's twat." The class did not laugh. Jon Silverman was losing his audience to humiliation on his behalf.

"I believe you're forgetting something," Mr. Allen said to Jon Silverman. The teacher would not be fazed by the jargon and would not be upstaged by a student.

"Show me where you were," Caz said, "when your house was broken into. Show me the dining-room table."

"I was under the table," Mary Elizabeth said quietly. "It's not . . ." She felt the softness of the skin on his penis, the hardness underneath, the warmth and the blood in his veins. He moved her hand up and down rapidly. "It's just a table. Maybe we should go to my room."

"Show me," he breathed into her hair.

"Under the table? There's nothing—"

His hand went into her waistband. He kicked her legs slightly apart with his foot. "You're making me crazy." He put his hand inside her underwear, stuck two fingers up her, and she gasped. He gasped. "Jesus, you're wet. Jesus. I guess that's for me." He moved her hand faster. The clock ticked. "Show me the table."

"The chick secretes a white, um . . . ," Jon Silverman stumbled.

"Vagina," said Mr. Allen. "Secretes discharge."

Jon Silverman had lost his smile. The class studied the faux wood of their desktops. "Discharge, yeah. It keeps the chick, um . . ."

"Lubricated during sexual activity."

"Yeah. Lubricated during sexual activity. So the dude's dick can pump, pump, pump." Jon Silverman pumped his fist in the air, one last attempt to regain his social standing, but the class had abandoned him. He was alone up there, in front of them all.

Caz pushed her slowly toward the dining-room table, away from the plate-glass door, his fingers dancing inside her so she stumbled with each step, his arm in the way of her legs, her hand pumping him up and down. She was a puppet. She was boneless.

"I'm making you crazy, too. I can feel it. Down here." She felt his fingers tap inside her, telling her something, heard the music of Alice in Chains streaming from the radio ("*I'm the man in the box . . . / won't you come and save me . . .*"). He pulled out a chair, pushed her shoulders so that she sat down hard, face-to-face with his crotch. She kept her eyes shut. She felt a potato on her cheek, gently caressing her. She wished they'd stayed out, under the bleachers like the other kids, somewhere they could be caught maybe, so that Mary would still be dressed and still be the talk of the school, but would not have her bra wrapped around her back with her breasts open to him, would not have a penis rubbing her cheek, would not be hearing the clock tick inside her head so loudly, would not fear the early and unexpected return of her parents.

*Say no,* she told herself. *Keep him guessing. Keep him wanting you.* But would he? That was the question. If she stopped him, would he leave? Or would they talk? Would he go to her room with her, laugh about the fight she had with her parents? Would he invite her to his house? Would he go to school the next day and tell everyone she was a tease? Would she ever get a date again? Get any boy at all to like her if she played this moment wrong? She wished she had even the tiniest bit more experience with all this. She remembered what Sofia said earlier in the library: *You can't pass up the chance with Caz, Mary. It might not come again, and then what would he tell people about you?*

"You're really cool. I didn't know how cool you were."

This made her heart wilt a little, and she didn't know what the wilting was from—that her plan had worked too well? Or that she hadn't had, she now realized, a solid plan at all?

His penis pushed into her cheek. "Go ahead. Give it a little kiss."

# Chapter 31

## 3:30 p.m.

Dan and Alicia Kowalski had just finished giving their prints at the police station and were headed back up the stairs when Dan asked her about the security contract she'd signed. He'd seen it just as they were walking out the door. "It hardly seems necessary at this point," he said, laughing a little at the irony.

"Yes, Dan. It would have been a great idea to have had an alarm system already, but we didn't, and so, yes, better late than never." Somehow the sleeves of her coat had twisted inside out and she stopped on the stairs to tussle with it.

He could hear the edge in her voice and he leaned toward her. "Are you actually blaming me for this, Alicia? Because that's what it feels like. What it's felt like since we got the call in Florida yesterday. Somehow I am to blame for the fucking house getting robbed."

"Dan—"

"Who's paying for this system? Where's the money coming from?"

They both knew that if necessary they could go to her parents. "It's discounted," she said, adding quietly, "because of the burglaries."

Dan took a step back and laughed. Alicia had finally sorted out the sleeves of her Windbreaker and put it on. "That's classic." He shook his head, rubbing his eyes as if he needed to clear out the sleep. "Talk about preying on the weak!"

Alicia glared at him for a moment, then stormed up the rest of the stairs.

"Vultures, right? Can't you see that? Didn't that *occur* to you?" He chased after her.

She knew what he meant; that was the thing of marriage. None of the subtext of history needed to be added. Even fights came with their own distinctive shorthand. She turned and poked him in the chest. "You don't *get* to call me weak, Dan. Don't you dare. I seem to remember a conversation about an alarm system when we first moved in, and someone—maybe it was, oh, I don't know, *you*— calling me paranoid. Assuring me that the chances were, let me see . . . what word did you use? Yes. *Infinitesimal*."

He held up his arms in a mock surrender. "I wasn't calling you weak." He truly believed this, though he knew somewhere that she wasn't entirely wrong either. He just didn't understand how everything she said seemed to come from such a place of hostility. Earlier, he'd taken Chester out on a walk to shake off their argument in the taxi; and then when he'd come home and she was still asleep, he'd wandered the house for a while. The place was cleaned up, buttoned up, and polished thanks to her parents, and he found himself jittery with nothing to do. (This also made him realize just how much time he probably spent playing *Halo* on his Xbox.) After a while, he sat at his desk and tried to think of what he could write for the *Oak Park Outlook*, a first-person account of the experience. But with so much already tidied up, he realized he hadn't experienced anything at all. Reporting would have to suffice for now, boots-on-the-ground interviewing of the police, the Village Hall folks he'd met over the years. Insurance would cover the material losses; Alicia's parents had taken care of the visuals, stacking up Dan and Alicia's lives so that normalcy at all costs could be maintained. But then a single thought wedged itself into his mind that he'd been unable to shake.

How could anything about their lives suggest normalcy?

What did it mean to have in-laws, parents, who were so skittish they tried to hold the world at bay, in all its pain and messiness? How could Alicia ever have the tools, the key, to her own survival with parents like hers? He felt something then that he hadn't felt in a long time, a shard of empathy for her, a clarity on why she'd signed the contract for the alarm system. Maybe it was her way of trying to do something, *anything*, in a family that refused to allow her to participate in her own life.

"Alicia"—his voice had softened slightly—"give me a minute. I'll meet you at the car."

"What? Why?"

He needed a moment to cool off, to let this empathy take root, but what he said was, "I just want to get a couple of phone numbers while we're here, make a couple of appointments for interviews and that." Village Hall was upstairs from the police station. Dan knew plenty of people from his weekly column, but more important, it began to dawn on him that the same compulsion that drove Alicia to sign the contract for an expensive alarm system also drove him to write something about the burglaries. To wrest back some kind of control.

It annoyed Alicia that he'd sprung this on her at the last minute. Dan promised her he'd be five minutes tops. He was doing this for them, he told her, for all of them. For his neighbors. For the whole town, really. Hadn't the burglaries put everyone on alert?

"What do you think you can do that the police aren't doing?"

"It has nothing to do with the police, Alicia. I'm sure they're doing a fine job." He looked away for a minute, at the outdated brickwork of the walls, a generic beige that ought to be plastered over and painted. "I'm investigating the . . . the . . ." He searched for the right word. "The impact. The sociology of it. How a bureaucracy like Village Hall deals with this; maybe they have some sort of partnership with the police. Some procedures that can be highlighted." He wasn't saying it right and didn't know how to phrase it because he didn't yet recognize that what he was doing was investigating his place in a life that had been purchased, wrapped up, presented, and then taken from him.

"Why does there have to be sociology in it at all? Why isn't it just a really bad thing that happened to a bunch of people?"

They stood for a second or two in a silent face-off. Alicia realized she wasn't sure what they were arguing about. They'd had such a nice time in Key West, swimming together, snorkeling, laughing on the boat as the sun dipped down the horizon. Away. When they'd been away from all of this. From their house and her parents and his job, such as it was, and her volunteering and their diversified-but-not-really community. Here, on land, they reverted back to familiar creatures. After another moment, Dan walked up the remainder of the stairs and left her standing in the foyer. He had the car keys, so she was forced to follow him up the five stairs to Village Hall, where she sat down on the first wooden bench she could find. Beside her was an abandoned real estate rag, and Alicia began to leaf through it.

----

Dan walked into the offices of various departments, trying to shake the argument with Alicia. All his contacts seemed to be locked in meetings or too busy to talk. The community development office and the citizens' complaint office and the community relations' office . . . he'd gotten nowhere. Among his more distant friends, he counted the assistant village clerk, Justin May, and he'd gotten at least a couple of minutes before Justin politely shooed Dan from the office to take a call.

"I just think people aren't looking at the bigger picture," Dan had told Justin. He'd knocked on five different doors and been met with five different versions of *not now.*

"Might be that it's too soon to tell what the fallout is, Dan." Justin adjusted his belt over a midsection of considerable girth. Dan had always believed Justin May's name suggested a youth that had abandoned Justin some years earlier. He had a trim, white beard and thin, tidy, white hair, with eyes the color of twilight.

"Yes, but this is unprecedented. This is . . . " Again, Dan wasn't sure what to call it, how to define it. In a way, he realized that he felt slightly less vulnerable than he might have otherwise, simply because so *many* of them were in the situation together.

"It is, Dan. But I think that's exactly my point. To think about it too much'll scare the hell out of people." Beyond Justin's door, a maintenance man pushed a gray, plastic garbage bin on wheels, rumbling as it passed by on the brick floor.

"Not thinking about it seems worse. We *need* to talk about it, don't you think, Justin? What about the FBI? Is this big enough for their involvement?"

Justin laughed out loud. "The FBI?"

"Justin—"

"Listen, Matlock. I appreciate what you're asking, but you're pissing on the wrong hydrant here."

Dan slumped against the doorframe. "You've got nothing to say?"

"Is this on or off the record?"

"Off."

"Off, then."

"No, wait. On. On the record."

"On the record? This is Oak Park."

"Okay, now off."

Justin had smiled. His phone rang. "Off the record? This is Oak Park, Dan."

Dan left Justin's office and simultaneously saw Alicia sitting on a bench in the atrium and thus *not* waiting in the car, and then Summer Schumerth, the *Oak Park Outlook*'s new "investigative" reporter. Summer was fresh out of j-school at Northwestern and wore her glossy brown hair in an earnest bun. Though she was only twenty-three, she had the demeanor of a middle-aged executive, all straight lines and hardness. She wore fall colors in the spring, oranges, browns, ochers. Dan offered an enthusiastic wave from across the large atrium, and then, when she seemed at first to ignore him, he waved both his hands in a kind of desperation.

"Summer! Hey, Summer! Over here . . ."

She finally turned her head in his direction. He could just make out her features through the plastic, green tropical plants under the atrium's skylights.

"Dan Kowalski!" he reminded her. Then, after she just stood looking at him, he said, "Your colleague. At the *Outlook*."

"Oh, yes," she said as Dan walked toward her. "You write the Life and Letters column, right?"

"That's right."

He'd reached her and was aware of Alicia, a dozen feet away, watching him in profile. Unlike his, Summer's notepad was filled with blue ink. She noted him glancing at it and moved to hold it to her chest.

"So, you're snooping around," Dan joked. Then, when she didn't answer: "Got any good scoops?"

"Seriously?"

He laughed awkwardly in what surely sounded too much like a snicker. Why had he gone so far out of his way to talk to Summer? He neither knew her nor was particularly interested in getting to know her. A strange inkling told him it was simply because he was in plain view of Alicia, whose shoulders slumped. Even her jawbone somehow looked angry to Dan.

"I'm covering the burglaries, Dan."

Dan went silent. Of *course* she was covering the burglaries. She was *the* investigative reporter. Had he even been considered for the story? he wondered. And now here he was, the victim, the calm in the damn center of the storm, and she was standing before him with a page full of notes.

"Care to give me a quote?" she asked.

Dan smiled at her. An inauthentic smile, tinged with a mixture of sadness, jealousy, and incredulity. He put the cap on his own pen, closed his notebook. Was he beaten? Was he giving up?

"Sure, why not? Here's my quote, Summer: Why do we feel so above it all?"

"*We*, who?"

"Why do we feel like these things can't, or shouldn't, happen to us because a small group of people were innovative and progressive forty years ago?"

"To whom are you referring?"

"Why do we think those people gave us a license to live as if they'd paid the tax for our lives, too? As if we don't have a part in our own undoing. I mean, really, come on . . . all that stuff that was taken? All that *stuff*? It was stuff, right? It was *shit*." He could sense a shift in Alicia, sitting up straight now. Listening.

Summer was writing furiously, shaking her head a little, not entirely sure what Dan was even talking about. A pigeon landed on the skylight above them with a loud plunk, as if it'd been bullied there by other pigeons.

"Stuff! Stuff we had, stuff we owned. Stuff everywhere! If we didn't have it, there'd be nothing to take, right? But here's the rub. We're *still* the haves. Take our shit and we'll *still be the haves*. I mean, that's crazy, isn't it? We don't want to believe it. We want to meditate and do yoga and eat our vegetables and tell ourselves we aren't the haves. Or we don't have to think about being the haves because you only think about *haves* when you're a *have not*, right?"

Dan dropped his pen, or it fell out of his hand. He hadn't noticed, but the light tap on the floor drew Summer's attention away from him momentarily.

"Or maybe a few of us *do* think about how we're the haves," Dan continued, "but the haves with social conscience, right? And this makes our *having* okay. But you know, all we lost, honestly, it really was just shit, Summer. Just crap. It wasn't like our houses burned down, like we'd lost family albums and that fucking Bible from our great-great-grandparents, and our kids' baby books. That stuff hurts when you lose it, but our stuff? Shit. The haves. What they really have are secrets. You know what I feel, Summer whatever-the-fuck-your-last-name-is? I feel free. I feel like if they hadn't taken it, I could give it all away. You need a TV? I had a great flatscreen. *Nice* fucking piece of kit. See my wife over there? Her parents gave it to us. *Gave.* That's a euphemism. But maybe this is the news flash. Maybe all that yoga and meditation and all those fucking vegetables are all part of the haves. They fucking *make* us the haves. They make us who we are." Dan was breathing heavily, frustrated by his inarticulate way of asking forgiveness. His way of giving it all back, everything he'd accepted from Alicia, everything he'd accepted from his fucking father- and mother-in-law. The flatscreen and the goddamned floral sofa set and the car. Even the house. Everything. He'd give it all back. Maybe even his wife.

"I'll . . . try and pull something out of that," Summer said, trotting away from him the minute he stopped for a breath. He barely noticed her leaving. He was suddenly aware of tears, rolling down his cheeks, a sensation he couldn't ever remember having as an adult. This, he realized, was what it felt like to *feel.* He turned, making no move to wipe his face, no attempt to calm his ragged breath, and there was Alicia, staring at him. His wife. The woman he wasn't sure had *ever* compelled him to feel in the way that this moment had, full of something. Full of anything at all. Alicia Dixon *cum* Kowalski. Ponytail, wisps around her face. Tanned. On the thin side. Light brown eyes like clay. Standing now, arms wrapped around herself. Watching her husband quietly cry, and she did the same right alongside him.

Neither of them noticed Michael McPherson come in the revolving door at the back entrance to Village Hall, followed by Arthur Gardenia, Helen Pappalardo, and Paja Coen, as Étienne Lenoir walked out.

*Wordpress Blog*, April 7, 2004, http://resmgr.wordpress
.com/2004/04/07/truth-of-diversity-hurts:

## The Truth of Diversity Hurts

### By Lola LOL, Anon., Residence Manager just west of Austin

Well, I don't know how to tell you this, Oak Park, but the truth
hurts. Maybe Shakespeare could put this better than me—in
fact, I'm sure he could—so rather than try, I'll just give you a few
spoonfuls of my building's statistics:

➢ **Demographic breakdown of building:**
  • 32 units. 1 Pan-Asian. 5 African-American. 26 Caucasian.

➢ **Noise complaints in past month: 3**
  • 1st offender, treadmill on 3rd floor (Black. Woman. Single.)
  • 2nd offender, dance instructor holding class in living room
    on 2nd floor (White. Man. Single.)
  • 3rd offender, born-again Christian speaking in tongues on
    1st floor (Black. Woman. Single.)

➢ **Police called by resident manager in past three months: 2**
  • 1st offender, crack addiction—taken from residence to
    psychiatric unit in restraints (Black. Girl. Teenager.)
  • 2nd offender, dealing drugs—taken from residence to
    juvenile detention center in handcuffs (Black. Boy. Teenager.)

➢ **Late rent in past three months: 2**
  • 1st offender/repeat offender. Still living in unit (Black.
    Woman. Single.)
  • 2nd offender/repeat offender. Evicted (White. Woman.
    Single.)

➢ **Fire in past four years: 1**
  • Offender, postcoital cigarette on mattress in laundry room
    (Black. Boy. Teenager with unidentified girl.)

➢ **Failure to take garbage from back deck to alley Dumpster in past month: too many to count**
  - Offenders—black, white, woman, man, single, married, teenager.
➢ **Demographic breakdown at last resident manager Sunday brunch:**
  - Of 32 units, 7 attended: 6 white, 1 black.
➢ **Demographic breakdown of tenants who attended last week's monthly building-wide walk:**
  - 4. White.

  -----------------------

  - Number of rehabbed apartments: 28
  - Number of units not rehabbed: 4
  - Number of blacks living in units not rehabbed: 4
  - Number of whites living in rehabbed units: 26
  - Number of "other" living in rehabbed units: 1
  - Number of complaints from tenants in non-rehabbed units to get units rehabbed: 3

  _____

I've been a resident manager in a building for four years now, going on five. You all know this. I write about it all the time! The rodents, the cockroaches, the parties, the gardening, the mopping and the sweeping and the apartment showing, and the moving in and moving out, and the lockouts, and the heat, and the air-conditioning, and the parking and all the follies and foibles of living in and managing a multi-unit residential building in this wonderful community we all call home. You've read about them all.

But I don't tell you about the real stuff. The hard stuff. The truth.

Diversity Assurance. Yes. I'm part of it. A BIG part of it. And I have to say that from a philosophical standpoint I am a believer in it—but a believer with one sweeping caveat:

Because we don't have something better.

Is my building diverse? Yes, indeed, it sure is, Dear Reader.

I've convinced whites and whites and more whites that this is a safe and lovely community to make one's home in—and I believe that. Five years ago, I was the third white tenant to move in. The demographics have shifted that much that quickly.

But what happens when one of the four black tenants who've all lived here more than fifteen years comes to my apartment with a complaint? Or for one of my quarterly Sunday brunches (to create community)?

Well, they see the truth. They see the beautiful hardwood floors I have, the new paint job, the newly outfitted kitchen. They see the rehabbed apartments that their landlord creates in part from their rent and in part from this village's grants program. And what do they think? Do they understand that in order to have a rehabbed apartment, they'd actually have to vacate for a month or two? No, they don't know that until they're told. And then, say they're willing . . . do they understand that their rent would increase by fifty, sixty, seventy percent? No. They don't get gentrification, which is really what D.A. is most of the time. This, Readers, is what they get:

Who's living in those nice rehabbed apartments?

. . . Everyone but them.

We have one rehabbed apartment with an African-American—a resident at a nearby hospital who is friendly to me, but not "friends" with me, and who appears to work 20 hours a day. This makes me sad. Just one. But I'm told I'm doing a good job; I'm told my building demographics mirror the country at large and that is the point. But the demographics don't take into account the staggering difference between standards of living of those in rehabbed units versus those not (who, admittedly, pay far less in rent).

I'm not saying it's not complicated, and I'm not saying we should kill D.A. But I am saying that if the Village of Oak Park thinks there's community here—real community, where we rely on each other, where we have each other's backs—then they're probably living in a dreamscape.

I don't know the answer. I don't believe we've found it—in D.A. or anywhere. I know what happened on Ilios Lane isn't something that should be pinned on the residents of the west side—even if it was residents from the west side who did it—and I know Oak Park isn't nearly the racial panacea that it believes itself to be—and that exists on both sides, blacks and whites. Because the blacks who live in my building and see my rehabbed apartment and curse at me when I call them to take out their garbage? They don't want to hang with me any more than I want to hang with them. They don't rely on me any more than I rely on them. Call this racist. Call it honest. Call it a factor of economics and culture and age, too. Call it all these things, because it probably is.

I wish it were different. I wish they were different. I wish I were different. I try. I truthfully, even in my darkest moments, believe I am trying. But mostly, I wish we were honest enough to come up with something better for ourselves, for all of us than, well, than our own devilish human nature.

Peace out, Readers.

*~Lola "LOL"*

# Chapter 32

## 3:38 p.m.

S usan McPherson was having trouble breathing. Her face was wet and her eyes were nearly blinded by tears and she was insanely thirsty. The boys were still following her. Why hadn't she told them off? Why hadn't she shouted, *What the hell do you think you're doing? You think you're funny? Go home to your mothers.*

Why hadn't she done what would have come so naturally in another place, with other boys? Other—she could not quite bring her mind to form the word—*white* boys, other *white* neighborhoods, where she was aware of the power brought by age. Here is the single thought that formed, as she ran, as she heard their laughter and hooting at the tears she could not contain: *Who am I kidding?*

All those years believing that proximity meant something, that her home just three blocks *from* the west side in any way at all resembled the west side. She'd driven through here. So many times she'd avoided the Eisenhower Expressway on the west and driven into the city down Chicago Avenue, down Lake Street, down Madison or Washington, and never once did she lock her car doors because she believed herself aligned with these people. She thought her life had been devoted to living among them, when, it was so terrifyingly clear to her now, she'd never even walked among them.

How could she have missed this?

The boys will get tired of her. The boys will get bored. If she yelled at them now, it would only highlight her weakness, her fear. The boys will slowly fall away like wolves, she thought. One after another. Just one. Just *one* needed to leave.

Imagine yourself running past the manicured lawns and mansions of Kenilworth, past the bank and then the Lake Theatre and all the way east past the library, she told herself. She wasn't far. She'd run here, after all, carried by her own two legs. That was the beauty of the grid system that was Chicago. She simply had to go west. But cul-de-sacs. Those could surprise you, and if she ended up turning down a cul-de-sac with an apartment building at the end and an alleyway the only escape, she'd be in real trouble. Stop your fucking crying, she told herself.

She ran past crumbling brownstones, large brick apartment buildings with busted windows and broken bottles sprinkled across the entryways. There were dirt lawns, no flowers, no children on the sidewalks pushing themselves on wobbly scooters. Through a few windows she could make out the flashes of television sets as she passed, she could hear the bass thumping of rap and hip-hop. She tripped in a pothole, landed hard on her foot, righted herself. The boys shook with laughter. She ran past an abandoned brick building with multicolored asphalt shingles. She slipped on a flattened paper sack from McDonald's, righted herself. Chain-link fences waist high ran along the sidewalk in front of nearly every house. But she heard no human sounds, save for the boys following her, collapsing with laughter. She could feel her leg muscles starting to vibrate from the effort, feel her lungs straining with each breath. Such thirst she had! *How much longer can I run?* She had to extricate herself. Go west. Surely Michael would be worried. Mary Elizabeth would be home from school. Was she closer to Oak Park in the west, or the Loop to the east? Garfield Park. There was a botanical garden there. If she could just get there, someone would let her use the phone. Let her sit down. Offer her some water.

*How can I be lost in a grid?* she thought. *How can I be lost so close to home?*

# Chapter 33

### 3:48 p.m.

É tienne saw Michael McPherson entering through the revolving door at the police station as he was exiting, and he offered a tentative smile.

"Where were you?" Michael's body was rigid, the tails of his beige trench coat flapping in the breeze. "Yesterday afternoon, where the hell were you?"

"Mr. McPherson," Helen Pappalardo said. But then she had nothing to follow it up with.

Étienne didn't answer.

"Get back from Paris early, then? Get the Concorde, maybe?"

"What's going on?" Arthur whispered to anyone in earshot. He wore his dark glasses, and an aging Members Only jacket in burgundy, thinning at the wrists, his gray hair fluttering in the soft wind.

"I saw you last night, Lenoir. Talking to Wasserman on your front porch, and I know you saw me. So I'm asking you, *neighbor,* where the hell were you?" Michael's index finger, straight as chalk, poked Étienne's chest.

Étienne was unused to confrontation. To be the object of anything was a revelation to him, that he could be the source of fervent emotion, of ire, fury, frustration.

"Yes," he told Michael McPherson, "I lied about Paris. I lied. I lied."

"Hey! You hear that news flash? You hear that, everyone? He *lied.* . . . My question isn't whether you lied, Lenoir, it's why? Where *were* you yesterday?"

Paja Coen, another Ilios Lane resident, walked around Helen, to stand next to Michael. Aldrin Rutherford had brought his estranged wife and children to the police station early that morning, and he was, at that moment, screwing in two kitchen cabinet doors that had been ripped off their hinges at the home he'd shared, until a month earlier, with his wife and children.

"Good lord, Michael. What does it matter?" Arthur said.

"Let him go," Paja Coen said. She had no idea what it was about Étienne Lenoir that seemed to incite Michael McPherson.

"No, it's fine . . . " Étienne wanted to say it was fine Ms. _____, but he didn't know her name. "Yes." Étienne turned to Michael. "Yes, I was at my restaurant yesterday. I lied about Paris. But I had nothing, *nothing whatsoever*, to do with the burglaries."

Michael McPherson's face was red, his fists were balled. Hoodlums were parked two doors down from his house. Cambodian hoodlums and their not-as-innocent-as-she-appears cousin. There was his wife, out there running a fucking marathon or whatever just to drive him crazy; there was his daughter skipping school and storming away from him as if *he* had been breaking the rules. There was his house, his street, his life, invaded right under his nose. There was everything, right there, before him in the eyes of Étienne Lenoir, his lying neighbor. Helen put her hand on Michael's shoulder. A police cruiser pulled up, parked in an open spot at the front reserved for officers on duty. A thick-waisted man with a shaved head and deep wrinkles around his eyes slid out from behind the driver's seat, holding a balled-up sack from Wendy's. He walked to the entrance where the five neighbors were gathered. The officer nodded, glanced at the five of them one at a time so quickly you'd never notice unless you were the noticing type. Slowly, because he sensed tension and was aware of his presence as a diffuser, he sauntered to the revolving door, stood in one of its quarters for a short but determined second, said "Afternoon" to them, and then began to push the door around.

Michael's body slackened. Helen took her hand off him.

There was so much more Étienne wanted to say to Michael. So much more explaining he wanted to do. About how he believed trips to Paris would lend credibility to his kitchen. About how it seemed like a place where he'd become someone other than whom he knew himself to be. About how it was always Paris he believed would bring on his mattering, and now he saw it was the illusion of Paris, it was the un-Parising of Paris. He mattered not because of something he'd done, but because of something he hadn't done. He mattered only as a measure of abstraction.

# Chapter 34

## 4:05 p.m.

D ara and Sary struggled to get the birdhouse from the back-seat of their Camry, then struggled to get it through their backyard and into the house. The box looked disproportionately large in the sparse living room. Sary turned on the floor lamp and heard the thumping of her nephews' music coming from their front yard. Then she took a six-pack of Coke from the refrigerator and went out to meet them.

Dara needed to get some tools from the basement to put the spirit house together, but he glanced out their living-room window and watched Sary walk toward Sofia and his nephews. Two yards over, Michael McPherson was standing on the sidewalk talking before a lone news camera, with some of their neighbors gathered around him. Dara wouldn't even have bothered to report Sary's lost cell phone if they hadn't been part of this larger problem on his street, and if anyone had asked, he'd have said, simply, that he wanted no part of the investigation. He didn't want his prints eternally filed away in a police station in America, in a country that had always felt temporary to him. Would he have a permanent file? What if someone misfiled it, from victim to perpetrator? What if, ten years from now, the government somehow used it against him, planted his fingerprints in some other crime scene? It wasn't unheard of, these kinds of things. Crooked cops. It happened in Cambodia all the time. And it happened in America, too. The only difference he believed was that Americans wouldn't admit it, while Cambodians had come to expect it.

So many things hadn't turned out the way he'd thought . . . America didn't offer him opportunity. In fact, it took away his chance to practice his profession as a pharmacist. It made his daughter a stranger to him. It robbed his wife of the last chance she had to live free of fear. He wondered what made his brother love the place so much. What made him stay year after year, decade after decade? Nimith hadn't been there in Phnom Penh, searching for their mad mother, watching the city get bigger and bigger and bigger, the foreign aid pouring in, the houses grander in scale. There was so much opportunity, it seemed to him now, in a city burgeoning with youth. When he'd begun work at a pharmacy, he manned the counter in a shop that didn't even have a working electric light. Pharmacy La Gare, the last place he'd worked before coming to America, had negotiated a contract with a Parisian pharmaceutical company a few years ago for the latest medicines to be airlifted to Cambodia. They'd gotten a refrigeration system with a generator, he'd heard.

He watched his daughter out the window, wearing jeans and a pale yellow sweater. How different would she be if they'd stayed in Cambodia? Would she become a pharmacist, too? Dispense medicines to foreigners and rich Khmers? Maybe now was not the time to leave, but Sofia was fifteen. Not a child anymore. Perhaps home was not so far as it felt. He realized he didn't want Sofia and his nephews hanging around outside in the front yard if there was a chance of even a single news camera still there, to take pictures, to publicize what had happened to them privately. He did not want to be visible. Not the kind of visible he felt himself to be now. He wanted to quietly go about taking care of his family, seen by them, but obscured from the rest of the world. And he knew—because he hadn't bought a house, because he hadn't acquired a piece of furniture, a utensil, a towel or a poster or a cell phone or a job or even a friend that he could not live without—he knew, because he hadn't done the things you do when you set down roots, that he would someday return to his real home.

Dara went into the kitchen and rinsed his face under the tap, then made his way out to the front yard, to gather his family and come back inside.

# Chapter 35

----

## 3:54 p.m.

They walked outside wordlessly, soundlessly, Dan's arm slung over Alicia's shoulder. She had his shirt bunched up in her hand, white-knuckling the cotton as if it might run free. The day had gone cloudy, but the air was fresh, the bite of late winter gone and the smell of buds everywhere. Wood chips from last year's mulch littered the curbs at the police station, and Alicia and Dan leaned up against their pale-blue Prius, breathing together, not quite ready to drive home to Chester.

"All these years," Dan said to her, "all these fucking years."

Alicia nodded.

His fleece collar tickled her chin. He pulled her hair out of its ponytail and let it fall down to her shoulders. She hadn't washed it since Florida and he smelled the sea in it. Dry trails from her tears feathered down her cheeks.

"To never once even talk about moving away, to never have the thought cross our minds?" he asked her.

"I thought you loved it here. I thought you never wanted to leave."

"Are you kidding? I thought it was you. I thought we needed to be close to your parents *for your sanity* or something." He laughed when he said "sanity."

Alicia laughed with him. "*My* sanity? Believe me, I'd be a lot more sane a thousand miles away from my parents."

"What were we thinking?"

"It's like a trance."

"How could it never dawn on us?"

"Doesn't it feel like a trance? Like we were in a trance?"

Dan didn't answer Alicia. Alicia didn't answer Dan. They had never even put forward the topic—leaving Oak Park and the long tether of her parents. They'd thought Oak Park was far enough away, a statement about their independence. Half an hour by car was the most they could muster, and they'd been proud of it. As if they were shaking off the shackles of their oppression by moving in to the house her parents had bought and furnished, and driving the car her parents got them.

"I went to Ann Arbor for the weekend once with my aunt and uncle," Alicia said. "It was fall. I remember the trees."

Dan noticed three or four gray hairs intermingled with her dishwater blond. He'd always been envious of how Alicia's blond was a sort of camouflage for gray, an unfair advantage against the collective inevitability of their aging.

"I'd never seen trees that color. The red wasn't just red, it was like *r-e-d*. Like someone had plugged in the trees."

"Champaign-Urbana's pretty nice. Bloomington, Indiana."

A sparrow landed near their feet, pecked at the cement, flew off in an instant. Dan watched a policeman emerge from the revolving door, climb into his squad car, and pull out slowly. Two older women, both black, came out arguing about parking tickets.

"Isn't there that famous deli in Ann Arbor? What's it called . . . Singers? Sangers?"

"Zingerman's," Alicia said. "I think I went there."

"Zingerman's."

"My cousin was going to school there. That's why we went. I think her major was history or something. Who majors in history?"

Dan rubbed his hands up and down Alicia's arms as she pulled away from him slightly, to look at his face. "You got something against history?"

She smiled. He couldn't remember the last time she'd smiled *at* him, as a result of him. "Nothing. I love history. But think about it. You're looking for a job at a time when the whole world is moving in the opposite direction of history. And really fast, right, with technology . . ."

"The future."

"Yes. The future. And you're talking about the past, your whole life is all about the past."

"Aren't we doomed to repeat the past if we don't learn from it?" he said. "How's that saying go?"

She laughed, reached up to push his hair back behind his ear. "I think we're doomed to repeat the past anyway."

"So why bother?"

"So why bother."

She stepped back away from him and ran her hands down the front of her own fleece top, smoothing it. Dan stood up from leaning against the car, clicked the unlock button on his fob.

"It's funny," Alicia said, "that thing about repeating the past." The quiet thump of the doors unlocking interrupted the ambient stillness. "It's not us repeating it, right? It's not our past, it's the past of our parents, or grandparents, or great-great-great-great-great- . . ."

"Yes?" Dan walked around to the driver's side, looked up, and saw Michael McPherson, Arthur Gardenia, Paja Coen, and Helen Pappalardo come out of the station. They saw him, too. Michael lifted a hand toward Dan and he nodded.

"How can it truly be the past," Alicia said, "if it's all new for us?"

# Chapter 36

## 4:07 p.m.

The sky above Étienne had turned thick and gray as the late-afternoon light began to surrender to evening. After his confrontation with Michael McPherson, he'd been shaken and didn't quite know what to do with himself. The thought of going home made his stomach churn; the thought of going to Frite was even less appealing. His life, he realized, had been whittled down to the marrow of just those two lonely spaces.

He found himself at McDonald's ordering a Big Mac and fries. He couldn't remember the last time a meal had been made *for* him, but he took no delight in this. The smell of oil and fried batter permeated every surface inside. The drive-through microphone screeched. Paradoxically, Étienne felt himself both ravenously hungry and strangely full, and he offered his order in a near whisper to the teenage boy behind the register. Carrying his tray to a Formica table, Étienne caught his reflection in the window, a slight stoop in his back, as if one of his customers might see him here, cavorting with the enemy. With Étienne's first bite, the middle bun slid out from the burger and fell onto his tray. Shredded lettuce and pickles began to spill out from the buns with his second and third bites, and Étienne watched as the warm, orange sauce oozed out onto his fingers. Why, he thought, with all the culinary advances of the twenty-first century, could not a soul in the world make a bun that didn't fall apart under the stress of a human mouth? He'd dropped the rest of the burger onto the tray and left it there, cleaning his hands off as he darted outside.

Étienne walked underneath the railroad tracks as the el thundered overhead, brimming with commuters. The sign in Frite's window announced a three-day closure so that he could organize his home, give himself some time off. But without the regular rhythm of work and home, Étienne found he had no idea where to go. He cut over to Taylor Street, to wander past one of his favorite houses. A gentle Victorian painted in plum hues with a turret and wraparound porch. A woman with dark curls was on the phone; he could see her wander from room to room, turning on soft-amber lights. Dressed in a dark suit, she must have just returned from work. The house was large, but not ostentatious; grand, but approachable. Years ago, perhaps before the dark-haired woman lived in the house, it had been painted white with gray trim, colors that obscured its real beauty. But then, he'd watched the house being repainted, a little more color each day. First the plum base went on. Then a darker plum on the patterned shingles around the turret. Goldenrod over the transom and on the window shutters accented with evergreen highlighted on the gutters and dormer. Étienne marveled as the house had come to life. In some sense, the house was like a thousand other houses in Oak Park. Not notable in size or in design, but he'd known it before its transformation, and that was the remarkable thing. This nothing into something.

And in that moment, Étienne suddenly knew exactly what he had to do.

He could sell off his two copper pots, certainly. The French café chairs and tables. Maybe the black-and-white reprints of Parisian scenes—the Seine at night, the Champs-Élysées in snowfall, the streets of Montparnasse. An estate sale for a restaurant. The death of a bad idea. Frite.

He would use the insurance money to start again, to take some time and get the recipe down just right, the interior design perfectly welcoming and warm. Long wood tables, that's what he'd need, like butcher blocks. And long benches. The kind of seating arrangement that compelled strangers to talk with one another.

He reached out his arm and softly stroked each oak tree as he passed, the thick hide of their bark rough against his fingertips. Open to the breeze, his bomber jacket flapped as he walked, but he didn't feel the least bit chilled. He could get rid of the bar that was there now, build a secure place in the corner for kids to play, with half walls and a gate so the parents could relax just a tiny bit and the kids could have some fun. He'd have beer. No wine, no hard liquor. Only beer, but good beer, interesting beer. *Local* beer, from Milwaukee and Goose Island. He'd serve it in mason jars.

Étienne felt a giddy energy that he was not familiar with in himself. The burgers would be interesting, free-range meat if he could afford it, with toppings such as bleu cheese or Havarti, roasted peppers or caramelized mushrooms and onions, avocado and arugula and tamarind. Maybe he'd have buns with cornmeal in them, or buttermilk. A pale-brown cat darted across the street and disappeared into a tree-filled backyard. Étienne watched its trajectory. Maybe in his new restaurant he'd play hip-hop. He'd even host artsy events. A poetry slam. Or an open-mic night. An exhibit of photography or art. Oak Parkers loved that kind of thing. And the key to it all? The bun. The ingredients for bread, he knew, simply had to be manipulated to make a bun that would work like pita bread, like conjoined Frisbees, keeping the hamburger and its ingredients firmly united. It wasn't a matter of engineering, the bun and the burger falling apart all the time. Not hardly. It was a matter of romance and chemistry. Why hadn't anyone ever done it before? Why hadn't *he*?

And he'd call it . . .

*Ed's: Our buns commit to your burgers.*

April 9, 2004

To: Jeanne Kirkpatrick, aka "Lola 'LOL'"
From: Oak Park Apartment Doctor, Inc.
Memo Re: Wordpress Blog "The Truth of Diversity Hurts"

Dear Ms. Kirkpatrick:

Your employment as Resident Manager at XXX Washington
Boulevard, Oak Park, Illinois 60302, is hereby
terminated, and your services are no longer needed,
effective immediately.

    You will have until the end of the month to vacate
the premises, or sign a lease and begin regular
rental payments to OPAD, Inc. Please let us know your
preference at your earliest convenience.

    We wish you the best of luck in your future
endeavors; however, we will be unable to provide you
with a reference, beyond verifying the dates of your
employment.

Sincerely,
Allison Cantor




Allison Cantor
Office Manager
Oak Park Apartment Doctor, Inc.

# Chapter 37

------

## 4:07 p.m.

Mary Elizabeth gagged and choked and felt uplifted once Caz removed his penis from her mouth. It disgusted her. It felt very much to her like suffocation, like being a captive, tortured for information. He pushed into her and she gagged. He pushed into her again and she gagged again. He tried for a third time and again she could not breathe and he pulled it out and said, "What are you, a fucking amateur?"

She didn't know what to say. She knew the word. Knew how to form it, how it was supposed to sound. She'd used it her whole life. Used it most often when talking to her parents:

*No.*

But she could not. It was as if Caz had stolen her voice. She was freezing, goose bumps temporarily scarring her entire body. Her arms were shafts, locked at her sides. Caz had turned up the kitchen radio so that loud, hissing heavy metal held her in a kind of noise box. If she sat here long enough, maybe he would just leave, maybe he would get bored with her. That was his reputation, right? Hook up with a girl and then dump her. It was the challenge of holding on to Caz that most attracted the girls, the reputation he carried of getting whatever he wanted whenever he wanted from whomever he wanted. The girls loved him because they wanted to fulfill all they'd learned of love from the movies—that is, that it takes one right girl to set straight a wayward boy. *One* girl who can make a difference, crack his shell, reach his heart. Because teenagers always believe in the One Girl Theory. Twentysomethings believe. Thirtysomethings believe. We all believe in such mythmaking.

Once, at a party, long after Cindy Hamilton had switched schools and the pictures of her stopped making the e-mail rounds, Caz had bet the boys $5 he could get Amber Belonsky to give Jeremy Busch, Jim Vigham, and Carl Lindorph blow jobs in front of everyone. Given what had happened with Cindy a year earlier, few doubted it, but there was something collectively titillating in the expectation. Amber was overweight, but not unattractive. She wore jeans with frayed bottoms and always needed a haircut. Caz had plied her with vodka and Hi-C fruit punch until she was wobbly and giggling. He kissed her in front of everyone, grabbed her breast as her head lolled back, and then asked her to kiss a few of his friends, his very good friends. Amber vomited halfway through Jim Vigham, and the others had gone home with tiny splashes of puke over their black motorcycle boots, but the damage had been done. Caz'd left the party $200 richer and secured his reputation. By the end of the year, Amber had transferred to Julian. Mary Elizabeth had laughed at Amber right along with the other kids.

Over the past few years Mary had pushed Susan away, but now she was trying to channel her. How would she keep Caz's interest without compromising her integrity?

"Caz. Caz, let's go to my room."

Mary Elizabeth wanted him to *sense* her *no* without having to say it. To hear it from the way her body failed to move, the way she shifted as if her limbs were a series of planks, unbalanced, toppling, unyielding. This was the difference between real life and the movies; in real life no one ever read other people's minds, even if they could, because to do so would mean concessions they were almost always unwilling to make, concessions that meant the inability to push one's own agenda. Caz had taken her clothes off. All of them except her socks and her bra, which remained hooked behind her, her breasts dangling out of it. The music was loud enough that she had to raise her voice to talk over it. He was dressed still, his penis jutting out from his pants, the only flesh he revealed to her.

"Caz," she whispered. "Caz. Please."

"I know. I know, baby." He told her to get on the floor, under the table. "I know you want it. I'm getting there, baby."

If they could only go up to her room. Escape the public space of the dining room. Led Zeppelin wafting into the dining room. "We can go upstairs."

"You gotta reclaim this space," he said. "Take charge of it."

Caz turned her over, pulled her up by the hips. She was half under the table, her head and shoulders in shadow and, from the waist down, open to him. She felt a pressure behind her. She thought momentarily of the kids at school, of lunch, of how her hips had seemed so aligned with Caz's then, so on fire, so joined. How she'd felt so beloved at that moment. *Beloved.*

Be.

Loved.

By someone who meant something. By someone whose presence was *noticed* at school. She belonged then, for a moment. And

in her belonging why hadn't she eaten the cookie? The whole fucking cookie? She could no longer remember. Had she thrown it away,
even?

She saw the dark posts of the chair legs. "I don't need to reclaim
this space." The words tumbled out of her quickly. "I was only here
for a minute yesterday. I was with Sofia Oum. Do you know her?
She's very popular. I didn't even know—"

The space. Under the table.

She felt a tearing, searing pain behind her.

Her breath came in sharp bursts, held then released, held then
released.

Felt the halves of herself separating, whittled away to thin, sharp
wedges.

She hit her head on the side of a chair seat. Tried to move her
legs, her knees closer together, so it wouldn't hurt so much. Caz
pushed her knees apart on the carpet. Pushed her head down so she
was kissing the rug.

Heard the hard slap of Caz's skin against hers.

The space. Under the table. *Reclaim. To demand the return or
restoration of.*

She would avoid this room until she left for college two years
later.

# Chapter 38

## 4:15 p.m.

A caravan of cars returned to Ilios Lane from the police station. Michael McPherson, Arthur Gardenia, the Kowalskis, Helen, and Paja poured into the street, and Michael invited them over to discuss the case, their insurance plans, but mostly to discuss their fear. As Michael expected (and hoped), Paul Patterson, the lingering reporter, tore an immediate path to him.

"Listen," Michael blocked Paul's tiny camera with his palms, "there isn't much to say here. The investigation is ongoing. The police have some interesting leads."

In his periphery, Michael McPherson could feel the Cambodian teenagers staring at him, mesmerized, it seemed. If only Paul Patterson weren't here, he'd march right up to that little Sofia and give her a piece of his mind. How dare she convince his daughter to skip school? Who did she think she was? She was lucky to be in America, and Michael McPherson had a fierce desire to remind her of that.

So far as he was concerned, the lot of them could march right back to where they came from.

"I've provided the police with a list of possibilities," Michael McPherson said. He had trouble keeping his eyes on the young reporter, his vision wandering left, wandering toward the Cambodians, the boys who leaned as graceful as ballerinas against their rusting car, their bodies lean and slim, all muscle and sinew. They wore bandannas. They wore torn jeans. They smirked at Michael.

"What do you mean, *possibilities*?" Paul Patterson asked.

Michael looked to Arthur and Helen. They were waiting to come in. Dan and Alicia were talking to Paja in a tight little trio, and the Cambodians were laughing to themselves, eating something. Chips maybe. "We thought we could go over the neighborhood-watch protocols again. Insurance. We ought to just . . . be there a bit. For each other."

"Yes, definitely," Helen said, touched by Michael's apparent inability to articulate whatever he was trying to say. "You know, Susan and Mary were such a big help to me yesterday, Michael. Cleaning up my house."

Michael nodded once and turned around. Arthur mumbled his assent and started back toward Michael's house with Helen following, saying, "Maybe we could help each other organize a bit, you know?" Helen noticed Michael's gaze had shifted and he was staring at the Cambodian boy with the roughest look. She, too, looked toward the Cambodians, but failed to see whatever it was that had caught Michael's attention.

Michael narrowed his eyes at the Cambodian boy down the street that he recognized from the day before, and the boy didn't look away. At least not immediately. The direct challenge of such a look! Michael thought. He felt the anger pooling. What did that punk do when he *wasn't* on Ilios Lane, Michael wondered. Loiter near their houses, watching, waiting perhaps? And learning. Oh, yes. This boy had been learning. Had been studying them, hadn't he? Had discovered who was who and what was what and where they all did what they did and when and with whom.

This boy, Michael McPherson suddenly suspected, knew everything.

Paul Patterson had sidled up to Michael once again and was asking him about possibilities and probabilities, lists and developments. This tiny, little husk of a reporter, this *freelancer*, this lone vulture trying to get ahead. Michael could see it now. How quickly they were all forgotten, how little anyone really cared. Their things scattered across some indistinct geography, their homes in disarray. They were all terrified, weren't they? That's why they agreed to come to the McPhersons'. No one wanted to go home. Michael couldn't remember what he'd been talking about to Paul Patterson and said, "That's all I can say for now. I'll give you an update when I can." Michael turned and motioned for his neighbors to follow. Up to his front door. He inserted his key, turned the knob, heard his daughter's music blasting from the small kitchen radio.

# Chapter 39

---

## 4:01 p.m.

Susan could hear traffic in the distance. The rush of tires on asphalt, quiet screeches from brakes in need of pads, the occasional horn. Toward the traffic. That's where she should go. Was she hearing the Eisenhower Expressway? She thought of Arthur, of how he believed his ears were better attuned to the world than the average person's because of his condition. Absolute-pitch theory, he had called it, except rather than music, he heard language. Eventually, he had told her, he could recognize and name the speaker without the use of references at all, if it was someone he'd heard enough, someone whose pattern of dialogue and dialect he had diagrammed himself. "Give me time," he'd told her, "and I'll know you from anyone with just a single phrase."

Absolute-pitch theory.

Would Arthur have been the one to recognize her scream?

The boys kept up around her. They were taunting her. They had

turned to the place all young boys turn to when they don't understand their own power: to ridicule and jest.

"Whatthefuckyoudoin'overinhere, layyyyddeeee?" one taunted.

Susan didn't know.

What the fuck *was* she doing over in here?

*Madison's zero*, Susan thought, trying to remember how the grid
system worked. *Move north by the hundreds. Chicago Avenue, eight
hundred north. Eight blocks north. Division Street, five hundred north.
Five blocks north. Washington and Randolph, one hundred, two hundred.* The boys quieted for a moment. She heard a mumble. She
heard their footsteps as they retreated somewhere behind her and
she nearly fainted with relief. She was so exhausted her breath was
ragged, her heart bursting inside her, her throat burning. Her right
ankle throbbed from slipping on the McDonald's bag; her hair was
damp with sweat.

On a stoop two houses up, another group. Young men, music
blaring from a boom box on one of the steps. Inside the house, a
young girl was screaming in rage: *You muthafucka, whatchyoumean
you ain't gotta. . . . You muthafucka . . .*

She heard more boys hollering from chipped maroon steps, and
her heart dropped and she knew they would not leave her. They kept
shouting at her that she was lost, just a little, lost white lady. They
kept telling her what she already knew. That she had come someplace
she wasn't welcome, and she didn't know what in the hell she was
doing. She had believed herself connected to them, to their world.

*She* had been connected, but they never were, never had been.

They'd never cared about her caring.

And she pictured them, then, as eternal boys, always around
her, in everything she would ever do. Eternal Boys running all the
way home with her, up her front lawn, and into her house. She pic-

tured the Eternal Boys in her kitchen, crowding her as she filled the dishwasher, squeezing into her car as she went to the grocery store, stealing the available oxygen around her. She pictured them sitting on her desk at the Housing Office laughing at her demographic spreadsheets, sprawled on the floor around her, moving ever closer like walls contracting, and she heard them cackling as she tried to tell a new client about life in east Oak Park. *Oh, yeah,* they'd say, *we can assure your diversity, baby. We can assure you a unique and satisfying living EX-PER-I-ENCE.* She felt them crowd her bed at night, lying beside her and on top of her so that she would always have to gasp for breath. She saw them, standing there, waiting, bent over in a runner's stance, ready to sprint, ready to pounce, ready for every moment. Asleep. Awake. Walking. Running. Talking. Reading. Ever present.

And then she pictured her daughter.

Mary Elizabeth McPherson.

And in her mind the Eternal Boys began to move, slowly, cautiously, away from Susan, to her daughter, their breath coming in short, sharp ringlets from their noses, their eyes narrowed, focusing, and she pictured her daughter taking steps backward, taking deep breaths, too, deeper and deeper, until she began to gasp for breath, until she, too, began to suffocate. And Susan would not let this happen to her daughter from these Eternal Boys. These pitiful, little, motherfucking, *small* boys. She would not. So she screamed a short, sharp, simple "No!"

She broke free of them and she ran and she tripped off the sidewalk and she never even noticed the bumper at all. Only knew that she was free of the boys. And her daughter would be free, too.

# Chapter 40

## 4:19 p.m.

At his front door, Michael glanced one last time at the Cambodians, standing around that beat-up Pontiac parked on the street in front of their house. Sofia gave him a tiny wave, and he balled and stretched his fists. What kind of illusion was she under that she had *any* right at all to wave to him? What kind of parents did she have? he wondered. If only he could give *them* a piece of his mind. But he knew this was not the time to confront her, to confront any of them, not with a news camera so nearby.

But those boys. Oh, he could see those cousins of hers, those three, with their torn jeans and their bandannas and how they'd never quite look you in the eye when you talked to them (not that he had ever tried). From afar they'd stare at him with a hardened bravado that amplified the distance.

And how, he wondered, how *had* Dara and Sary escaped the burglaries so completely? Not a single electronic stolen beyond the wife's cell phone? Not a TV or a DVD player or a computer? Why had he and Susan let them off so easily about this? Why hadn't he confronted them? Or Sofia? Why had he spared the girl's feelings? After all, she'd been the one to ditch school with Mary Elizabeth. She'd been the one high on ecstasy with his daughter.

And it all made sense now. The boys, Sofia's cousins from the city, surely they'd been the source of Mary Elizabeth's drugs. Surely they'd passed them to Sofia, who'd convinced Mary Elizabeth to take part, and now here those boys were, loitering like the hoodlums he knew them to be, right in front of Paul Patterson's news camera. What did the others think? Was he the only one who could see them for who they were? The only one bold enough to stand up to them? He could feel the same rage he'd felt just an hour or so earlier, standing in front of the police station with Étienne, a sharp, dark clot of anger that began somewhere in his abdomen and spiraled out through the rest of his body. One of the boys, the middle one, widened his eyes and lifted his gaze and met Michael's for one split second. One tiny moment that only the two of them shared, and there was nothing there, no understanding, no attempt at camara-derie. Michael despised him. And he, in turn, despised Michael. *The camera,* Michael thought, *is saving your ass, little man.*

He turned and walked in his front door. Arthur, Dan, Alicia, Paja, and Helen followed. He heard the music from the Loop, louder than Mary usually played it. He was surprised Susan let her keep it this loud. Why was she playing the kitchen radio anyway and not hiding out in her room as she usually did? He recognized the drums, the angry melody of one of Mary's favorite bands. He'd heard it coming from his daughter's room a hundred times. Lincoln Park. Like the north-side neighborhood where wealthy white urbanites lived in their tree-lined Chicago brownstones. But, no, it wasn't *Lincoln,* Mary had said (why such scorn in her voice?), it was *Linkin.*

*Linkin Park.* "Just because you're a rock star doesn't mean you are required to have bad grammar," her mother had said. Laughing. Diffusing the moment. That was Susan's role. The Grand Diffuser. A meteorological force for peace and harmony in the house.

Where were they? Susan and Mary Elizabeth?

It seemed that something had gone haywire with Michael's family, with his life. Shouldn't he be further along by now? Vice president of *something*, director of such and such? Healthy pension fund growing exponentially? Wasn't middle age supposed to be one's golden years? Where was he on this scale? Another decade of house payments, college tuition still to come for Mary Elizabeth. Susan pulled in a pittance from the Housing Office, and his salary, so dependent on sales, was volatile. His pension? Nine-eleven had taken care of that, and who knew when, or if, the market would ever recover? He didn't even own his car outright.

Michael stood on the foyer's tile for a moment.

He listened to the music streaming from the kitchen, a solid wall of instruments, he thought. No nuance. No subtlety. Just noise. He felt himself recoil at the sound: *"All I want to do is be more like me and be less like you . . ."* Behind him, Michael heard Helen mention something about children to Paja. Dan put his hand in the small of Alicia's back.

Michael took two steps into the dining room.

He would recall only colors later. And the sound of Linkin Park.

Blue jeans.

Black boots with thick soles.

The roundness of his daughter's hip.

The bottom of her socks.

She was under the table, most of her hidden, visible from the waist down, as she knelt on all fours in front of a boy Michael had never before seen. A boy with dirty-blond hair that hung long and limp past his shoulders. An olive-green T-shirt, faded with age around the shoulder blades, jean jacket tossed in a bundle to the floor. Michael thought he heard the tinkle of a belt, prong against buckle, prong against buckle, prong-buckle, moving, moving, moving. His daughter's knuckles, gone white with her fingers grabbing at the rug.

Then the boy was on the wall. His neck under the forearm of Michael McPherson, the sweat from his tryst with Mary mixing with the sweat of his surprise. The shock not just of her father, but of *all these people*. Everyone in the room flushed with a mutual, breathless shock.

*Who the hell are all these people?* Caz thought. The ground was not beneath his feet. His penis, slick and hard, bobbed in the air, and he first tried to find his pants, his zipper, then reached to get out from Michael's forearm. He hung there, one hand clutching Michael's forearm, the other trying to tuck his penis back into his underwear.

He gasped, "She fucking asked for it, you asshole."

Michael stumbled backward. The boy slid down the wall, collapsed, righted himself. Had a boy, had *this* boy, said what Michael heard? Had a boy ever said such a thing to an adult?

Michael's voice was a growl. "What. Did. You. Say. To. Me?" His flesh was red, his hands clenched, his legs shook. He could not look down toward the table, toward his daughter, sobbing, scrambling, screaming for her clothes.

Alicia covered her eyes.

Arthur recognized the scream. Reached for it.

Dan stared at Mary Elizabeth's feet as they frantically searched for the leg openings of her jeans. The front door had been left open.

Helen bent down to help Mary Elizabeth put her clothes on.

"Mr. McPherson," Paja Coen said cautiously, holding out one arm, looking first at Michael, then at the boy, who was heaving, who was trying to buckle his belt, but his hands were shaking too furiously and he couldn't find the holes. The rage of adults had long since ceased to terrify him.

"I said," Caz spoke slowly, matching the sinister quiet of Michael's tone, "she fucking asked for it." Caz turned, glanced under the table for a fraction of a second.

Mary Elizabeth saw it all then, the entirety of her immediate future wrapped up in an infinite black tunnel. Caz's eyes, glazed over as he glanced in her direction, unfocused. It was as if she were camouflaged inside her own dining-room wall. She suddenly knew the answer to a hundred questions, some she had asked, many she had not.

"No," Mary Elizabeth screamed. "No, I did not, you fucking asshole."

"You sure as fuck did, you bitch."

Mary snapped her mouth shut, could not look at Caz, who seemed to her to have morphed into some kind of animal. Helen was kneeling over Mary, brushing her hair back with her hands, telling her it would be all right, and Mary wanted Helen to stop.

Michael McPherson got hold of a clump of Caz's T-shirt. He was saying nonsensical things: "pissant" and "learn a lesson" and "invade my family." Mary had never heard her father like this, so angry he couldn't finish a sentence. The collective sound was overpowering, everyone hollering at once, and Mary was trying to decipher whose words belonged to what voice, and it seemed to her that noise could carry a physical weight.

Paja and Arthur would remember Michael's scream later. Paja

would compare it to a bear, Arthur to a volcano. Dan pushed Alicia out of the way, back into the living room where the front door stood open.

Wrapping her arms around Mary Elizabeth, Helen pulled the girl up.

"Where is my mom? Where is my mom?" Mary Elizabeth sobbed. *Whereismymommymymommymom?*

No one would know for several hours.

Michael had Caz by the back of his jeans now, by the belt, by the loops (the seams of a pair of Levi's had a tensile strength of 142 pounds. They would learn this in court). Caz was bent over, clawing at the floor, clawing his way out toward the front door, a flailing, downward dog. Michael tripped after him, holding tight to his jeans. Someone was screaming for Michael to let go. For Michael to calm down. For Mary Elizabeth not to look. For Caz to get out. For everyone to calm down. Only Arthur stayed silent, focused on the voices, trying to find Mary Elizabeth by the sound of her sobs.

Caz made it to the door.

He made it outside.

He tumbled, rolled. With Michael on top of him. Around him. Holding on. Dan left Alicia and ran toward Michael.

Paul Patterson's little camera sprang to life. "What the hell's going on?" he shouted, running across the lawn, one of his shoelaces flapping ominously.

Dara and his nephews ran toward Michael. Sofia and Sary followed across the yard. Sofia felt a kind of sickness spread through her body because she recognized the boy as Caz and she knew immediately what had happened, that Mary's father had walked in, had seen too much. Sofia had encouraged Mary Elizabeth to hook up with Caz, and nausea rose from Sofia's stomach. Mary's dad tackled Caz in a rage, and for a moment Sofia feared for Caz's life. One of her cousins threw a protective arm across her body, and Dara yelled at her to stay away. There were too many voices, too many bodies running toward and away, and she could not make out who anyone was, what anyone was doing. She stopped at the edge of the McPherson lawn and felt her mother come and encircle her with her arms. The shame, the terrific, horrible thing she had done, burrowed into her. She never said a word. Would never tell Mary how wrong she had been, how terribly, terribly wrong.

Blood bloomed across the face of the blond boy with the dangling belt. Spread like drops of water blown across glass.

Dan Kowalski could not get a grip on Michael. Dan was not given to physicality in any way, and so his arms felt uncoordinated and perhaps a little rebellious, suggesting through returned impulses from his brain that he was ill prepared for this kind of fight. He was wearing boat shoes and they slipped off his feet, and then someone—maybe Caz, maybe Paul Patterson—tripped over one and yelped.

Paja Coen stood on the stoop at the front door and yelled for Michael to stop.

Aldrin Rutherford came running out of his house at the commotion, stopped short at the end of Helen's lawn, and watched, his mouth agape, his T-shirt damp with sweat and dark with dirt. Before the summer was over, a RE/MAX FOR SALE sign would appear on the Rutherford lawn.

Alicia Kowalski went to Helen and Mary Elizabeth. Alicia held on to the other side of the girl, linking her arms around Helen's, the two women forming a circle, cocooning Mary Elizabeth, who was crying so hard Helen feared she would hyperventilate, so she simply said, "Sssshhhhhh, I know. Ssssshhhhhh. Sssssshhhhh . . ." But she didn't know.

Mary Elizabeth took no comfort from these women. No safety. She felt trapped, held there against her will. She would not remember their names, these strangers who would populate her life for just this moment and then, one by one, slowly dissolve from the frame. She would remember feeling as if her mother were nearby, arm's distance away, and these women seemed to be keeping her from Susan, trapping her there between them, and she had an irrational, fleeting thought that Caz had somehow managed this, too. Her continued captivity.

"Sssshhhhhh," Alicia joined Helen. "Sssshhhhhh."

Because there was nothing else that could be said.

For a long, long time.

For years.

Paul Patterson ran to Arthur. "What happened in there?"

Arthur adjusted his dark glasses, but did not respond.

"Sir. Can you tell me anything?"

Arthur stood. Silent. He was used to his own silence. He could outsilence anyone. He thought of Mary Elizabeth. Who cleaned his house. Who read to him. Her voice had always been soothing. He'd loved that voice. He'd know it anywhere, even now as it was. Sobbing, screaming. It had always carried heat to him, a rich, quiet softness. He'd loved how her statements often ended in a kind of gentle question. *Tell me,* she might have said, *tell me about what is to come. Tell me what to expect. Tell me what it'll be like.* Adulthood, she wanted to know. His theory of questions. *Is it bad that I can answer for you, but not for me?* Her real question, he knew but had never articulated until this moment, was whether there was ever a moment in your life when you felt you had control? It was another way of asking about happiness. When it would come. If it would come. If it demanded a high price. If you could survive enough to eventually make your way toward it. He thought back to that night when he'd first run into her near the 7-Eleven last fall. How he'd leaned on the mailbox and she'd sat on the ground. So limber. So free to move as she desired. The young own their bodies in ways they don't fully grasp, Arthur thought, until they are forced to give up ownership, as he had done, as everyone must someday do. He did not have a daughter, but he knew if he had, he would do exactly what Michael McPherson was doing now. And so he remained silent.

Not for Mary, this time.

But for Michael.

The three Cambodian boys were the first to reach Michael, after Dan fell back from the force of Michael's arm.

The camera never stopped.

Michael's nose was broken.

Mary saw Arthur then, who had come to stand beside her, and she reached for the collar of his Members Only jacket and was suddenly released by Helen and Alicia into Arthur's arms. She did not think of his blindness then. Not that day. But for every day after. How in all the noise, all the chaos, all the injuries and confusion and rage, he had found his way to her.

"Arthur," she said. "Arthur."

He did not say, *Ssshhhhhh*. Instead, he whispered in her ear, "Close your eyes."

And she did.

Caz tore a ligament in his left ankle tripping over the doorframe with Michael McPherson atop his back, and Caz heard a familiar sound, emanating from somewhere behind him though he would not be able to place it for a long time to come. Michael dislocated

Caz's jaw and left shoulder, cracked two ribs, and Caz would be unable to talk in his own defense in court. This would understandably make the jury more sympathetic, and so for those few weeks he was thankful for the injury. It was the only time in his life he would be given the benefit of the doubt, the only time in his life he would be the recipient of empathy. His jaw would heal cockeyed, just two small millimeters off course, so that he appeared always to be grinding his teeth, to be thinking every possible thing through, even the smallest, most inconsequential thing (rum and Coke, or Jack and Coke? Marlboro Reds or Camels? Doggy or missionary?). Later, driving a truck across country just as his father had, he would earn the nickname Gnarly, not as in cool dude, but as in gnarled. As in twisted limb and jagged root. He would never tell the story of Michael McPherson, of how he got a gnarled jaw, and that sound— what *was* that sound? Both familiar and distant—would haunt him. Of his scar, he would fabricate a story about an ice-hockey pickup game, the fucking puck coming right toward him. Bam! *Into the jaw.* Bam! The story he told. The story would feel real after a dozen tellings, after he'd lived a dozen years, after a woman whose name he couldn't at first remember would give birth to a little girl she claimed was his, and it would turn out to be true, and he would remember that afternoon and he would finally know that if he couldn't ever forgive Michael McPherson, he could at least understand. He'd feel the urge to find Mary, to search for her and look her up and apologize, and every few years the urge would overtake him, but he would drink it away. He'd visit with his daughter as she grew and he'd vow to protect her in his quiet moments, in front of mirrors, or driving down long stretches of highway parting Midwestern cornfields. He'd keep her away from boys like him. He would make this vow as Mary's father had once done, and so many other fathers across time and history, because they believe themselves somehow stronger than the forces of the world. They make their vows and still their daughters are never safe.

Then one day in a flash it would come to him. The sound he'd heard. The familiarity. Mary's screaming, Mary's sobbing. He'd heard it once before. From another woman he'd known. His mother. No one would have to tell him that trauma and memory were not false, not for the weakhearted. No one would have to tell him what he'd done and what he'd lived through. It would come to him at once, a weight so overpowering and so overwhelming he would suddenly understand them all—his mother, his father, his own past, his daughter and her future, and what he'd taken from Mary, and he would give in. Give up. His body would not be found for days.

The police were quick to come. This was Ilios Lane, after all. This was one day past *the* day. This was a street, Sary would later say, where the ghosts were thick with rage. Sofia watched her three cousins make their way to Michael McPherson with determined strides. *I should stop them,* she thought, one second too late.

"Get off me, you goddamned dropouts," Michael yelled to the Cambodian boys. The boys who were winners of merit scholarships and travel grants. The boys who were bilingual and averaged, collectively, 3.8 GPAs. "Get the hell off me." He swung his arm just to break free, he would tell the police, would tell Detective Wasserman. He wasn't trying to harm the boys. His only focus was on Caz, the rapist. The word would make Mary Elizabeth flinch. She wouldn't know if it was an accurate description of Caz for many years.

The three Cambodians converged on Michael, pulled him off Caz, who sat dazed on the cold ground in front of the McPherson house with his belt unbuckled and blood splattered down his olive-green T-shirt, his jaw slack and hanging, dizziness surrounding him.

An ambulance was called. The cousins jumped Michael, and in a rush of adrenaline he lashed through the air. Ken, who weighed no more than 110 pounds (less than the tensile strength of a pair of Levi's), flew off Michael's arm like a balled-up wad of paper and hit his head on the sidewalk, and it bounced up once and came to rest at the foot of Paul Patterson, whose camera panned over Ken's body from his tennis shoes, up his torn jeans and across his unbuttoned flannel shirt, and up to his blood-soaked bandanna.

His concussion was the opposite of minor. A blunt-trauma head wound. A hospital stay and a high school career extended by one semester. His concussion would slur his speech, blur his vision for months. It would end the budding friendship between Mary Elizabeth and his cousin, Sofia, and render Michael McPherson—from the standpoint of American actuaries and their risk graphs and their forecasting charts—an uninsurable homeowner for the rest of his life.

Wasserman arrived moments after the first police cruiser, followed immediately by one ambulance and then another (the following month, Paul Patterson would be offered a job on WGN news).

"It's not what it looks like," Michael said to Wasserman. He was out of breath, but already his hands had been cuffed behind him, his face sheened in sweat, blood spattered from his nose down his shirt, one eye bloodshot.

"You can open your eyes now," Arthur whispered to Mary.

The human cacophony stopped abruptly.

"I'd advise you to keep quiet, Mr. McPherson," Detective Wasserman said.

"That *boy*—"

"For your *own* good. Take my advice now on this, Mr. McPherson."

Wasserman scanned the scene. The McPherson girl looked disheveled, her eyes—clenched shut when he'd arrived—were open now and staring at her father. The blind man across the street was beside her, gently holding her hand. A young Asian boy Wasserman had never before seen had paramedics hovering over him. They shone a light first in one eye, then the other. Another boy with long, stringy hair lay strapped to a gurney, his head secured in a neck brace. It was, Wasserman knew, *exactly* what it looked like. He nodded toward the officer holding Michael's arm. The officer led Michael to the police cruiser, and Michael turned around and saw that Mary was beside Arthur, and even though Michael knew Arthur could not see him do so, he mouthed a thank-you to the old man.

The verdict was guilty.

Caz was a minor by a year. His prior record made the judge go easy on Michael McPherson. The lack of a prior record for Ken, in turn, made the judge go harder on Michael McPherson. His wife's long-standing favor in the community coupled with her injury would also make the judge go easy on Michael McPherson. The loss of his daughter, wholly and completely, went unnoticed by anyone except Michael McPherson. At the end, the score would be even—two easies, two hards. Two boys injured. Two women lost.

Probation. Two years. Thirty days' jail time. The judge let Mary Elizabeth, after pleading and begging and writing a letter on her own behalf, have Arthur stay with her for those thirty days, and in that time she learned to live in the dark, and eventually she would seek out the darkest places she could find. She'd write a dissertation about Bosnian women refugees in Chicago, about how trauma skips a generation and embeds itself in the generational memories of grandsons and granddaughters, and she would be given a grant from the National Science Foundation to continue her research on women from Burma, from Iraq, from Syria and Afghanistan and Somalia and Rwanda, and always she would seek out the darkness. She would replace her own story with the stories of women she met who'd lived through worse. She'd think of Arthur. All the time, Arthur. But she'd never ask the question again. Of herself. Of anyone.

The burglaries were forgotten in the wake of an adult's beating—*beating*—two minors. The minors were never named. Alleged sexual assault was never proven.

Mary Elizabeth would recognize in herself the inability to speak at moments of heightened tension. She would warn would-be suitors about this characteristic. She would avoid action movies and horror movies because they made her too tense. She would engage in yoga and meditation, in college and then in graduate school. She would always want quiet. Music rarely played in her house. She lived on quiet streets, on dead ends or in buildings set back from the road. Nightclubs, concerts, and sporting events were generally off-putting to her. She lived in a calm and steady darkness that she'd learned from Arthur Gardenia.

"It's almost," she later said, "it's almost like noise erases me."

But on that day she stood in the foyer, watching first with the arms of her neighbors around her, then Arthur's hand in hers, and she knew her father had said, in fists and in rage, what she had been unable to: *No. Not this time. Not Mary Elizabeth McPherson.* This wouldn't heal her. This wouldn't make their relationship smooth and easy, but it would be an image, a moment for her to remember, to recall in times of doubt. To Mary, it seemed suddenly that her father fought a lot of things. He fought people and their ideas, he fought his wife, his children. He fought her. He fought his career and his inertia of failure and much of the movement of life around him. He fought his boss, he fought his clients, he fought utility companies and bureaucracy and neighbors. He fought illness in others, and in himself. He fought crabgrass and weeds and overheated radiators. He fought banks and credit-card charges. He fought his own heart, his own mind, his own desires. Sometimes, it seemed, he'd take on the sun if he thought it might fight fairly. But this moment, this day, captured digitally and played over and over again in evening-news cycles—a man collapsing under the pressure of his home's burglary, said the media's logic—on this afternoon before news of her mother reached them, before her father's arrest and sentencing, before they moved and everything changed and she never saw a single Ilios Lane resident again, she had this image:

Her father.

One single afternoon.

Enraged.

And fighting for her.

# Epilogue

## Thursday, April 8, 2004, 6:30 p.m.

When Susan finally opened her eyes, she could feel a crust around her eyelashes, and someone had removed her contacts so that the whole room was blurry. To her right, her daughter sat in a chair staring at her own knees, her shoulders arching forward as if the weight of her body were too much to hold up. She wore her winter fleece, even though Susan thought the room was too warm. She wanted to tell her daughter to sit up straight, to look ahead, but a searing pain in her thigh caught her breath and she inhaled sharply, and Mary suddenly looked up at her, and that's when Susan noticed someone else in the room, someone who wasn't Michael, though she could not make out who it was until he spoke.

"It's best if you lie still," Arthur said. "Just try to relax, Susan."

Mary seemed to be vibrating in her chair, her whole body in a kind of quiet movement. Arthur Gardenia sat next to her, and Susan had no idea why. She could feel the irritation of a breathing tube in her nose, and her thighs itched furiously, which was a result of the morphine, though she did not yet know this.

Arthur told her about her injuries. A dislocated hip and broken femur. A cracked rib, a small tear in her earlobe. Pins in her leg. A smooth-as-could-be-expected operation. A long road ahead of her, certainly, but no reason she couldn't expect to make a full recovery. On a far table she could see colorful blobs, flower baskets it seemed, and a couple of pink and yellow balloons.

"Your cheek," Mary said, "it's like really swollen. But don't freak out. The doctor said it'll be fine."

Susan finally managed a word: "Cheek."

"It was pretty bloody."

Susan nodded. "Water."

Mary took a plastic cup from the bedside table and bent a straw toward her mother's mouth. Susan tried not to gulp, but she was so very, very thirsty. Outside her door she heard someone call out, "That's okay, honey," and break into laughter. Footsteps faded away. This was the first time, Susan realized, that she'd been in a hospital bed since Mary had been born, and now here was that same tiny baby, grown-up and helping her own mother drink. Susan had to concentrate hard not to cry. What had she done with all those years? She could not remember anything between that seven-pound baby and this fifteen-year-old girl. Nothing of Mary's childhood came into her mind, and she felt a tiny panic spring in her belly. Then an image came to her, a mermaid cake, a child's birthday, and she relaxed a little.

Susan could feel her hair matted to her forehead, to the pillow. Pastel wallpaper spanned the room, a peach curtain separating her bed from another patient's. She smelled dried sweat and ammonia and then something else, something delicious, like garlic and cheese and other things she had no names for in her blurry state.

"I slept at Arthur's last night," Mary said.

Susan understood that her daughter was speaking to her, but the room was strange, as if the walls were unsound, as if they might collapse on her. Where was Michael? she wondered. Talking to the doctor? Looking for a parking spot? Out getting coffee in the hospital's cafeteria? She began to remember, to put it all together. The burglaries. Her daughter home. Safe. And not safe. It seeped back in. The missing pieces of her recent life, how she'd rushed home from the office and run toward Mary, even as she saw that her daughter was unharmed. How she felt for a moment as if she'd always be running, trying to outrun, outmaneuver, outsmart, anything that came near her daughter. Then the boys. And the wolves. And she remembered, all of it.

"It's just temporary," Arthur said. "Until you're home." They'd move a bed into the living room of the McPherson home, he said, so Susan wouldn't have to navigate the stairs. And Arthur would be there. Yes, he would. Even a blind man could stick dishes in the dishwasher, he'd said, and smiled. Toss some clothes into a machine. Michael, well. That's all Arthur could say about him.

"It's been quite a while since I had the great opportunity to offer help to someone else," he told her. "I'm not much of a cook, but I'm quite adept at opening cans." Then he pushed a small bag toward her on her tray table and the food smells grew stronger. She noticed Mary nodding at everything Arthur said. She was wearing an oversize men's flannel shirt that Susan recognized from Michael's closet.

"And Étien—Edward. Mr. Lenoir. He brought over a bunch of

food earlier today. Tons, actually," Mary said. "He's starting a whole new restaurant. He told me and Arthur. It's like some kind of fancy hamburger place."

"He knew the hospital food would be ghastly," said Arthur. "He's asked us all to be culinary guinea pigs for some new grand idea he's not quite unveiled."

"Michael, well?" Susan said. Such small talk. What was it all about? A machine beeped rhythmically, something squeaked in the hallway.

Arthur and Mary exchanged looks, and Susan suddenly suspected that the conversation they were having had nothing to do with food or beds or care, and that her husband, Michael, was not speaking with the doctor or getting coffee in the cafeteria or trying to find a spot on the street to avoid a large parking fee. The specifics were lost on her, but she felt a heaviness in the room, as if the edges of the television and the tray table and the bed, and the doorframe and even her neighbor and her daughter, had trailed off into the distance. What might have happened if she hadn't gone for a run? If she had just once remembered to bring her cell phone? The smallest decision, the smallest step to the left, or to the right, the smallest remembrance, the smallest moment, in anyone's life can upend so much more. One small inch. Could change everything. If she reached out, if she touched her daughter on the knee, on the leg, on the hand, just anywhere she could reach, could her daughter hold that tiny touch forever?

"You were very lucky," Arthur told Susan. "Very lucky someone was right there when you were hit. Called 911 immediately after the damn driver sped off. Do you remember being hit by the car?"

A nurse barreled into the room and announced himself as Todd. "Glad to see you're awake, Mrs. McPherson."

Susan managed a half smile, but she was trying to remember what Arthur had just said. About someone calling 911.

Todd looked at her chart, lifted one side of her blanket, and peeked at the cast. He took her pulse.

"You'll surely be feeling yourself soon, so don't you be afraid to ask for something, you got me? That pain'll hit you like a train wreck."

Susan nodded. She understood, then. Not that she'd be feeling *like* herself soon, but that she'd be *feeling* herself soon, her broken body. She found herself wanting to say, almost like a confession to Todd, that she had not quite felt herself for a little while now.

Todd winked at Mary, said he'd be back in a while, and disappeared out the door.

Then Susan allowed her mind to remember, the secret she would never share. The Eternal Boys. The wolves. "Who called 911?" she slurred, her lips thick and dry.

"I don't know," Arthur said. "A young boy. Stayed with you till the ambulance came. The driver said he had you in his lap, talking to you like you were his own mother. Telling you to keep yourself strong, keep on breathing. Said he'd learned CPR after his brother was shot, some years back. Didn't need it for you, thank God."

Just one. Eternal Boy. Who would not leave her.

She saw her head in his lap.

She heard him talk to her.

Susan felt her eyes grow warm, felt the tears rise up from where she lay.

"You're cracking again, Mom." Mary's voice was dry and monotone, and Susan realized that Mary, too, was crying.

Mary had never seen her mother cry like this. It made her think of a cavern, the endless space of something hollow and shapeless and infinite.

"I don't believe they got the boy's name," Arthur said.

Of course they didn't. The world was full of ghosts and spirits, things they once held that were gone, and things intangible, equally gone. Because it wasn't the items in their homes they'd lost, Susan would someday think, it was their own tiny empires. Their own lost cities.

Mary reached out and covered her mother's hand with her own, then scooted her chair over and lay, forehead down, on the mattress at Susan's shoulder. Mary's body shuddered. Susan could not remember the last time her daughter had reached for her.

"Tell me," Susan said, reaching her left hand across her own body and touching Mary's kinky, curly hair, the thick mass her daughter hated so much, the strength of Samson, which was—they both knew—just the kind of tall tale a child believes for far too long, "tell me everything that happened."

# Author's Note

Though the characters and events of this book are entirely fictional, the Oak Park Community Housing Office is inspired by the real-life Oak Park Regional Housing Center. Oak Park's Diversity Assurance program is similarly based on an actual program in the Village (one of many throughout the years). I have collapsed several different programs under the umbrella of Diversity Assurance here for the sake of narrative clarity. Oak Park itself has been the study of demographers worldwide for many years. In the years it took to write this book, I read blogs, letters, Listservs, and community articles that discussed the diversity programs, and the area's longtime integration efforts, with more detail than any casual reader is likely interested in. But those sites showed me that while the methodology might not be agreed upon, the heart and soul of the real Oak Park community shares a deep and abiding commitment to inclusion.

My interest was more than academic, however. I first moved to Oak Park in 1992, right out of college, into a building on Austin Boulevard owned by Russell and Kevin Schuman, who had a company called RK Management. They believed in the mission of integration, and still do today, and I am profoundly grateful to have crossed paths with them. They owned several large buildings on Oak Park's east side, and had hired a resident manager for each. The woman who managed my building—Ann Maxwell—was also fresh out of college. Ann was the first community activist I'd ever met, the first person to show me that a neighborhood with diverse faces and voices and viewpoints offered a much richer experience, a better world, than one of homogeneity. In the early nineties, Ann used to hold potluck dinners for the tenants of the building so we'd get to know one another. She started what was then a radical program: having renters in a multi-unit building recycle their waste. She swept the alleyways and picked up trash and calmed tenants during stressful times. Once, when the power went out during a storm, she invited all the neighbors she could find to play cards by candlelight in her apartment. It is hard to capture all that she has added to my life over the past two decades. She is my soul sister, my closest confidant, and the person I most aspire to be like: humble, curious, brilliant, empathic, steadfast, and hilarious.

Eventually, I became a resident manager myself for RK Management, at a building three blocks west of Austin Boulevard, and just around the corner from Ann. On paper, my job was to clean the building, show apartments, and be a point of contact for complaints or issues. But my real job was to create community. We managers were the most visible and present manifestation of a belief system that said all people had a right to live where they choose, free from crime and racial intolerance. We tried to make neighbors known to neighbors, to foster friendships and relationships—things that often prove challenging among renters. Everything one could imagine happened during my five years in that job: fires, floods, break-ins, drug dealing, domestic violence. One girl who'd gotten addicted to crack was wheeled out of the building on a gurney multiple times; she was fifteen years old. When she eventually moved, we found locking mechanisms outside her bedroom—the sign of a mother perhaps in equal measures abusive and terrified. Another woman was regularly beaten by her boyfriend, but refused to cooperate with police when they were called to the scene—an act I only later discovered was likely her means of self-protection when the officers left. Those were some of the worst moments. We had many, many beautiful ones, too. One tenant taught his neighbors how to dance. Another group began an annual camping trip together. We planted a collective herb and vegetable garden, and held building-wide courtyard parties and potlucks. Of the many, many lessons I garnered while in that job, perhaps none has been more profound than the realization that if you come from the majority culture you have the luxury of racial oblivion, by which I mean you need not think that race is part of everything; minorities very often do not know such luxury. It is a lesson I try to impart on my daughter. Though she is only five, when I walk into a classroom—my own or hers—or an event or a party, I find myself instantly scanning the faces for diversity—in race, in culture, in gender. Too often, I am disappointed by what I see.

Though the mission of the Housing Center is controversial to some, at its core it was begun by a group of idealistic people who believed integration was a primary marker of both social progress and a rich and varied life, and who fervently espoused the view that decent housing in a safe community with a good school district was a basic human right. Even in the late sixties in Oak Park, it was entirely legal for Realtors to refuse to show properties to minority families. Roberta "Bobbie" Raymond began the Housing Center out of a church classroom, with the aim of correcting some of the grave injustices committed under the discriminatory practices of redlining and blockbusting—practices rampant in Chicago and many other cities across the U.S. in the early part of the twentieth century. Recently, she completed a DVD for the Oak Park Library's historical archives about what it was like to start the Center forty years ago. She and her colleagues received death threats at the time. But the question, she said in the interview, is the same today as it was four decades earlier: "How much do you intervene? . . . You wish that it all were not necessary."

Indeed.

But as a writer and a humanist, I am grateful for the legacy—and the challenge to do better—that she and so many others have left me.

# Acknowledgments

I am thankful to my incredible support system of early readers: Ann Maxwell, David Corey, Andre Dubus III, David Keplinger, Danielle Evans, Stephanie Grant, Glenn Moomau, and Gayle Forman (who deserves extra kudos for answering a panicked call from me in the middle of the night from South Korea). For research help on police procedures and common burglary patterns, Deputy Chief Robert Scianna, Detective Robert Wile, Marcello Muzzatti, and Betty Ballester were integral. Dr. Arthur Shapiro deserves thanks for allowing me into his lab at American University and devising an experiment that enabled me to experience hemeralopia. Steve Carr taught me more about bridges than I could possibly include here, and I think of him every time I cross one. For all public radio wisdom: John Barth, Israel Smith, Vidal Guzman, and Nancy Robertson. Joellyn Powers and Bryan Freeland were fantastic research assistants; Debby Preiser of the Oak Park Public Library and Rob Breymaier of the Oak Park Regional Housing Center both offered eleventh-hour help. Bobbie Raymond took time from her holiday to keep me from embarrassing myself with historical inaccuracies; thanks to her fact-checking, but especially to her vision and passion.

I would also like to thank the following: Ted Conover, Richard McCann, Kyle Dargan, Elise Levine, Mia Jordanwood, Bree Fitzgerald, Alison Brower, Elizabeth Becker, Sarah Pollock, and Caroline Alexander, who first told me of a mass burglary in Georgia back in the 1980s while we were standing on a hilltop in South Vietnam with the U.S. Army, and which later became the seed for this novel. For twenty years, my agent, Susan Ramer, has fought for me and believed in me and cheered for me, and I wish for everyone to have someone like her fighting their corner. My team at Scribner was so beautifully engaged and enthusiastic that I feel both undeserving and profoundly grateful: John Glynn, Gwyneth Stansfield, Steve Boldt, and Dan Cuddy. My family has the fortune—good or bad—to be filled with writers and in particular my cousin, the poet Lance Lee, provides eternal inspiration and advice. My brother, David, inherited the best of my family while often enduring the worst. My Aunt Barbara and Uncle Wes have been surrogate parents to me. Thanks, also, to my father, Richard Snyder, my stepmother, Barbara Snyder, and my siblings: John, Josh, Kristi, and Doug. Finally, I thank my husband, Paul, for continuing to believe in me and for giving me the greatest gift I've ever received: my daughter, Jazz. The harmony and rhythm of my life. Who knew you could love someone this much?

# About the Author

---

**Rachel Louise Snyder**'s work has appeared in the *New Yorker*, the *New York Times Magazine*, the *Washington Post*, the *New Republic*, and the *Atlantic*. She is the author of three books—*No Visible Bruises: What We Don't Know About Domestic Violence Can Kill Us*, winner of a J. Anthony Lukas Work-in-Progress Award, a 2019 National Book Critics Circle Award finalist, one of the *New York Times* 10 Best Books of 2019, and a 2019 Kirkus Award finalist; *Fugitive Denim*; and the novel *What We've Lost Is Nothing*. Snyder is the recipient of an Overseas Press Award for her work on *This American Life*. An associate professor at American University, Snyder lives in Washington, DC. Follow her on Twitter at @RLSWrites.